"Answer me, Erin. Do you believe I'm your enemy?"

Tears gathered in her eyes. How could she believe that, when she was so spent from loving him, and from being so loved by him?

"No." She took Colin's arm from around her and began to get dressed. Even though she denied that Colin was her enemy, the question of her faith in him was one she had planted over and over again herself.

Colin ran his hand up her back. "If you mean that, Erin, you'll stop what you're doing and stay here with me."

She made her choice. Time and again, Colin's actions had served to dispel her doubts, but still the questions remained. How did he know what he knew? Was he responsible for murder, or worse? And what nightmares lurked that a few sweet dreams might forestall?

Dear Reader,

Do you remember Florence Nightingale? The mystique, the drama, the romance of a woman in the trenches, fighting overwhelming odds to save the lives of real flesh-and-blood men? In my heart, a certain fascination about men and women in medicine lingers, for in medicine the aura of boldness and sensuality, of dark secrets of life and death and the power to control them, abides. The excitement takes hold, as fresh and vivid now as for the medicine men and women of our ancestors.

Doctors have always been my heroes. Having spent twenty years in laboratory medicine, living the real-life, day-to-day drama of it all, I wanted to write about these heroes and heroines, our modern-day healers, caught up in their passion for saving lives, wrapped up in mystery and in danger and intrigue, and of course, falling in love.

Hot Blooded, as well as my next two upcoming Intrigue titles, *Breathless* and *Heart Throb,* which will be available in April and May, form the Pulse series. I hope they'll make your pulse pound!

And I hope you love them.

Carly Bishop

Hot Blooded
Carly Bishop

Harlequin Books

TORONTO • NEW YORK • LONDON
AMSTERDAM • PARIS • SYDNEY • HAMBURG
STOCKHOLM • ATHENS • TOKYO • MILAN
MADRID • WARSAW • BUDAPEST • AUCKLAND

For my brother, Rick,
who knows a great deal about heroic measures.
Namaste.

ISBN 0-373-22314-5

HOT BLOODED

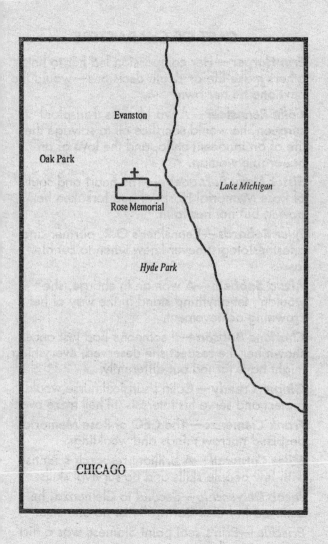

Evanston

Oak Park

Lake Michigan

Rose Memorial

Hyde Park

CHICAGO

CAST OF CHARACTERS

Erin Harper—Her compassion led her to help others make life-or-death decisions—would the next one be her own?

Colin Rennslaer—A world-class transplant surgeon, he would sacrifice all to salvage the life of an innocent child, and the love of an honorable woman.

Sister Mary Bernadette—The heart and soul of Rose Memorial Hospital had forsaken her power, but not her faith.

Tyler Robards—Rennslaer's O.R. partner and anesthesiologist never knew when to cut his losses.

Alexa Sabbeth—A woman in charge, she wouldn't let anything stand in the way of her crowning achievement.

Charlene Babson—If someone had just once shown her the respect she deserved, everything might have turned out differently.

Ginger Creedy—Colin's surgical nurse would protect and serve his interests 'til hell froze over.

Frank Clemenza—The CEO of Rose Memorial despised narrow minds and weaklings.

Miles Cornwall—A brilliant research scientist with few people skills and *no* survival skills.

Jacob Delvecchio—Second to Clemenza, he believed in Miles Cornwall like no one else.

Priscilla—Erin's seal point Siamese was a flirt and a tattletale.

Prologue

So *this* was the stench of betrayal.

He watched the door to his office close on the most unlikely of culprits and fought an overwhelming urge to gag. The project had taken on a murderous life of its own. Now he would have to kill it himself. In his entire forty-nine years, Miles Cornwall, M.D., Ph.D., had never been so angry.

He'd been so certain of success in developing an artificial blood. Only the discovery of penicillin rivaled HemSynon for such potential to advance the practice of modern medicine. A life-giving blood substitute, it could be transfused with no risk of hepatitis or AIDS. The ramifications were explosive without considering the sales projections.

Miles had spent the past four years directing the development of the blood substitute, and only one obstacle remained—how to remove the artificial cells once the body replaced them on its own.

But now people were dead or dying. Certain irresponsible jackasses had jumped the gun and transfused HemSynon months ago. Far ahead of schedule.

He couldn't help thinking of Erin Harper, former student, former fiancée, the woman whose doctoral degree he'd denied for reasons he couldn't even remember now.

Her work had always been above reproach, compassionate and strong—without ever forgetting that human nature was invariably the weak link in research situations.

Erin was a perfectionist, but if she had been in charge of the HemSynon project, a betrayal such as this would have been impossible.

Miles almost laughed.

A part of him stood back in clinical detachment, observing the signs and symptoms of his own rage. The ringing in his ears, the thunder of his pulse, molars gnashing, skin mottling. He swept together the piles on his desk—the evidence of murder.

He couldn't in all conscience call it anything else. Clutching the damning patient charts to his chest, he locked his desk drawers, grabbed up his briefcase, departed his office and locked the door. He made a detour through to the main hospital, near the surgical lounges and the secured offices of the medical librarians.

There must be medical abstracters working, but no one answered the summons of the doorbell he rang.

"Bloody hell!"

He felt agitated, like a rat in an indecipherable maze. The patient charts—the records of murder—were thick and heavy, and he could no longer tolerate them in any case. He dumped them summarily in a transfer bin and never gave them another thought.

The time neared nine o'clock. He headed to the executive board meeting. He should have been able to report HemSynon ready for market in less than six months.

People were willing to attend late-night meetings for good news. God help him, he didn't know what he would tell the board now that the project had been compromised.

He'd called Erin, though they hadn't spoken in years. He had asked her to come because he believed she would be able to see how the project had gone wrong. If Erin Harper had ever refused to help a colleague in such dire need, Miles had never heard tale of it.

People were dead. The thought kept circling in his head.

Though he no longer had the charts in his possession, their names were etched in his brain. Candace Hobbs. Ralph Costigan. Enos Polonoski. All surgical patients of one Colin Rennslaer. Dead as doornails, every one. Only the child, Molly Beecham, remained alive. Miles would gladly have convened a firing squad for Rennslaer and his sidekick anesthesiologist.

He knuckled the elevator button. When it arrived, he got on and punched P1, which emptied at street-level parking. He would walk across the street to the Rose Memorial Hospital and Research Center boardrooms.

Erin's flight from Phoenix should already have landed. Miles had told the Rose Memorial administrator flat out to send a limousine to collect her. Jacob Delvecchio had nearly swallowed his tongue when Miles told him he'd called Erin in as his replacement as director of the project.

Erin didn't know that last part herself. She'd never have agreed to come at all had he been straightforward about that. But the bottom line was that if the HemSynon project required Louis Pasteur, Delvecchio would have resurrected him, so flying Erin Harper in wasn't such a huge step, really.

Any moment the limousine would deliver her to the suite of offices across the street.

Miles heartily wished that he had not sent for her now, because humiliation was all that awaited him.

He exited the parking garage, which was as steeped in automobile exhaust fumes as he was in his own sick-at-heart fantasies of revenge. He strode to the corner and saw that the limousine had pulled up in front of the corporate offices. Erin stepped out and waited for the driver to retrieve her bags.

Seeing her for the first time in four years—or was it five now?—Miles felt a fresh wave of regret for having treated her so shabbily. But mostly for himself, because he'd lost her. She wore a silvery blue trench coat and had her full, sandy-colored hair in a becoming straight, short style. The beams from the bright streetlights glinted off her hair. She had a way about her that invited people around her to abandon moods and cranky attitudes, but Miles knew that disguised how very driven she was.

A massive food delivery truck was approaching, but he had time to wave and call out to Erin. Time enough for her to wave back before the delivery truck blocked her from his view. He stepped out into the street. Seeing Erin could make him feel almost hopeful again.

He never had a chance. He was already into the lane when he heard the protesting peal of tires and the roar of a powerful engine bearing down on him. He was struck first in the knees.

Time warped. He flew into the air and crashed down onto the windshield. In the split second in which he registered Erin's scream, Miles saw the face of his assailant, and the stench of betrayal assailed him again before his brief-case flew out of his grasp and he hit the ground, suffering the mortal blows.

The car disappeared. A siren wailed around from the emergency-room corner. Faces he'd never seen before hovered over him, talking to him, insisting he answer them. Miles wanted to know how the ambulance had arrived so quickly. But of course the limo that had delivered Erin would have a telephone. The paramedics had decided he was nearly a lost cause. *Circling the drain,* they said, in their ghastly lingo.

Then he saw Erin's face. He couldn't seem to hear anymore, but her lips moved and the paramedics seemed to leap to her bidding. He saw her dash tears from her cheeks and grab a stethoscope from one of the medics.

He clutched at her hand and tried to speak. He could taste his own blood and knew that it gurgled from his lips, but he would not be placated. He had to tell her now... now.... "Erin, listen..." he croaked.

"Miles, please! Whatever it is, *it can wait!*"

"No...can't..." He clung to her wrist like a madman. Choking in his own body fluids, he fought to make Erin understand.

"Less...project...tell...Erin...tell...less...sabo—"

He saw through his blinding pain that Erin had heard him. "Tell Les? What, Miles?" she cried. "That the project has been sabotaged?"

He gave a bittersweet smile. *Not... exactly,* but her face faded into the blackness, and he gave up the ghost of consciousness.

Not exactly...

Chapter One

The trauma team in the emergency room of Rose Memorial was on hand at the swinging glass doors. The facility would have been ultramodern in the early eighties. Now it appeared tired but clearly beloved. The Hippocratic oath, hand embroidered on a fragile square of linen, was encased in a small, nondescript wooden frame, and near it hung a photo of the original hospital built by the Sisters of Mercy.

One entire wall was devoted to photos of staff, and over the years the nurses' garb changed from the habits of nuns to starched white uniforms and caps to unisex surgical scrubs.

At some level Erin noted all of that, the history, the progression of years upon years in photos, the poignant seediness, but Miles's critical condition consumed her attention.

Keeping pace alongside the gurney transferring his body from the ambulance, Erin listened intently to the gurgling, suffocating sounds in his chest with a stethoscope. One of the paramedics busied himself protecting the precarious vein access he'd gained. The other, a burly, competent black woman, held the oxygen tank in place beside Miles's body.

Erin had never intended to take charge, but the paramedics were more than grateful for another pair of hands. Maybe they thought she was a doctor, or maybe they'd already put in too many grueling hours.

Erin hadn't bothered correcting whatever assumptions led them to defer to her expertise. Rattling off orders left and right was all that saved her from curling into a ball to block out the horror of the hit and run.

If she stopped for one moment to consider how close she'd come to throwing up, or that this crumpled mass of bone and flesh was Miles's body, she would surely come apart at the seams. The lead trauma doctor, his scraggly gray eyebrows clashing over faded blue eyes, listened intently as Erin first introduced herself and then fired off her triage evaluations.

"Pericardium is flooded, lungs and abdomen filling and turgid. No pulse in either femoral artery... Pupils are dilated and irregular...."

Dr. Bayless nodded his understanding and set his staff into motion. "Get me a pericardial tap. Carson, get the blood bank on this. Ten units whole blood, O neg, STAT to pre-op. I want some Plasmonate in the meantime, and hang a Protocol 2 IV of antibiotics. Let's move it, people! We've got about ten minutes before our John Doe bleeds out."

"His name is Cornwall," Erin said softly. "Miles Cornwall. He's on research staff here." She knew people always tried harder when patients had a name, and a little harder still when the bleeding body was one of their own.

One of the nurses, enlisting Erin's hands to unravel the tangle of IV lines, looked up at her with surprise. "You know him?"

Erin nodded. "I did, a long time ago."

The information sharpened the edge on Dr. Bayless's interest, as well. Thumping at Miles's abdomen, he gave Erin a studied glance. "Irene, see if Colin Rennslaer is available—for *surgery,*" he amended tiredly, as if the name of Colin Rennslaer and "available" in the same breath could be counted upon to be misunderstood.

Erin smiled briefly, though she wasn't in on this private joke. She was grateful that she could still smile, because that meant she was still functioning in a professional mode where humor was accepted—even necessary—to relieve the tension. Family and friends wouldn't appreciate it.

The nurse at Erin's side explained all the females future, present and past who had ever sighed over Rennslaer, all the while slathering Miles's chest with Betadine so Bayless could perform the pericardial tap. "It's an awful cliché, I know. But the man has got to be seen to be believed."

Erin nodded, though all the swooning meant nothing to her. The important thing was that as a surgeon, this Colin Rennslaer had the respect of the emergency-room physician, which was no small achievement. She just prayed now that his surgical skills were at least the match of the skills he used to induce such naughty smiles—which was when she knew her sense of humor and professional objectivity had begun to wane.

RENNSLAER WASN'T available. He was in the middle of a heart-lung transplant on a young woman whose family filled the surgical waiting room. The O.R. was already a beehive of activity with the transplant going on. Another surgeon took Miles to the operating room, and Erin was told it might be several hours.

She joined the small crowd in the waiting room and tried unsuccessfully to read the newspaper, dozing on and off for a couple of uncomfortable hours. At last she poured a cup of hot water, dunked a packet of Earl Grey and admitted to herself that she didn't really know where to go or what to do. Despite her familiarity with hospitals, she didn't know Rose Memorial, or even how to get to the administration offices, where she thought her bags might have been taken.

How could she be worried about her luggage at a time like this? She felt sick at heart and then at loose ends again. She discarded the tea bag and, when she turned, she found a tiny, wizened nun at her side in a full, old-fashioned black habit.

"You must be Erin," she said, and smiled, a Mona Lisa sort of smile that young girls learned when their teeth weren't pretty. "Such a grand old Irish name. And I am Sister Mary Bernadette, of no official capacity here anymore."

The little nun rolled every *r*—in fact seemed to choose her words for their *r*'s. The lilt in her voice was musical and quite deliberate, and Erin was charmed.

Sister Mary Bernadette had a pretty, girlish pink complexion made fragile and old by her wrinkles, and her eyes were brown, clear and shiny as polished mahogany. Erin guessed by the way she spoke of "no official capacity anymore" that she had probably once been very much in charge.

"Yes. I am Erin Harper. I'm very pleased to meet you," she said. "And to hear such a beautiful brogue again. My grandfather—" The lump in her throat was so sudden. Between the shock of Miles being struck down and the little nun's achingly familiar accent, Erin was almost in tears.

"You've had quite a day, haven't you, girl?" Mary Bernadette stuck her birdlike arm around Erin's waist and gave a hug. "Come walk along awhile, drink your tea and I'll apologize for makin' you cry."

Erin took a deep breath and gave Sister Mary Bernadette a determined smile as they started down the hallway. "There's no need to apologize—"

"Oh, but I'm not sure the dear Lord would see it that way," Mary Bernadette interrupted, telling on herself with a gleam in her eyes. "When they hold the *real* bonfire of vanities, I'm certain it'll be my brogue that'll have to burn. In the meanwhile, it's all that's left me. You know I've been sent 'round to collect you?" she continued. "Jacob is off on some tangent or other, but Alexa asked me to see you to her office."

Erin combed a handful of hair away from her face as they got onto the elevator down. "I know this doesn't seem possible, Sister, but I've never heard of Jacob or Alexa. The only person I know in Chicago is Miles, and until this morning I hadn't spoken to him in nearly five years." And, put that way, Erin thought, leaving the elevator, what was she doing here at all?

The sister frowned. "According to Jacob— Oh. I forgot. You've never heard of Jacob. Mr. Delvecchio is the president of Rose Memorial's board of directors. Alexa Sabbeth is executive vice-president."

Sister Mary Bernadette hesitated as they came upon the medical-records department, which was locked up and dark as could be. A pile of medical charts in a transfer bin outside the door had snagged her attention. "What in the world?"

Erin knew instantly what troubled Mary Bernadette. Unattended patient records violated the regulations of half a dozen hospital governing agencies. Mary Bernadette muttered something very unsisterly about the way things were run these days and snatched up the armload of charts.

Erin stretched out her hands. "May I carry those for you?"

Mary Bernadette didn't think twice about it before thrusting the charts into Erin's arms. "You're a dear girl, Erin."

She pushed through an almost hidden doorway into the original lobby of the Sisters of Mercy Rose Memorial Hospital. Straight ahead two admissions clerks worked quietly, and an operator sat monitoring an incongruously modern communications system. "Surgical resident to ICU South" came the soothing, lilting voice. "Respiratory therapy, five..."

To Erin's left, ultra modern glass-and-chrome sliding doors triggered by electric eyes encased the aging pillars of the old, original entry into the hospital.

Though in recent years the facility had been bought out by private investors, it retained the heart and soul of its rich ecumenical history. A hardwood floor, darkened with age and the footfalls of many thousands, creaked under Erin's step. A carved wooden crucifix hung in the small lobby, and it was of such an age that the wood of the Savior's thighs had dried and cracked.

Standing beneath the original gas lamps, transfixed by the weight of a hundred years of history and an atmosphere of untold compassion, Erin prompted the sister on their conversation. "According to Mr. Delvecchio..."

Mary Bernadette crossed herself and then turned back to Erin. "According to Jacob, you are Dr. Cornwall's candidate to take over as director of his blood project."

Erin shook her head and took an unconscious step back, clutching the pile of patient charts to her chest. "Sister, that is not at all why I'm here! How can they—how can Mr. Delvecchio believe—" She stopped short. What had Miles done?

The sister shrugged. "One never really knows with Jacob. Perhaps Alexa can explain."

Erin searched Mary Bernadette's expression, but she could find no indication that the sister knew what had caused Miles to tell Erin one thing and the hospital administration another. Nor did she understand the hint of impatience when Mary Bernadette spoke of Alexa Sabbeth.

"Then's it's Ms. Sabbeth's misunderstanding?" she asked.

The sister's lips pursed. "Impossible. Alexa never misunderstands a thing. I believe she is aggravated that, though Dr. Cornwall reported to her, he went to Jacob with his request concerning you."

Erin sighed. Miles was ordinarily a politically adept man, but it sounded as if he had deliberately gone over Alexa Sabbeth's head. "Do you think he can have mistrusted her?"

"Not likely." Sister Mary Bernadette frowned. "Don't get me wrong, Erin. I am actually quite fond of Alexa, but her ambition puts a great many people off—and 'tis one of the seven deadly sins." She paused, considering, causing her wrinkled face to prune up even more. "Or is it? I don't know. I'm not up on my sins anymore. But the girl works day and night. Can't be persuaded to go home. I thought she had, earlier," the sister confided, "but she's back in her office."

Erin felt a little defensive about working day and night. "Maybe it's only that there is so much to do."

"Or perhaps too little faith in the abilities of others." The sister's eyes twinkled, and Erin laughed softly, understanding how thoroughly she had just lumped herself in with Alexa Sabbeth.

Mary Bernadette indicated a shaft of light coming from an office halfway down the darkened hallway. "There you are, dear girl. If you'll kindly hand over the charts to Alexa, I'll leave you now. So much to do, you know."

It wasn't until the birdlike little nun with her habit flapping disappeared around the next corner that Erin caught her tongue-in-cheek admission. *So much to do...* Sister Mary Bernadette was guilty of the same deadly sin.

Erin turned, feeling her weariness eased a little by those few minutes with Sister Mary Bernadette. As she approached the light, a woman appeared in the doorway.

Alexa Sabbeth. A crisp, stylish, cream-colored linen suit flattered her thin frame. Her build was one that always made Erin feel chunky by comparison. She wore her sleek brown hair in a pageboy and, though surely exhausted, she projected the careful blend of efficiency and control Erin valued herself.

Erin transferred the weight of the patient charts onto her left arm and held out her hand. "Alexa Sabbeth?"

"Yes. And you are?"

"Erin Harper. Sister Mary Bernadette brought me down from the O.R. waiting room."

"Oh, Erin! Hello! I'm so sorry. I guess I didn't expect it to be you when I saw the armload of charts." Erin held them out to Alexa, who glanced at the names as she took them. Her brow furrowed unpleasantly. "Where did you get these?"

In no mood to answer for someone else's carelessness, Erin indulged a flash of irritation. "Sister Mary Bernadette picked them up from a bin outside your medical-records department."

"Well, then," Alexa remarked, brightening visibly, "all's well that ends well."

Not really, Erin thought. No one in Alexa Sabbeth's position could afford to dismiss untended confidential records so lightly. But Erin reminded herself the problem wasn't hers—but Miles's problems weren't hers, either, and yet here she was.

Alexa turned back into her office. "Mr. Delvecchio will be gratified that we've connected at last. We've been in somewhat of an uproar here since Miles was struck."

Erin nodded. "Have you had any word from security or the police? I should have thought they might want to talk to me."

Alexa put the charts into a deep desk drawer and locked it. "They're currently tracking down the driver of the food-delivery truck. They did ask to see you as soon as it could be arranged. Tell me, Erin, are you planning to assume Miles's responsibilities on the HemSynon project, or is Jacob out in left field somewhere?"

Erin sensed a level of anxiety to equal her own in Alexa Sabbeth's question. "I was hoping you could tell me. I don't know what Miles said to lead anyone to believe that, but—"

"Then you didn't come here to take over as director of the project?"

"No. Miles told me that his project was at a critical juncture and that he couldn't look at it objectively anymore."

"Meaning what, exactly?" Alexa asked. "He's been reporting to me—and to the board—for months that the research is right on target."

Erin found herself automatically placating. "I'm sure it is. Miles Cornwall is a top-notch research director. It's not that uncommon to ask for an outside audit of a research project—"

"Except that this project requires absolute confidentiality. Not that you would compromise that in any way," Alexa amended. "It's just unnerving that Miles would spring this on me so suddenly."

Erin thought it was actually very in keeping with Miles's style. But even if he had brought her here under false pretenses and then misrepresented what that meant to the Rose Memorial administration, it was still the middle of the night, and Miles was still fighting for his life in surgery.

"Truthfully I don't know what Miles expected. I know the project is vital to him, but unless he survives to explain his reasoning," Erin said, "we have nothing to discuss."

Alexa sighed and shook her head. "You're right. I'm really very sorry. Talk of the project is entirely inappropriate right now." She jerked when her telephone rang. Plucking the receiver out of its cradle, she sank into her deep leather chair and removed an earring. "Sabbeth here."

She glanced quickly up at Erin and nodded to convey that the call concerned Miles. She hung up, then settled back into her chair. Clasping her hands together, she rested her elbows on the desk and touched a forefinger to her lips. Her eyes glistened.

"Miles survived the surgery, but the prognosis isn't good at all. Would you like me to take you to the surgical ICU?"

What Erin would have liked was to awaken in her own bed in her house in Phoenix. To see her aging, snobby little seal point Siamese cat, Priscilla, snarling at her for waking in the middle of the night from a nightmare.

For a woman who kept her world very carefully ordered, Erin thought miserably, for a woman who matched her decor to her cat, the past hours had been pure hell.

She should go home. Ask for the limo or a cab back to O'Hare, get on the first plane heading southwest and go home. She didn't owe Miles Cornwall anything, really. Not her loyalty or even her presence at his deathbed.

But he'd asked for her professional input on a vitally important medical-research project. She had agreed. It was really that simple. She couldn't go without doing what she had agreed to do.

THE HEART-LUNG TRANSPLANT in Operating Room 23 had reached its thirteenth hour by midnight. Staff had rotated twice by then—all but the lead surgeon, Colin Rennslaer, the anesthesiologist, Gordon Munson, substituting for Colin's usual man, Tyler Robards, and Colin's surgical nurse, Ginger Creedy, Texan to her marrow. Everyone knew Ginger to be Rennslaer's right hand, aptly enough, since he was left-handed.

Colin Rennslaer's concentration was absolute. Hours passed. He was aware of a part of his mind following the strains of the Pachelbel Canon, which he chose because it was cultured, classical, cadent and because it said something about him. But the surgical team buzzing around him, serving him, had no doubt of his attention to every crucial detail. They all knew surgeons who were razzle-dazzle, ain't-I-swell? hacks. He wasn't one of them. He had an ego, but he was never too big for his britches and never holier-than-thou.

At the end he tossed the last hemostat into the basin filled with antiseptic solution, stepped back and gave the surgical resident the opportunity to close.

Colin regarded his twenty-year-old patient. No surgery of this duration went without unexpected twists and turns, but nothing gave Colin a high, a surge of pure satisfaction, like coming up roses from a position of pure manure. His patient, Nina Tobias, had her best shot now at living and breathing easily for the first time in her young life.

He shared a quick exchange of glances with Gordon Munson, who had set aside his *Mad Magazine* in deference to winding up this procedure, then hung around long enough to see Nina stabilized in the recovery room. He went to the surgeon's lounge and dictated his postoperative notes. No one ever got on his case for not keeping up with his dictation. He wanted to be the best and brightest and he went on record within the hour of concluding his surgeries.

He snapped open the locker he never bothered locking, threw his jacket on over his scrubs and shouldered his duffel bag. He could have showered then and there, but he wanted to throw together an omelet, wash it down with a glass of sauvignon and soak in his own hot tub.

And he wanted to jet through the rare cool Chicago night in his antique cherry red convertible Jaguar. Run off a little more steam so he could savor his quiet time, play his sax awhile, and sleep.

Light on his feet, he skipped down the stairwell to the first floor. Nearly colliding with Sister Mary Bernadette on his way through the door, Colin treated the old nun to an ill-behaved smile and pecked her on the cheek. "Don't you ever sleep, darlin'?"

The sister drew herself up to her full four feet ten and a half inches. The top of her head hit somewhere around Colin's biceps. "Certainly. But I'm older than the Methuselah, my dear boy." Colin groaned. "I know. Old enough to have bounced St. Peter on your knee. But—"

She smiled. "So, you would agree, beauty rest is rather a lost cause."

He clamped a hand against his chest and leaned theatrically against the wall in the darkened empty hallway. "Another quandary!"

He knew she didn't expect him to agree or disagree. Even in her youth, the sister would not have benefited from beauty rest, but her voice was angelic and Irish and sultry as the lowest note he could achieve on the alto sax he played in a chamber-music ensemble.

He was a sucker for comely sounds. She was pleased that he had recognized the damned-if-you-do, damned-if-you-

don't dilemma, which by now he knew was her chief spor
in life.

She congratulated his surgical success with Nina To
bias—not much that went on in Rose Memorial escape
her—then patted his hand and sent him on his way.

He was feeling somewhat mellowed by his encounter wit
her when he rounded the corner in the physician's garag
and discovered his beloved cherry red Jag missing.

THE HEART MONITOR GLOWED an eerie amber in the dark
ened postoperative ICU 17. Yards of tubing hung from
multiple IV med bags and fed into the needles positione
in Miles's veins.

Flexible, pleated tubing the diameter of a garden hos
was strung from his slackened mouth to the whooshing
ventilator. His hapless body was covered by crisp whit
hospital linens, and his thinning blond hair seemed plas
tered to his head.

Erin's throat throbbed. It didn't matter that she ha
worked in a room like this before, that she had taken car
of patients like this or that this intensive-care unit was a
familiar to her as if she'd worked here her whole life.

Miles lay dying in that bed, and medicine was still suc
a barbaric practice—invading, stitching, stapling. Sh
couldn't seem to breathe. He'd been her friend and men
tor and fiancé, and though he'd finally betrayed her, she'
once respected him. Even loved him.

Thinking now of the things that made him so mortal, s
human, Erin clamped her lips together. He might be
world-class researcher, but he couldn't manage a simpl
checking account, and his attention span at a special din
ner out was no better than that of a second-grader.

He had respected her work but denied her doctoral dissertation. And now he needed her. He was a first-rate louse, but he didn't deserve this end.

She could smell death on him. Her hands curled tightly around the cold metal bed rail. He would want them to fight for his life to the last blip on the monitor. It wasn't that she didn't believe in saving lives. She did. But the truth was, the high-tech life support engulfing him now only prolonged his death.

She swept a tear from her cheek with her forefinger, then covered Miles's hand with her own. His skin felt hot and dry. He made no unconscious move to grasp her fingers with his own, but seemed all at once to be fighting the respirator. Her heart twisted painfully. She'd seen countless patients do that before—struggling to take one last breath on their own.

Her own throat swelled. "Hang in there, Miles," she whispered. But in her most guarded professional judgment, she knew Miles wouldn't last until dawn no matter how hard he tried. "Who are you?"

Erin straightened and looked toward the sliding glass door, thinking this might be Miles's surgeon. A man—tall and lean and broad shouldered—filled the entrance. The harsh fluorescent lighting behind him cast a halo on his silhouette, and his shoulders tilted as he leaned into the frame of the door.

"Well?" His body language was clear to her. He expected an answer to his question, and he was used to getting exactly what he wanted when he wanted it.

"Erin Harper. Who—"

"Colin Rennslaer," he supplied, moving into the room. "I'm looking for Delvecchio. I was told he would be here."

In spite of herself, Erin felt the stab of feminine interest. *The walking cliché who had to be seen to be believed....*

The quintessentially dangerous, prowling male. His features were clean-cut and strong. A full masculine jaw, dark, heavy eyebrows that accented a fine bone structure, a head of dark, shiny, razor-cut hair. The imperfections made him human, and more dangerous.... The night's growth of whiskers, the way a surgical cap had compressed his hair, the wrinkled, raw linen sport coat he'd thrown over sweat-stained raspberry surgical scrubs.

Erin knew Colin Rennslaer's type. The world was expected to revolve around him, and most of the time it did. She wasn't prepared to fall into his orbit, or for her own nerves to react like a small pile of iron filings streaming toward a magnet.

"I haven't seen Mr. Delvecchio," she answered at last. "I haven't seen anyone. My best guess is that he's out looking—"

"For my car?" Rennslaer gave a quick, curt nod. "Good."

"Your car?" "Yeah." He moved into the room and gave a weary grin. "A cherry red antique Jaguar. They don't come any sweeter."

Erin shook her head. If Miles hadn't been lying there near to death, she would have teased, given him a hard time for having lost his pretty toy and needing someone to find it. But it annoyed her to be standing over Miles's deathbed and finding Rennslaer's grin the least bit engaging. "Is Miles's surgeon anywhere around?"

"Miles?" Frowning, he went for the patient chart slotted just outside the door and held up the covered clipboard to the light behind him. "This is Miles Cornwall?"

"Yes." Erin nodded, thinking Rennslaer must have been directed to ICU 17 without benefit of a name.

He flipped through pages of chart notes, then strode into the room and stood across Miles's bed from Erin. He wore silent, rubber-soled clogs, and his feet were bare inside them. She wished she hadn't noticed.

He tossed the chart on the foot of the bed and pulled a stethoscope out of his suit-coat pocket. Staring off into space, he listened at several points to Miles's sutured chest and abdomen, then fixed his eyes on her as he listened some more. "What happened, do you know?"

"Yes." It unnerved her that he paid attention to her while she answered rather than hearing the reply and nodding vaguely. That he was still regarding her with his shadowed eyes, waiting for her to explain. "A hit-and-run accident, at about nine o'clock."

"You were there?"

"Yes. Do you know Miles?"

"Yeah." Straightening, he pulled the stethoscope from his ears, tucked it back into his pocket and then palpated Miles's abdomen gently. "We're on a couple of committees together—morbidity and mortality. Transfusion services." His heavy eyebrows came together. "Wasn't he supposed to be presenting the board with the final FDA recommendations on HemSynon tonight?"

"That's what I've been told."

"Are you family, Erin Harper?"

"No. An old friend... a colleague of Miles."

"Which is it?" he asked, narrowing his shadowed eyes.

"We... It doesn't matter."

He gave her an odd look. Speculative. Then a slow half smile, as if to agree that it didn't matter. "How did you happen to be here at exactly the right moment to see Miles run down?"

She didn't want to be attracted to Colin Rennslaer, but he had a way about him that made her feel very much... attended. Even while he was evaluating Miles's condition. Almost as if he cared.

"Miles asked me to come."

Rennslaer replaced the sheet over Miles's chest. "Why?"

"To do an outside evaluation of his research project."

"On HemSynon? I wasn't aware we needed an outside audit." Scraping the backs of his knuckles over his eyes, he looked very, very tired. "Look, I'm going to go get a dose of the sludge they call coffee down here. Can I bring you a cup?"

"I'd like that very much. Thanks." The offer surprised her. Colin Rennslaer might be the hunk of Rose Memorial, full of himself and bent out of shape over having lost his car, but Erin was never tempted to ignore the fact that he was a man with the rare skill—and the sheer nerve—to transplant a human heart and lungs. Entitled to the ego that the job required, but not above going for the coffee himself.

She took the coffee gratefully when he returned.

"A smile. That's better." He studied Miles's breathing for a moment, then went back for another chair. "Take a load off."

Erin gave Miles another brief once-over herself, then sat and sipped the thick brew of coffee.

"So what do you know about the project?"

"Almost nothing." Erin settled her arms onto the armrests and leaned back into the easy chair. "Synthetic blood is a hot topic right now. There are probably half a dozen research teams fully funded and committed to getting a product on the market."

"Exactly." Colin slumped in the hard plastic chair he had retrieved, crossing a bare ankle over his knee. "Not a moment to spare. Delvecchio would sell his soul for Rose Memorial to bring out the first artificial blood product."

"It's that close, then?"

"We think so. The meeting tonight was on my schedule, but when a heart-lung comes available, you don't stand on prior commitments."

"No," Erin reflected. She glanced over her shoulder at the cardiac monitor. "I guess you don't." Miles's heart rhythms were thready, threatening to collapse. She slid her hand atop Miles's again, but when an IV monitor beeped, signaling a break in the flow, she reached automatically to shut it off and check the drip-rate valves.

Rennslaer gave her a questioning lift of his elegantly masculine eyebrows.

She gave the monitor one last check, then sat down again. "I'm an R.N. I've been moonlighting in intensive care off and on since I got out of college."

"Then I'm really confused. How are you qualified to consult on a research project of this importance?"

Vaguely annoyed at the implication that she wasn't qualified, she knew his question was a legitimate one and should be asked.

"I worked in clinical research in order to afford graduate school in hospital risk management."

"Ahh. Making sure the doctors don't spend too much money trying to save lives."

"Money is part of it, of course. But making sure people get the care they need is just as important. Anyway, Miles was my boss, and I directed research teams of my own."

"Any major successes?"

Erin nodded. "Yes. One of my teams managed to bring an insulin-delivery project to completion—through the FDA maze, that kind of thing."

"Managed?" Colin grinned. "You say that as if it were an odd skill you picked up somewhere."

"Well, it is, sort of."

"Not unlike heart surgery," he remarked. "Take it apart, fix it, put it back together. What could be more simple than that?"

Erin laughed softly. Heaven help her, Colin Rennslaer was extraordinarily talented, handsome, arrogant, purely male, careless enough of custom to get the coffee himself and . . . funny.

"Okay. But directing research just paid the bills."

"The bane of postgraduate school." Colin drained the last of his coffee. "We used to call it slave labor."

"Exactly. But you think I should take credit for what amounts to getting people to do what they should have been doing anyway?"

Colin smirked. "Yes."

"Glory-monger."

"Unabashed."

But if he were, Erin thought, he wouldn't be sitting around a darkened intensive-care unit, taking note of every blip on Miles's monitors. "Is it hard, making yourself appear to be so shallow?"

"All part of my inimitable charm." He gave a smile his mother was surely only the first to weep for. "No more difficult, anyway, than for you to take the credit for making your team the success it was."

Erin sighed. The achievement hadn't made a fig's difference in the end. Miles had still blocked her degree. She rose from the chair and went to stand by the floor-to-ceiling window. In the silence the hiss of the respirator seemed magnified. The black of night reflected Miles's deathbed and the relentless life-sustaining equipment surrounding him, and Erin felt the old resentments surfacing once more.

"I don't get it, Harper," Colin said, missing nothing, his voice low and probing. "Why aren't you out making the life-and-death, dollars-and-cents decisions about health care with your fancy risk-management credentials?''

Erin stiffened and turned toward him. "Because I never completed the degree."

"Why not?"

"I quit."

But she must have given herself away, glanced too quickly at Miles or studied the IV drip too intently, because Rennslaer shook his head slowly, his gesture calling her on the lie.

Her resentment over what Miles had done transferred all too easily to Colin Rennslaer. He had no business slitting into her feelings. *Her* emotions. Her history. But in one deft, uncanny moment he had managed to carve away from her every protection she had ever invented.

He might as well have stripped her bare.

Chapter Two

Light glinted off the dark chest hairs spilling from the V-neck of his scrubs. The scrub pants that should have hung loose fitted him too snugly by far, but in all the right places.

His eyes, whose color she had still not seen, were deep in shadows. She felt them on her. Her breasts tightened as if he had touched her. He had done nothing more than ask his question, but Erin was neither naive nor unwitting enough to believe he hadn't intended his question to expose her.

She shivered and gave a mocking half smile. "Didn't you get enough practice with your scalpel tonight, Dr. Rennslaer?"

He gave her the same sort of smile in answer, but he wasn't going to let her off. "How did he do it, Erin?"

She shook her head and turned to stare at the reflections in the window. It surprised her to feel the resentments she had thought long since buried.

She'd been enamored with Miles Cornwall, with his incredible energy and wit and brilliance. When he had asked her to marry him, she agreed. Within weeks he'd begun to scare her with his intensity and his attempts to control every waking thought she had, and with his habit of sitting night after night editing her dissertation for her until she didn't recognize her own work.

"He was in love with you, wasn't he?" Colin asked, somehow taking from her silence how complicated her history with Miles was. And again his insight took her breath away.

She pursed her lips. There was an intimacy that sitting together in a darkened room with a man's life at stake fostered. Rennslaer sat there quietly expecting that because he had bared part of her soul, she would reveal the rest of it.

Something in her wanted to take the chance, once and for all, of letting it all go. Or maybe she was simply too worn-out from the strain of the night's events to keep her mouth shut.

She swallowed and met Colin's shadowed, waiting eyes. "Yes. He was in love with me. Whatever that meant to him."

"What happened?"

"He persuaded the jury to delay the decision on my dissertation pending certain . . . revisions."

"Which were?"

She shrugged and returned to her chair. "All he really wanted was for me to present the draft he had edited."

"You refused?"

"Yes."

"Why?"

"Because it wouldn't have been my work. Does that sound terribly vain?"

"No," he answered. "Stubborn, maybe. A little expensive." He sat forward and reached out to prevent her biting at a ragged fingernail. Only he didn't let go of her fingers. He just held them lightly in the warmth of his hand.

His touch made the awareness between them soar. Erin tilted her head. Intimacy like this never lasted beyond the moment, in a darkened room where confidences seemed to come so indiscreetly, and she knew the exquisite sensation would fade, as well.

"Well, anyway. There you are. You cut, I bleed. See what happens when you forget you've got a scalpel in your hand?"

He laughed and let go of her, which she told herself was what she had wanted. "I should apologize. It's just...well, cutting is what I do best."

"Yeah," she returned softly. "I see. But I'm not your patient, Colin."

He tilted his head. "I'll try not to think of you like that again."

Ahh, the dangerous flirtation, Erin thought. He wasn't thinking of her as a patient at all. Did he think that staring into his shadowed eyes and whiskered jaw was enough to make her lose her head?

This was either the most evolved come-on in history—or the most primitive *me Tarzan, you Jane.* In either case she was not falling for it.

She thought to tell him not to bother thinking of her at all, but he let the fierce awareness between them fade and asked, "So what have you done since?"

She reached for her handbag and pulled out a nail file to take care of the edge she'd been tempted to bite, thinking about the twists and turns her life had taken since Miles. The truth was she owed him a debt of gratitude because she'd finally discovered what she'd been searching for all along.

"I've almost completed my work for a doctorate in medical ethics."

"Not, I assume, to decide whether we should clone human beings," Colin joked.

"Well, I have an opinion on that, but no. To practice in a hospital setting."

A nurse came by to check on the status of Miles's IV medications. She was clearly surprised that Colin was still around. He reminded her that his car was missing, gave her a smile and told her he'd be right here in case anything came up. When she'd gone, he turned back to his conversation with Erin. "How did you get interested in ethics?"

"I worked with a firm of attorneys for a couple of years, helping evaluate malpractice claims. There are a hundred frivolous cases for every one that deserves the scrutiny."

"Two hundred."

"Spoken like a true physician." Erin smiled. "But after a while I got involved with the cases brought by people who were forced into life-and-death decisions about loved ones—judgments that most of us have no experience in making."

Colin shifted in his seat. "Come on, Erin. You don't really think it's any easier for doctors to make those judgment calls."

"Not easier at all."

People got sick and died, and doctors were the ones who got to stand up and admit that no matter what they tried, nothing was likely to work. She knew that too well.

"Harder, maybe," she continued, "because families want the doctors to tell them what to do. But if you have to put someone on life support, the family suddenly has the press second-guessing them, the hospital bean counters worrying about their liability, lawyers fighting, judges issuing orders. It isn't only doctors, you know. None of us knows where to draw the line anymore."

"And you really want to get in the middle of all that?"

"Someone has to."

"Like *someone* has to step in and save the HemSynon project?" He didn't wait for her answer. "Don't you ever ask yourself, why me?"

"Hardly ever," she returned. "My housemate, who is also a therapist, says I am a classic codependent rescuer scanning my environment at every moment for a desperate situation into which I can throw myself. Feature presentation, *Erin and the Volcano.*"

Colin laughed. "So, okay. You reject Miles, he rejects you, but meanwhile he's figured out that you can't be bought, bribed or blackmailed. He was obviously familiar with your work. If he thought he needed an outside evaluation this late in the game, it makes sense that he would ask you."

"Superficially I suppose it does." Erin ran her fingers anxiously through her hair, already caught up again in Miles's scheme. The constant mechanical hiss of the respirator was numbing, and this room was a haven compared to the frenzy of activity around the rest of the surgical ICU. Patients were streaming in now from the overfilled trauma rooms of the medical unit.

Against that background she thought she could detect an attempt to allay her confusion.

"Why superficial?"

Erin straightened. Thirty minutes ago she'd have thought Colin was surely only sticking around in hopes that Delvecchio would soon come around to announce that Colin's missing Jag was not missing at all, but someone's twisted idea of a practical joke. But that wasn't true. Colin seemed to care very much what became of the HemSynon project.

Too much?

So much that he could ignore the exhaustion of seventeen hours in surgery, not to mention his missing Jag?

She had no way of knowing. Perhaps he *was* just killing time while someone turned up his car. "For one thing, I have only a vague idea what HemSynon is about."

Colin shook his head. "You know more than you think, Erin," he said. "It's risk management at the most basic level. Transfusing blood is dangerous. You're a nurse. You know that. First we have to cross-match—and there are hundreds more antigens than the ABO and Rh types everyone knows. Every time we transfuse we run the risk of sensitizing the patient with one of the subtypes."

"And being synthetic, HemSynon can be transfused regardless of the patient's blood type?" Erin queried.

"Exactly." He sat up out of his slump. "Doesn't matter whether you're an AB pos or an O negative."

"Which," Erin mused, "makes it invaluable even before you throw in the risk of transfusion-transmitted diseases."

Colin nodded his approval of her appreciation of the issues. He pinched the bridge of his nose, his attentive glance passing over the monitors connected to Miles. "Of course, every unit of blood is tested, but in the case of AIDS, one in every quarter-million negative tests is going to be wrong."

Mistakes, Erin thought, that seemed coldly clinical when reduced to numbers. For labs to be wrong only once in two hundred and fifty thousand tests was nearly impossible. In human terms that *one* was staggering.

"Not very comforting, is it, if you're the one who gets that unit of blood?"

"No." Colin grimaced. "There's something almost... menacing about it."

"A death lottery." Erin shivered. People would rather take almost any chance than risk getting infected by the AIDS virus. Two months ago she'd had the care of a man who was the sole support of his family. He had refused any blood transfusion, and though he survived the surgery to repair his esophagus and stomach ulcers, he hadn't survived his loss of blood. His heart had worked too hard pumping too little blood, and the thirty-seven-year-old had died of cardiac arrest.

"Will it really work?" she asked softly, wondering again if Colin had a personal stake in Miles's project.

"HemSynon? It'll transform the practice of medicine. Cancer patients, kidney-dialysis patients, surgical, trauma. It's hard to believe Miles told you nothing about it."

Erin said nothing. In her experience physicians often responded to new treatments with the same kind of enthusiasm as Colin's soft baritone conveyed. He wouldn't need a personal stake in the HemSynon project to be excited about its potential. What if he had one anyway? And why did it matter?

But it did matter. Miles had spent his last conscious breath to tell her the project had been sabotaged. But what did that mean? Theft? Reporting false test results? Concealing side effects? Obstructing progress? The list of possibilities here was very long indeed, and the only thing Erin could know for sure was that Miles no longer trusted anyone involved with HemSynon.

Colin's familiarity with the project aroused a warning alarm in her. He had been sitting with her in Miles's room for well over an hour. The nurse who'd come in a little while ago had been dumbfounded to find him still waiting there, and the truth was, Erin didn't believe it was his missing Jaguar that kept him waiting, either.

Colin looked steadily at her, stroking his long, lean surgeon's fingers over taut muscles in his neck. "Erin, what are you doing here?"

She wanted to believe that he was asking because he knew she had a life and important career aspirations of her own, and not because he had anything to do with the sabotage of the HemSynon project. His question made her uneasy, but she couldn't imagine his being involved in anything like sabotage to a major research project.

She shrugged and answered indifferently. "I had a week before the semester begins."

"A few free days isn't a reason, Erin. Based on what you've told me, you don't owe Miles Cornwall the time of day."

"That's probably why," she answered.

"You've lost me."

She got out of her chair and went once more to the window. The reflections from inside prevented her seeing much of the trees and flowers. Her own feelings about being here seemed equally veiled, and she didn't know if she could explain them at all.

"Miles called me in the middle of the night. He said he had arranged for a flight here and that it was absolutely vital I be on that plane."

Colin had gotten up, as well, and stretched. He came to stand near her and leaned into the glass with one shoulder. Her eyes were on the level of the hair curling above the V-neck of his scrub top.

"He didn't say why?"

She shook her head. "No, other than that he needed an outside audit of a very critical project. I told him—God, I couldn't even believe it was him—I told him it was impossible." Her stomach burned, exactly as it had when she first recognized Miles's voice. "He said he knew he didn't have any right to ask—but that's exactly the reason I should see how important this was."

"So in other words, if he thought he had a choice, he would rather have shot himself in the foot than ask you for anything."

Colin's pithy metaphor went straight to the heart of all her frustration and weariness and anger, and Erin was

mortified because a small cry escaped her and tears prickled her already scratchy eyelids.

Why hadn't she told Miles what he could do with his
precious project? She was angry at herself, at Miles, at the
hit and run... and Colin Rennslaer made a handy scapegoat. She didn't want his sympathy or his touch, but he
took the fist she'd pressed to her lips and held it against his
chest in both his hands. She let him. Worse, she liked it.

"What is it, Erin?"

She felt the vibrations of his voice in his chest, and she
had to fight liking that, too. "He made this mangled analogy about how my cat would never ask a sardine if it
minded serving as her lunch. So if she did, I would know
something was terribly wrong."

He let go with one hand and circled her shoulders with
his arm, overcoming her resistance, pulling her close. She
rested her forehead against Colin Rennslaer's whiskered
chin, telling herself she was too tired and emotionally
drained to do anything else....

He smelled of sweat and a hazelnut-scented scrub solution. She closed her eyes and inhaled the scent again, los-
ing herself in the soothing, subtle pleasure of his arms
around her. His body radiated heat, and hers absorbed it.
He breathed, and she felt his pectorals rise and fall beneath her hand.

He kissed her temple and then the corner of her mouth.
Desire rippled through her, lingering even after he had
ended the kiss.

She reminded herself one more time that she must be
immune where Colin was concerned. Straightening, she
backed out of his embrace and groped for something, anything to say to dispel her startling attraction.

"Do you know why Miles believed that something had
gone so terribly wrong?"

Colin frowned. "No. None. Did you think I would?"

"For a surgeon, you seem very familiar with the project." Her body still hummed, and she felt defensive. "That kind of involvement seems unusual before a product goes into clinical trials, doesn't it?" He wasn't answerable to her, and she knew her question would provoke him.

But he was not defenseless. He stared hard at her for a moment, as if he knew her harsh questions had more to do with her reaction to him than with Miles's project. His head went up, and he gave her a private sort of smile. "It was only a kiss, Erin."

"My mistake," she returned, despising herself for feeling cheated.

Whatever he'd expected, that response wasn't it. He seemed chastened. He fixed his eyes on hers. "I'm sorry. That was a cheap shot." He shrugged, and his gaze fell to the corner of her mouth. "It wasn't even the truth."

She felt the ripple of desire pass through her again, stronger. "Will you answer the question? Please?"

"We worked very closely on computer models. Miles wanted clinical input. He wanted to know in minute detail how the HemSynon molecule compared with current blood-oxygenating technologies. Frankly he asked for my opinion every step of the way. As far as I was concerned, the project was on target."

"Then why did he think he needed me?"

"We're left with two choices, Erin. Either he'd gone over the edge, or he knew exactly what he was doing. Considering what HemSynon meant to him, which is it, do you think?"

"Neither," Erin snapped. She didn't know. More importantly at the moment, she didn't know why or how Colin Rennslaer had turned her inside out.

Why a man who shouldn't have had the time or inclination sat with her anyway.... Why he kissed her, acted as if it meant nothing and then bothered to admit that wasn't true.... Why he persisted in believing Miles was right to have called her when he didn't really know her from Eve, and then acted as if she should go home anyway.

She refused to feel flattered. "It was never a simple case of *this* or *that,* and—" Erin broke off. Miles might very well die without ever having the chance to explain, but she could never say that in his presence. "It's really none of your business anyway, is it?"

Colin took the easy chair that Erin had been sitting in, folded his hands over his abdomen, dropped a leather clog and rested a bare foot on his knee. "Why don't you tell me what you really think, Erin?"

"I think you should go home."

"You're the one who should go home, Erin. I can assure you the project will go on without you." He glared impatiently at her, remembering why he was sitting with her in the first place. "Besides, I would go if I had a car. *My* car."

She glared back. "There are taxis, just for occasions like this. Or maybe Delvecchio will order up a limousine—"

Mile's heart monitor went silent, flat-lined and then wailed. Colin was out of his slump and his flash of anger in a split second. Watching the monitor, throwing down the bed rail, he delivered an expert, glancing blow of his fist to Miles's chest. Another, then again.

Again. Again.

On her feet, as well, Erin glanced with practiced efficiency at the status of his IVs and the placement of the respirator tube. She punched on the overhead light. Anticipating Colin, she held the respirator mouthpiece in place and the chest tube draining into the Hemovac unit.

"Get a crash cart in here. Procaine. Now!"

"Colin, wait. He's already getting intravenous procaine." She knew he knew that. He was no green intern, but she wanted him to think twice about putting Miles through a resuscitation attempt when they both knew he wouldn't survive it.

She knew he knew that, too.

"Anybody die and appoint you God, Harper?" he snapped, and for the first time she could see that his eyes were an unlikely piercing hazel blue. And that he was absolutely serious.

So was she. "No, but—"

"Then either glove up and help, or get your pretty little fanny out of my way. Your choice, but get the damn crash cart in here *now*."

Erin turned on her heel and went for the cart. It wasn't hard to recognize. All crash carts came on wheels for easy movement to the bedside and were stocked with life-saving meds and equipment. Dressed in her gray stirrup slacks and a navy silk blouse, she ought to have been challenged for touching the cart, but every nurse, orderly and doctor in the place seemed up to his or her elbows in some critical procedure on some other patient.

All she wanted was for Miles to have the dignity of a peaceful death, but she brushed a tear aside and went into her professional role. The decision had been made by a physician to resuscitate. She didn't have to like it. She *didn't* like it, but she would assist as ordered.

She wheeled the cart around, manhandled it into Miles's room and jerked open one narrow drawer after another, searching for the megadose procaine with a needle long enough to deliver it straight into Miles's heart.

She ripped open a sterile pair of gloves and grabbed a pair for Colin. These days, where blood was likely, you didn't perform any procedure without them. Not if you wanted a job, not even if you were a doctor.

Colin snatched the gloves up and had them on instantly. She struggled with her left one, then handed him the prepackaged procaine. He felt a moment for a landmark—ribs above the heart, moved outside the field for Erin to swab Miles's chest with Betadine, then drove the long needle straight through the chest wall to Miles's heart.

Colin was rewarded with a pathetic blip, followed by a pattern of more useless blips. Nothing the most hopeful bystander could call a cardiac rhythm. Knowing the danger of repeated blows to the chest, he tore aside the sheet and called for the paddles.

Erin squeezed a dollop of gel directly onto one paddle. Colin slapped them together to spread the gel, then applied them to Miles's chest, one directly over his sternum, the other just below Miles's left nipple.

"Stand clear."

He delivered the jolt, focused on the monitor, ordered Erin to adjust for a higher dose, then zapped Miles again with another jolt of current.

Miraculously a thready rhythm returned.

"Yes! Yes!" Colin whispered under his breath, urging Miles to live.

But Miles chose not to. At least, that was what Erin wanted to believe. Knowing his time was up, Miles had gathered himself together for one last moment of life, a moment of choice, and let go.

Even Colin, who would do whatever it took, had to see that. Erin couldn't blame him. Physicians fought off death. That's what they were trained to do, and that's what they did. But for all Colin's trouble, for all his skill and might and determination, Miles had flat-lined, just as she had known he would.

He'd have died no matter what, and Erin resented the necessity of making Miles's last moments of life so godawfully traumatic.

Colin set aside the paddles, silenced the ventilator and pulled off his gloves, discarding them in the biohazard trash. Dark smudges like hematomas lurked beneath Colin's eyes, and she could see now the day's growth of mahogany whiskers sprinkled with silver that had darkened his jaw.

He must have seen the helpless anger in her. He fixed his surprising hazel-blue eyes on her. His words seemed to scrape by his throat. "He wasn't a DNR, Erin. I had to—"

He was interrupted by a small knot of men and Alexa Sabbeth gathering at the door.

"Dr. Rennslaer, Ms. Harper. I'm Jacob Delvecchio." Accompanied by a couple of uniformed security guards, he was dressed exactly as Erin had imagined him—pinstripes, paisley tie, brown wing tips. He was shorter than Alexa by a scant inch, stocky and unrelentingly Italian in his darkly handsome features and animated gestures.

Colin turned, a frown of irritation at the interruption on his face. "Yes?"

"Doctor, I just wanted first to welcome Ms. Harper aboard." He turned to Erin. "I'm in your debt for coming. Alexa has filled me in on your qualifications, and I'm sure you'll manage to bring Miles's project in."

She had no chance either to acknowledge the introductions or correct his assumptions. The uniformed security men were shifting anxiously from foot to foot, Alexa looked grave, and Delvecchio turned to Colin.

"Doctor, I have some unfortunate news. Security and the Chicago police have identified your Jaguar as the vehicle that struck down and killed Miles Cornwall."

Chapter Three

It seemed to Colin that every able body in the surgical intensive-care unit had stopped in midsentence. He didn't
think this was a practical joke, twisted or not. His car, his
precious cherry red Jag, had been filched from the physician's lot and dealt Miles Cornwall's death. He didn't believe it.

He couldn't believe it.

Apparently everyone else could, though Erin Harper
looked more disoriented now than at the moment Miles had
died.

"My car," he repeated.

One of the security team, the pencil-necked one with
blond hair, chimed in. "There were two eyewitnesses,
Doctor. The men in the delivery truck. The driver is a real
nut case on antique sports cars, and he recognized a '69
Jag. Not to mention your license plate—Too Cool. Nobody forgets that, I don't imagine."

"Too Cool?" Erin repeated, looking up at him for some
redeeming explanation. "You paid money to send that kind
of message?"

"The car, not me," Colin snapped. He swallowed hard.
If he thought Sister Mary Bernadette had a comely voice,
Erin Harper's made him hum inside like a string on a cello,

but the sensation clashed with her meaning. He didn't want to be responsible for Cornwall's death, even in the most roundabout way, and he didn't want to get into justifying a damn license plate. How could anyone have used his car to kill Miles Cornwall? "Where is it now?"

Delvecchio started to reassure Colin the way any hospital administrator caters to his physicians, but the second security guard cleared his throat. Tugging thoughtfully at his double chin, he interrupted Delvecchio's placating. "We were hoping you could tell us, Doctor."

Even in her dazed, weary state Erin thought there must be some mistake. Why would security be asking him what he knew about where his car was when he'd been in surgery half the night?

The tendons in Colin's muscular neck stuck out like inch-thick rope, and he towered over Delvecchio.

"Did you bother informing these gentlemen that I just wound up a seventeen-hour transplant?"

"Colin, for goodness' sake, calm down," Alexa interjected. "Nobody is accusing you of being the hit-and-run driver. These men simply need to know if you lent your car to anyone—"

"No, I didn't lend my car to anyone." He scowled. "Isn't parking security your job, Alexa?"

"Yes," she retorted. "But that's kind of irrelevant now, isn't it? The question now is, could someone have borrowed the car without your permis—"

"Not if they valued their damn necks."

"Did anyone unauthorized have access to your keys, sir?" the pencil neck asked.

Colin looked at him as if he'd lost his mind. The car was gone, which necessarily meant that someone bloody "unauthorized" had the keys or the skills germane to stealing the Jag without them.

"Come on. It's their job to ask these things, Colin."

He gave Alexa a hard, bottom-line, this-is-your-fault sort of look, then reached for the duffel bag he'd stashed under the nurses' station desk. He pulled from a zippered pocket a set of keys on a brass ring.

"Satisfied?" He drew a deep breath. Clearly no epithet was equal to his frustration. The keys were accounted for, but the vintage Jag was gone.

"Think about access, Colin," Alexa persisted, subtly shifting blame away from herself. "You've never bothered getting a lock on your locker. Isn't it possible that someone might have taken the keys and returned them during the night?"

"Yeah," Colin answered, glowering. "And it's equally possible that someone hot-wired the engine and took off out of the 'secured' area."

Erin sympathized with him. After so many sleepless hours, and after Miles's death, Colin Rennslaer had had one beast of a night and now he was being held answerable for his car.

"Well, that's the problem with vintage cars," the more substantial guard said. "They don't have the keypad locks or any modern security measures built in. Anyway, the police strongly suspect the hit and run was incidental to the theft of your car."

"Incidental?" Erin echoed. Miles's death was *incidental?*

"Yes, ma'am. A vintage vehicle this caliber is a prime target for theft. No one would deliberately commit a hit and run in a high-profile custom Jaguar. Dr. Cornwall was just in the wrong place at the wrong time."

Or else, Erin thought darkly, Miles had been in precisely the right place at the expected time. He had discovered the sabotage. Someone had a vital interest in seeing that Miles never made it to that board meeting.

AFTERWARD, NEAR DAWN, Sister Mary Bernadette took charge of Erin's comfort. Delvecchio and Alexa left for a breakfast meeting with their department directors. Colin departed to shower, check on his transplant patient and begin his teaching rounds. Sister Mary Bernadette volunteered to make the call to Miles's daughter, but Erin felt obligated to relay the news.

It was in the sister's little corner office, a room the size of a cell with a plain desk, two straight chairs, a crucifix and a lovely ivy needlepoint by Mary Bernadette's own hand, that Erin sat to make the call. Though it was early yet, only six-thirty in the morning where Miles's eldest daughter, Joyce, lived in Stockton, California, Erin felt the call shouldn't wait. She retrieved the number Alexa had provided from Miles's personnel file while the sister called the hospital operator for a WATS line.

Mary Bernadette broke into an infectious grin. "Modern doodads! Think what Abbott and Costello could have done with WATS lines."

Smiling, Erin suspected that the tiny little old nun went about easing bleak hearts wherever she was called upon to go, and places she wasn't. The very soul of Rose Memorial, everything to everyone. Her presence had broken Erin's tension, but the task ahead of her remained.

Erin gave the operator the number and waited. Joyce Crabtree was only three years younger than Erin, and she had already been in and out of three failed marriages. The last Erin knew, she had moved into a shelter for battered wives. Even if she was on her feet again now, four years later, the news of her father's death was going to hurt.

Two thousand miles away Joyce answered the telephone. Erin held Sister Mary Bernadette's hand across the scarred desk. "Joyce, this is Erin Harper calling. Do you remember—"

"Oh, my God. Something has happened to Daddy, hasn't it?"

"Yes.... Joyce, I... He died this morning, less than an hour ago."

"Are you there, in Chicago?"

"Yes. I—"

"Then Daddy called you?"

Distractedly Erin let go of Mary Bernadette's hand and sat back. "Did you know he was going to call me, Joyce?"

"I'm not surprised," she answered, her voice wavering. "He phoned me, too. Probably just before he called you. I thought he sounded terribly depressed. He asked me if he thought you would hang up on him if he called."

Trying to understand what had gone on, Erin studied Mary Bernadette's gnarled fingers caressing her rosary beads. "Joyce, none of this makes any sense to me. Did your father tell you why he wanted to speak to me?"

"In a way." Joyce's voice broke on a small sob. It took her a moment to compose herself over the whining of children in the background. "Did you know he had been seeing someone there? Someone who also worked at Rose Memorial?"

"No. But—"

"Well, he was. I think he was very hopeful for this relationship, Erin. But when he called he said that now he knew exactly what he had put you through."

The sister's rosary beads clicked in a slow cadence as she progressed along the length of the strand. Erin wished for one tenth the peacefulness they seemed to impart to Mary Bernadette. "Joyce, that's all ancient history."

"Maybe. But I don't think so, Erin. I think he was terribly in love with someone who betrayed him, and he wanted to apologize to you because he finally understood."

Miles had conveyed nothing like that when he had called Erin. "Did he *say* that?"

"Not in so many words, but—" She broke off, and Erin could hear a child crying in the background, then Joyce's muffled voice summoning another child to look after her brother. "Erin, why are you in Chicago?"

"He asked me to consult on his research project, but apparently he told the administration here that I would be assuming responsibility for it."

Joyce laughed, but it wasn't a pleasant sound. "How typical. Will you do it?" she asked. "Because, after all, what was the point of Dad's existence if all his precious work is lost?"

His daughter's bitterness came as no surprise to Erin. Even in her own short relationship with Miles, the research had always come first. Foremost and always. People didn't matter in the larger scheme of things, and their feelings mattered even less. Even his own, Erin guessed, because he hadn't said one word to her about having been betrayed by someone he loved.

"Joyce, I don't think—"

"Erin," Joyce interrupted tersely. "I have to go now. I'll just say this. The only reason Dad would have called you was that he didn't trust his precious Hem-whatever to anyone else. God knows, that's all he really cared about. I'll make the arrangements, but I won't be flying out for the funeral. Goodbye, Erin."

Sister Mary Bernadette took the receiver from Erin when she let it fall away from her ear, and recradled it. "Shall I call her again in a few hours?'' Mary Bernadette asked. ''Perhaps to help her with the arrangements?''

Erin nodded. ''I'm sure Joyce would appreciate that very much,'' she replied, thinking Mary Bernadette would most certainly handle the details with dispatch. ''She doesn't intend to be here for the funeral.''

''Is she taking her father's death very hard?''

''I suppose so, in her own way. She'd like her father's life to have gone for something. Miles was never available, never there for anyone, even his girls.''

The sister rose and glided around her desk to stroke Erin's short hair with her gnarled hand. She smelled of soap and hand cream, and her habit flowed so near to Erin that she felt nearly enveloped. She knew the respite was temporary, though. There had been something ominous in the truth of Joyce's remark.

Miles would not have left his project to the slightest mischance.

''What is troubling you so, Erin?''

''This all seems so...bizarre.'' Despite the soothing touch of the sister's hand on her head, Erin felt a sense of foreboding that Miles was accomplishing in death what he hadn't in life—bringing Erin Harper to heel at last. ''It's as if I've wandered into this dark, twisted nightmare. I know if I wake up it'll go away, but...I can't, because someone has set something into motion that I can't escape.''

Sister Mary Bernadette spoke quietly. ''I have lived a very long time, my dear, and found that it is most often easiest to bow to these things than to fight them. But you have honored your friend's request, and perhaps you are not meant to stay.''

''You know very well that does nothing to ease my mind,'' Erin scolded in Mary Bernadette's droll spirit.

The sister gave Erin's head a final pat, then moved to give a turn to an age-thickened violet plant sitting on the old granite window ledge. "It is a dilemma. One always worries about the road not taken. A favorite pastime in my old age is thinking back on the forks in my journey through life that I thought were simple detours.

"Would you like some quiet time to yourself?" the sister asked. "The sanctuary is almost always empty at this time of the morning. I should think a scrap of quiet contemplation might serve you just now."

Erin smiled wearily at the tiny Mary Bernadette. She didn't think time or the silence of the Rose Memorial sanctuary could dispel her foreboding. It was the worst kind of self-deception to tell herself she didn't know what that was about.

Already she felt compelled to stay.

She needed the time and quiet to convince herself that remaining wasn't in the greater scheme of things. Her resolve didn't last beyond the next hallway, where the old asphalt tiles were wearing thin and the gas lamps served no real purpose anymore but as a reminder of enduring times.

"Sister Mary Bernadette, did you know Miles?"

"Not personally. His tenure here began the year after my retirement as administrator. Why?"

"Did you ever notice a...a romantic involvement?"

The sister's dark eyebrows lifted, her brown eyes gleamed like candlelight on an altar of antique pecan, and when she spoke, her brogue was rich with irony. "No need to broach the subject of romance so delicately with me, dear Erin. It's a fact of life in a hospital, and the bare truth of the matter is, the signs of it are rarely lost on me."

A fact of life in a hospital. For the barest instant Erin fell back into the pungent, male scent of Colin Rennslaer, the size of him, the way the surgical scrubs fitted him, how he had cradled her in his arms and kissed her. She imagined that the sister knew Colin had kissed her in the dark of the intensive-care unit. And curiously, that she approved.

An old-fashioned steam heat register in the hallway banged and hissed and clanked to life, and Erin jerked her thoughts off their guilty course. It would surely be impossible for the sister to know or care about every kiss Colin Rennslaer stole in the dark.

"As for Dr. Cornwall," Mary Bernadette continued thoughtfully, "if he was involved with anyone here at Rose Memorial, he and she were very circumspect. Is it important?"

"It could be."

Miles had given his daughter to understand that he had been betrayed. Whether that had anything to do with the HemSynon project was the only real question. He'd told Joyce he knew what he'd put Erin through, but that could mean that he'd simply been dumped by a woman he loved.

But Miles had always been literal minded to a fault, and Erin was tempted to believe that he meant his comment to Joyce. Whomever he had been in love with had also betrayed his research efforts. Or at least he believed that.

Sister Mary Bernadette rounded another corner to immense, beautifully carved old wooden doors that guarded the sanctuary. She pulled the right one open easily and gestured inside. "Here we are, dear child. The house of the Lord. Ask, and it shall be given you."

"Divine guidance?" Erin asked.

"If you're very, very lucky indeed," the sister answered, nothing droll left in the tone of her sweet voice.

INSIDE, THE HARDWOOD floors and pews and pulpit, even the communion rail, had darkened to near black with age though polished to a rich sheen. Traditional stained-glass

windows adorned the walls on both sides, filtering the outside light through prisms of oyster-shell white, burgundy
reds, periwinkle blues. The craftsmanship left Erin in awe.
Candles, which she thought must be left burning day and
night, provided the only inside lighting.

She sat in the third pew, trying to match in her mind the
deep silence of the sanctuary. Mostly the tranquility was
wasted on her. When Alexa Sabbeth and Jacob Delvecchio entered, it was lost anyway.

Neither one of them had gotten an hour's sleep or a
change of clothes, either. Heavy, dark bags had gathered
under Delvecchio's eyes, and the crispness had left Alexa's
suit.

"Ms. Harper," Delvecchio greeted her. He sat in the pew
beside her, and Alexa, carrying a large, flat manila envelope, took a seat directly in front of them. "Sister Mary
Bernadette told me that you might be found here."

Erin thought from Delvecchio's tone that the sister had
been reluctant to impart the information to him, but it was
equally clear that he and Alexa were intent on their mission. He didn't waste a moment.

"I understand that Miles's death has been a tremendous
shock to you," he began, "as it has been to all of us. The
HemSynon project, as you must know, is at a critical stage.
Sister Mary Bernadette confided that you were not given to
understand that Miles wanted you to assume his responsibilities."

"That's right," Erin answered. "I would not have come
and I'm certain Miles knew that. The truth is, I think you
would be better off—"

"Please." Delvecchio waved off her protest. His fingers
were thick as cigars, but pale and pampered looking.
"Show her," he instructed Alexa.

"Erin, perhaps you will reconsider when you've seen this." She pulled two sheets of paper with the Rose Memorial logo and Miles's own letterhead from the envelope and handed them to Erin.

A chill passed over Erin. The first sheet was Miles's resignation. Short, to the point and without any clear explanation.

The HemSynon project has assumed a life all its own. I regret to admit that I am no longer in control. My failure in this regard has facilitated the abuses of trusted members of the HemSynon team, which makes it imperative that Erin Harper be immediately instituted as project director.

Miles had signed the letter and attached a second page documenting in flattering detail Erin's credentials so that the board could act without delay.

"What abuses?" Erin asked. "And what 'trusted' team members is he talking about?"

Alexa shook her head. "In retrospect I suppose that Miles had been anxiety ridden of late. I chalked it up to the rigors of the project. He was a morose sort of man anyway, but he never spoke of abuses by anyone."

"So you don't know who—"

"No. There's no one. In fact, Jacob and I feel that Miles may have been suffering an emotional breakdown that was causing him to overreact. Frankly, from the tone of his resignation, I am tempted to believe that he may well have thrown himself in front of the first oncoming vehicle."

"Suicide?" Erin asked, feeling blindsided. "By stepping in front of a vehicle that might as easily crippled him for life as kill him?" No. Miles would never have left the HemSynon project to chance. He was a morose man. Erin had more reason to know that than anyone. But he wouldn't have left his death to chance like that, either. "If Miles had chosen suicide, he would have used one of a countless number of fatal injections available to him. I don't believe it."

Alexa shrugged. "It's still a possibility."

"Look," Delvecchio charged in impatiently, "Miles Cornwall's death is regrettable, but the project must go forward. I am prepared, Ms. Harper, to offer you his salary, a VIP suite for whatever length of time is required to bring the project to fruition and whatever administrative support becomes necessary. In short, whatever you need."

Regrettable. The death of a butterfly was regrettable. Miles Cornwall was a human being. "Mr. Delvecchio, if you suspected that Miles was suffering an emotional crisis, or even that he was simply overreacting—"

"Then why am I willing to take his recommendation that you replace him? What are the odds that the behavior of even one member of the HemSynon team is less than lily-white? Whatever they are, I can't afford to take the chance."

He got up, followed like a shadow by Alexa. "I'll need your answer by noon, Ms. Harper," he continued. "Needless to say, if you agree, you will have the gratitude not only of myself and Alexa, but of the entire board of directors of Rose Memorial. Good morning."

After they had gone and the sanctuary door closed behind them, Erin shivered, more from exhaustion than anything. She couldn't buy into a suicide theory, but too many other unlikely, unexplained events crowded her thoughts.

That Miles would call upon her at all... That he would have been betrayed exactly as he had betrayed her... That he could have been struck down and killed at the exact moment when he could still have explained... That a thief could have the monumental bad luck to turn a spectacular getaway in Colin Rennslaer's precious vintage Jag into a fatal hit and run . . .

And most of all she thought about why the fate of Miles Cornwall's HemSynon project should loom larger in her mind than dreams that were so near she could reach out and grab them at last.

She talked all of the time to her psychotherapist housemate, Sidney, and she thought she'd learned not to constantly be coming to the rescue, offering help no one had asked for.

Miles had asked.

And Delvecchio had asked, quite nicely.

Erin stared at the unwavering flames of a dozen candles and sighed deeply. Medicine had changed too fast. Twenty years ago you didn't want to get yourself admitted to a teaching hospital because medical students and interns might practice procedures on you that you didn't need.

Now students and interns were the least of anyone's worries. Life-and-death decisions were being made according to technology and cost—by bureaucrats and insurers and lawyers.

She believed passionately that patients needed a break. An advocate. And she intended to become one.

But then a synthetic blood would change all the rules, too. It was an idea whose time had come. Whose time was now. And Miles had asked.

Sidney would be perversely amused that she still hadn't progressed to the life lessons on saying no when someone asked for her help. Miles had apparently counted on that.

He hadn't counted on dying, but there was no way she could walk blindly into such a guarded research enclave expecting to salvage anything without inviting mutiny.

The thought provoked a shake of her head. Miles would have expected she should anyway, and she resented it. He had been a man of whims, however scientifically brilliant. He'd denied her Ph.D. on his personal whim and he had wanted what he wanted with his dying breath—which was the protégé he had lost when he indulged his whims.

"Oh, Miles. Why me?" she murmured.

"What have we here, Erin Harper? A persecution complex in the making?"

Erin turned slowly toward the lightly cynical baritone behind her. She recognized Colin Rennslaer's voice, but she was unprepared for the sight of him, leaning indolently against the heavy wooden sanctuary doors, freshly showered and dressed in civilian clothes. Expensive, tailored raw silk civilian clothes. She wanted to discount him for all vanity and no substance, but she'd seen the substance first in the physician, the healer.

And she couldn't so easily dismiss him, but she wouldn't let him see that.

"Haven't they delivered you a new Jag, yet?"

He sauntered toward her and sank loose limbed into the pew behind her, subtly forcing her to turn toward him.

"As a matter of fact, they have. Hunter green, I understand. Haven't they seen to your return flight?"

Erin gave a smile. "I don't think that's on the official agenda. Are you so sure I should go?"

"Yeah." He massaged his eyes with a thumb and forefinger, then opened them again. In the muted light of the sanctuary, his hair shone like varnished mahogany, and the shades of his hazel blue eyes reminded Erin of frost on bare oak limbs. "Ever heard the expression 'follow your bliss'?"

She curled up sideways on the pew and wrapped her arms around her knees. Colin continued to surprise her with dimensions she wouldn't have imagined. "Sure. What's your point?'' She must have been more tired than she thought, not to have seen this one coming.

"That hell is following someone else's bliss. No one's indispensable, Erin. Not Miles and not you." He seemed curiously reluctant to be discouraging her, but his expression became shrewd. Guarded. "HemSynon will get onto the market without you."

She rested her chin on her knees, wondering at his detached interest. Why should it matter to him one way or another? Why should Colin Rennslaer care how she spent her life? Why would a busy, exhausted transplant surgeon, robbed of his beloved Jaguar, spend even two minutes making a case for her to leave?

Was he threatening her with hell or just making a point? "Is it true, what Alexa Sabbeth said? Are you really so careless about your locker?"

He grinned, but the frost got severe and Erin didn't know which to trust. "Is there something relevant in your question?"

"Well, maybe," Erin returned. "You know, I've been thinking that the assumption the police made—that the hit and run was secondary to the theft, might be off base."

Colin crossed an ankle over his knee and sat back, extending his arm along the top of the pew. His bare feet were clad now in pricey Italian leather loafers. "Why?"

"Why not?" Erin answered, more than irritated with herself for noticing bare ankles sprinkled with very dark hair. "If someone knew that you would be in surgery all night, and that Miles would be crossing the street for a nine-o'clock meeting—"

"Are you suggesting someone planned to run Cornwall down like this? With *my* Jag?" he demanded, incredulous.

"Yes." She shrugged, gratified in some perverse way to have thrown him a curve. Colin Rennslaer stole her breath in daylight filtered through stained glass depicting the Virgin Mother with her infant Son. "I think it's a possibility."

"Who would want to kill Cornwall?"

Chapter Four

We were hoping you could tell us, Doctor. She wanted to echo the security guard, but Colin sounded genuinely doubtful that anyone would have reason to kill Miles. And she was too tired to be flippant anymore.

"I don't know who had reason to want Miles dead. But his daughter thinks he was jilted, and he died before he could brief me on exactly what he thought had gone wrong with the HemSynon project. I'm no detective, but the timing bothers me, Colin."

Still resting his arm on the back of the pew, Colin raised his hand to massage the tension from his forehead. "I'm not tracking this very well, Erin. Freak accidents never happen when it's convenient for the victim. It seems like a pretty big stretch to link Miles getting run over with whatever he thought was going on in his research. I mean, did Miles give you any reason to think somebody was going to kill him?"

"No." Erin found herself rubbing her own brow. This whole train of events was freakish, but she wasn't given to an overactive imagination. And the fact remained. Miles was dead.

"Think about it, though. If what you told me about HemSynon is true, and I'm sure that it is, the potential for sabotage or industrial theft or even dry-labbed results is darn high."

"Still a far cry from murder, Erin. I've got to get out of here," he said, straightening his body in the pew, "but I'll say this once more because I think you need to hear it.

"There are at least three people on the project right now who could assume Miles's responsibilities. Project directors are a dime a dozen. There will never be enough people with the training and perception and compassion to do what you can do with your degree—to balance what's medically possible against a patient's highest interests."

"I know. It's so important. But—"

"If you know, why are you beating yourself up about this?"

She gave a half smile. "I wasn't aware that I was beating myself up over it."

"You're sitting here talking to Miles as if he were alive and had a clue what you'll have to give up to stay!"

"Miles never had a clue."

"Take one yourself," he warned, rising from the pew. "I have a feeling I'm going to regret saying this..." His gaze fell to the corner of her mouth where he had kissed her, then back to her eyes, and his smile faded. "Go home, Erin. Life is too short."

If she didn't trust Colin's motives in lobbying on behalf of her bliss, she trusted herself even less in his presence. Half the night he'd sat with her, anticipating her, comforting her, half reading her mind. The truth was, even now while he was walking blithely out of the sanctuary, she knew he had really been arguing her case.

And deliberately evoking in her with his glance the memory of that kiss stolen in the dark.

Life is too short.

The trouble, Erin thought, was that Miles's untimely death proved Colin's point. And it was that more than anything else that convinced her to give Delvecchio the answer he wanted.

PREDICTABLY Sidney laughed his head off when Erin called the house they shared in Scottsdale, Arizona. She would have spared herself his twisted sense of humor if she hadn't needed him to pack clothes and take care of getting her cat, Priscilla, into her travel kennel for the flight to Chicago.

Alexa Sabbeth provided Erin with a temporary Rose Memorial identification badge and the keys and entrance codes to the locks at the clinical research area, which included Miles's office and the labs. Sister Mary Bernadette took her to the staff cafeteria for a bite to eat, and the city police questioned Erin there.

She described what little she had seen and the aftermath. It wasn't much help, but Erin thought the police hadn't expected much anyway. They'd already gleaned every detail of the hit and run Erin could provide.

At last Sister Mary Bernadette took Erin to the VIP suite in the tenth-floor penthouse of an old brick building connected to the hospital.

The suite was usually reserved for families of whatever dignitaries were patients in Rose Memorial. Though very old, the suite rivaled any accommodations Erin had ever seen.

An antique parquet entry gave way to an exquisitely furnished living room. A richly embroidered carpet was worn in a few places, but Erin knew it must be very old. A decanter of brandy sat atop the coffee table with half a dozen miniature snifters. Vast Italian vases were filled with a collection of jade plants whose trunks were thick as an arm and equally old.

Pris would have to be on her best behavior.

The bedroom was furnished in antiques that had probably arrived new at Rose Memorial. A four-poster bed high off the floor was covered with a handmade quilt. She sat for a moment on the upholstered bench that went with a vanity and three-way mirror. Delicate lace curtains with filmy sheers covered the windows, which looked out onto Lake Michigan.

An enormous claw-foot bathtub stood in the center of the bathroom, and Swedish ivies spilled over an old pedestal sink.

The lingering scent of lilacs reminded Erin of sleep-overs at her Grandma Anne's house in an old section of Phoenix. And she longed to fall asleep to memories like those.

Sister Mary Bernadette had gone to the picture window with a view of Lake Michigan and sailboats out for an early run. Erin put an arm around the tiny nun's shoulders and rested her head atop the sister's.

"From my rooms I can see the lake, as well," Mary Bernadette commented. "I spend hours these days dreaming of sailing along on the water."

"Have you ever been?" Erin asked.

"No," Mary Bernadette answered wistfully, her "no" sounding more like a "nigh." "But if the Buddhists turn out to be right, and we come back to another life, I'll be a big, strappin' man and I'll have one of those fine sailboats."

Erin laughed softly and stood back to see the sister's face. "But will you have any say in the matter?"

A troubled expression passed over the nun's wizened old features and took hold in her eyes. "I'm afraid, in my heart, Erin, that you've had no real say in your coming and your going here."

Erin shrugged. "I have. It was a very tough decision, really, but—"

"Well, I've a feeling there's some . . . some evil afoot, Erin. Some manifestation of man's inhumanity to man going on, and I'm sure I don't like it." She gave Erin a hug and made her way to the door. "Be careful, dear child. God bless your endeavors."

SHE SLEPT for nearly ten hours beneath the quilt. By the time she awoke, it was dark outside and the old ceramic clock at the bedside read 7:40. Alexa Sabbeth had promised toiletries and a set of fresh clothing. The delivery, in a bag from an upscale department store, sat just inside the door of the suite.

Erin started a bath and emptied the bag. A white lab coat, a temporary Rose Memorial identification badge and a pager were on top. A pair of beige linen slacks had been selected along with a sleeveless navy blue ribbed silk sweater. The lingerie was a bit too ample. People were always surprised by her generous contours into thinking she weighed ten or fifteen pounds more than she actually did.

She tossed a few bath granules from a crystal jar into the running water and climbed over the lip of the old-fashioned tub into bubbles and hot water up to her neck.

She emerged from the suite an hour later feeling far better but a bit moody. Scared maybe. Alone and in a strange place. Alexa had volunteered to show her Miles's research facilities, but since Erin preferred seeing them on her own, she really had no one to blame for feeling isolated and crabby.

She attached the pager to her waistband and the ID badge to the breast pocket of the lab coat, which she tossed over her arm. With Miles's office keys in hand, she departed the penthouse building, determined to shake her mood.

Though the twisted maze of hallways through Rose Memorial actually linked the research facility to the hospital, she chose the outside route. She walked in the balmy night past clumps of flowers and planters for nearly three city blocks to the outer entrance of the Rose Memorial Hospital Research Laboratories.

A burly, good-looking, Nordic blond security guard approached while Erin punched in the security code that would unlock the doors.

"Tony Bugen, ma'am," he offered. "May I see some identification?"

The walk had helped to restore her. Erin handed Bugen her ID and stood propping open the door, explaining that she would be working in the building for the next several weeks.

"Did you hear about the hit and run last night?" When he indicated that he had, Erin continued. "The victim was the project director."

"Dr. Cornwall?" he asked, surprised. "I heard the guy died, but I didn't know it was him."

Erin took a deep breath and nodded. "Yes. He did die, very early this morning." When would the reality of Miles's death finally sink in for her? "You haven't heard anything more?"

"Not a thing. Funny, too. You'd have thought I would, one way or another."

"Yes. One would think so," Erin said. "Anyway, I'll be taking over for him."

"Be careful no one follows you through the doors, Ms. Harper. People are in and out of this building at all hours, and I've got to cover all entrances."

"I'll do that—and thanks for the warning. Tony, do you know much about what goes on here?"

"Not a lot. Why?"

"I was just wondering if you've noticed a change in the routine, different people, odd hours, that sort of thing."

He reached in the breast pocket of his uniform, pulled out a cedar toothpick and popped it between his teeth. "Well, like I told you, people do come and go at all hours. Less so in the past couple of months, I guess, since they put the production crew on one ten-hour shift. Not much activity after, say, nine or ten at night."

"Have there been any break-ins in the past few weeks— or cases of anyone being followed inside?"

"Once. Last winter. I'm always worried about the addicts. You know. Looking to find something to shoot up. Turned out to be a homeless drunk looking for a boiler room to curl up in."

Erin looked for a side arm, but he only wore a billy club and a small cellular phone. In Phoenix the security staff carried handguns. "Shouldn't you be armed?"

The guard shrugged. "My opinion? Damn straight. This isn't what you'd call the safest neighborhood, but the Rose Memorial administration don't hold with guns."

Erin nodded. There were compelling arguments on both sides of the handgun issue, she knew. Especially in a hospital environment, where the inventory of drugs invited trouble.

"Tony, I wonder if you would do me a favor?"

"What's that?"

"The project is on its last leg. There really shouldn't be anyone here after ten o'clock. Would you mind taking my pager number and giving me a call if someone does come after that?"

"You won't mind if I clear that with Ms. Sabbeth?"

"Not at all," Erin answered. "In fact, she should know."

Tony shoved the toothpick from one side of his mouth to the other and took out a pencil to take the pager number.

Erin gave him the number, thanked him for his help and went inside. The door swung closed and locked again automatically behind her. The project administrative offices, she knew, were on the third floor. She took the stairs from one dimly lit hallway to one just like it four half flights up. Miles's office was at the far end of the hall.

When she reached it, she saw that the door was not firmly shut, only closed without having latched.

Erin stood back and swallowed hard. It seemed such a small thing, but it wasn't. Carelessness like this proved that things weren't quite as they should be.

She gave a fleeting thought to going back outside for the guard, but she had heard nothing from inside Miles's office. Nothing so innocent and noisy as cleaning staff, nor any furtive riffling through file cabinets.

She gave the door a push with her fingertips, and it swung silently open. Still nothing. Part of her reacted to the lingering scent of perfume, which would have annoyed Miles to no end. She leaned to one side until she could see that the door led into an anteroom with only a coffee pot on a table and a couple of stark Danish chairs. But when her eyes adjusted to the dark, she could see there was a vaguely gray light coming from the office beyond, like the light of a television set.

Or a computer monitor, because TV images would flicker.

She knew people who always left their computers on. Miles hadn't been one of them, unless he had changed his very set ways. Erin shivered violently and then straightened her shoulders, commanding herself not to behave like such a ninny. She crossed the small anteroom and stepped into Miles's carpeted office.

Angled away from her, Colin Rennslaer sat staring off into space, his profile sharply delineated by the light of the computer monitor.

His hair was full, thick and straight, razor cut so that it fell perfectly over his brow, and his nose and lips and chin were cleanly, powerfully sculpted.

Deep in concentration, he sat with one leg stretched out beneath the computer stand and the other hiked up with his heel on the edge of Miles's chair.

"Bet this looks real bad, huh?"

Erin jumped. Gnawing on the tip of a pen, he'd given no signs of recognizing that he was no longer alone. When he spoke, she was the one knocked off guard instead of the other way around, as she would have preferred. But Colin Rennslaer wasn't going to murder her midstep, either.

She let relief drizzle through her, dumped the keys and lab coat onto the credenza at her side and let the anger spill out in her tone of voice. "What are you doing here?"

He turned in the chair and switched on a green library lamp at the corner of Miles's desk. "Moonlighting?" His smile was the most gifted blend of guilt and who-me? charm she had ever seen. She pitied the man's poor mother, but on the other hand, she wasn't at all amused to find him here, where Miles should have been. She glanced at the monitor behind him, which had an on-screen menu of some sort.

"On who, or what?"

"Whom."

He had the most gorgeous lips. "Whom, then," Erin snapped. "This really isn't smart, you know."

He tilted the swivel chair back and laced his fingers over his flat abdomen. He'd discarded the suit jacket, and she saw now that he had pulled his tie way loose and undone over half the buttons on his tailored shirt, which left it hanging open.

"I know."

"You know," she repeated. Sinking into a chair that resembled the Danish pair in the outer office, she crossed her arms and legs.

The truly despicable part was, she suspected he'd only half undressed because he wasn't expecting anyone else to come around. The air-conditioning was off for the night, making the entire building stiflingly hot. But he wasn't unaware that he'd done it, either.

He made no attempt to repair it. And from the shadow of a smirk on his lips, she knew he didn't mind if it bothered her.

"I'm still waiting. What are you doing here?"

He sat forward again, all traces of his disarming grin gone, his broad, handsome brow furrowing. "Erin, I've been thinking. It bothers me."

"Thinking?"

"Will you give me a little slack here? I'm trying to explain. Please?" Seeing that she might relent, he went on. "What disturbs me is not knowing why Miles wanted to resign, why he called you, how he had it all set up with the dragon lady and Delvecchio that you would take over—"

"The dragon lady?"

"Sabbeth. Dear Alexa. She used to be head of surgical nursing. Queen B of the O.R. And I don't mean insect variety."

"Is that how she knew you don't have a lock on your locker?"

"A perfect example. I got a weekly memo from her. Why the hell should she care if I locked my things up?"

"So your keys would be safe?"

Colin scowled. "That's another thing. Cornwall is dead, the timing sucks, and the worst part is, some jerk used my Jag to kill him."

"No." Erin shook her head. "The worst thing is that he is dead."

"You know what I mean, Erin."

She lowered her eyes. She did know what he'd meant, but he provoked her into wanting to be hard to get along with. Maybe because he'd felt so certain no one would discover his moonlight spying that he'd half undressed.

Still, Miles's death weighed heavily on her mind, as well. She took a deep breath and met Colin's eyes again. "This morning, before you came into the sanctuary, Alexa was making the case that Miles may have been trying to get himself killed."

"To commit suicide? Cornwall?"

"Yes. I suggested that it would have been stupid to risk getting badly injured instead of dying—if that's what he'd intended. And Miles wasn't stupid. But later I thought why would someone intent on killing him risk that, either?"

Colin dragged a hand through his hair, and despite the heat, it fell perfectly back into place. His shirt didn't. Erin promised herself she would stop noticing.

"Maybe whoever it was didn't intend to kill him," he suggested. "What if someone just needed to get him out of the way for a while? It wouldn't matter if he recognized my car because I was in surgery."

Exactly. Colin Rennslaer had an alibi. So why was she thinking his grasp of all of this was a little too ready? Too...pat and prepared. But again she knew why. He was the one she'd come upon where he shouldn't have been, scrolling through Miles's computer files.

Her eyes caught on the slackened knot of his tie. She couldn't fail to ask him the hard question just because the shadow beneath his pectorals and his pristine white shirt made her mouth go dry.

She sucked at her cheeks for moisture to bathe her tongue so she could ask. "Are you the one who needed him out of the way for a while?"

"No."

His intensity made her hurry on. "Because it was your car, and you're the one sitting in Miles's office in the dark, Colin."

"No. Do you believe me?"

She wanted to believe him. She didn't want to make him stop looking at her with more than ordinary courtesy, but she had to know why he was here. She tilted her head in the direction of Miles's computer. "Did you find what you were looking for?"

"Answer me, Erin." He looked hard at her, demanding an answer that meant something to him. "Are you going to believe what I tell you?"

He wanted her to believe him because she believed she could trust him, and not because he could give her a reasonable excuse. There was an undeniable sexual attraction between him and Erin Harper, which was fine...but he didn't want to start out with her making excuses for anything.

He respected her for asking the question. He found that he wanted her respect in return.

Erin nodded at last. "All right. I believe you."

Colin smiled briefly. He was so used to getting what he wanted when he wanted it that her agreement was almost anticlimactic. "Should I ask why?"

Erin smiled as briefly. "I'll try any fool thing...once."

Colin laughed. "Fair enough. Where do we go from here?"

"Tell me what you thought you would find in Miles's computer—and if you found it."

"Some explanation, I guess. What I found bothers me, Erin. A lot."

"What is it?"

"Here." He gestured for her to come around the desk and sit where he had been sitting in Miles's chair. His long legs stretched out beside her, he sat on the edge of the desk behind her. He reached out and tapped the Enter key for the screen to come up again.

"What am I looking at?"

"This is a menu Miles developed so we could all play around with the variables in the HemSynon research. Once any of us came up with a viable development angle, he would duplicate disks, send them out to the key team members and wait till somebody came up with another idea."

"Okay." Erin was familiar with the concept. Trading data in the way Colin described allowed for brainstorming at all stages of research and development. She'd never seen it implemented like this in a clinical setting, though. "So?"

"So look." Colin leaned forward again, and Erin could feel the heat his body gave off and notice the scent. She forced her concentration to the computer. "The menu lists the various development tasks and the applications. Cue up that one."

Erin brought up the applications menu. Colin continued. "I'm familiar with one through five on this menu."

Erin examined the first five: Surgical/Transplant; Surgical/Routine; Surgical/Trauma; Medical/Renal; Medical/Anemias. "I presume all of these are blood-transfusion categories? Possible uses for HemSynon?"

"Exactly."

"What about the last one, number six, 'Scenario'?"

Colin grimaced. "I've never seen it before." He reached for the keyboard and typed "6" at the cursor. A list of fifty-seven names came up, in the order of last name, first name, middle initial. "Every name on this list is that of a transplant or cardiac-bypass patient. All but six of them were mine, right up to last week."

Erin frowned. "What do you think it means? Did Miles go back and apply the HemSynon model to old cases?"

"That would be my guess."

"Well, it wouldn't be an unusual way to test a model, Colin. What bothers you about this? That he used your old surgical cases or—"

"Ethically this stinks, Erin! A second-year law student could make a case for a wholesale invasion of the doctor-patient privilege, and—"

"Come on, Colin," Erin interrupted. "Every patient signs waivers to allow their cases to be brought up for study."

"With the consent of the physician," Colin answered. "Which is why I was sought out for the team. But no one asked me, and Cornwall never told me. Worst of all, these are in protected files."

"They won't be hard to get into. Not for—"

"That's not the point, Erin," he protested, "and you know it. Don't you think it's a little odd that every file on this disk is open but the one with my former patients? Or that they were never included on the disks I received?"

"I suppose it is. Yes. Especially since your cases should fit into the Surgical/Transplant applications." Erin paused, still uncertain what the issue was with Colin. Still uncertain, in fact, as to whether she had already misplaced her trust in believing him.

On the other side of it, though, she knew he could as easily have wiped out the offending files if he were guilty of the sabotage. And he could have done it right in front of her.

"So tell me exactly what it is that worries you."

"That my patients' names are coming up in the middle of a project that's been sabotaged. Miles might have been forecasting how the surgeries would have turned out with HemSynon, but there wouldn't be any reason to hide that from me." He looked away, thinking, then returned his gaze to her. "What was he hiding? Or what did he uncover that someone else had been hiding?"

Erin shook her head. The Scenario files proved nothing, only raised more questions about sabotage and secrets in the medical research. But she couldn't quite believe the innocent explanations—that Miles may only have been tinkering . . . or that file with Colin's patients was what had prompted Miles to bring Colin into the project to begin with. Either way, Colin would have been told, or should have been. If she couldn't accept such reasoning, why should he?

So why *were* his surgical patients' names in the Scenario category at all? She would have to store away the question until she had seen more, understood more of what had been going on in Miles's research project.

"Colin, who has access to this computer?"

He shrugged and stuck his hands into his pants pockets. "I'm here, but I have the lock codes to the building, and most of the security people know me by sight at least."

"Who else?"

He angled his head toward another door, which was in the shadows far to the right of the computer desk. "That leads to the lab facilities. Anyone regularly in the lab has access. But if the Scenario file is someone's nasty little secret, why put it right there on a menu that everyone could get at?" He drew a deep breath and let it out in frustration, then rubbed his eyes with the heels of both hands. "I don't have an answer for that, and it bugs the hell out of me."

"I can see why," she answered. The possibilities seemed endless. "Colin, I know you're not going to like this, but I'm going to have to ask you to back off from this. I can't have a member of the research team involved—"

"Save your breath," he interrupted, fixing her with a hard stare. "I'm not sitting around a hot, stale, tacky little office trying to figure out what's going on out of idle curiosity, Erin."

"Exactly my point. You are a member of the research team—which gives you a vested interest and which makes it inappropriate for you to be anywhere near my inquiry into Miles's concerns."

"*Inquiry?* It's my reputation tied up in this project, and my Jag tied to Cornwall's death. I'm not about to back off. Whatever it takes, Erin. Remember?"

"Your reputation isn't my concern, Colin. The project is."

"And that's exactly my point," he returned. "But I'll make you a deal. You're into this because you caved in to Delvecchio and said yes when you meant no. If you want to back off and go home, I'll do the same."

She started to protest that she hadn't done any such thing, but she had and she knew it. She leaned back in Miles's chair and lifted her sweater at the shoulders. Even the silk knit had begun to cling to her in the stifling heat.

For a moment his eyes focused on the sweater as it settled back against her breasts. Erin swallowed and wetted her lips and she looked up at Colin, waiting for him to lift his gaze. When he finally did, she found that she had lost her train of thought.

The silence grew between them. Only the fan inside the computer whirred. A light sheen of sweat glistened on Colin's brow. Erin felt a bead of it trickling down beneath her sweater, between her breasts. She couldn't look away.

The startling, intense awareness just kept erupting between them despite the importance of the things they had to say or the conflict between them. Like who caved in, who said yes or no and why. Erin swallowed, hoping he would smile or make some remark, anything to discount what was happening between them and simmering beneath the surface of what was happening around them.

He said nothing, but after a few moments he looked away. His head sank until his chin nearly rested on his chest, and he let the intensity go. Still resting against the desk, he began to button his shirt.

"Erin, look. I—" He broke off suddenly when a narrow strip of light caught his attention beneath the door leading to the labs. "Someone else felt the need of a little moonlight marauding."

Erin turned to the door and saw the faint light, as well.

Colin finished buttoning his shirt and wrenched the knot of his tie carelessly back into place. He got up and crossed to the door. Listening for a moment, he gestured for Erin to join him, then pulled the door open and took the lead.

The lab was still mostly dark through the rows of counters organized in rows and carrels. Millions of dollars of complex electronic equipment stood silently in shut-down modes. The light they'd detected beneath the door came from a walled-off room in the middle of the lab, perhaps seven or eight lab stations from the door that led to Miles's office.

Erin reached out to catch Colin's attention. "Is that someone's office?"

"Yeah. Charlene Babson, Miles's administrative—"

"Hey, Babs. Baby," another masculine voice called out, interrupting Colin's soft-spoken response. "Have I got a case for you. Another candidate for our most precious blood."

Midstep, concealed by the shadows and shelves and analyzers, Erin and Colin stopped and exchanged glances.

"Most precious blood?" she murmured. "Does he mean HemSynon?" When Colin nodded, she continued, "Isn't that a little . . ."

"Sacrilegious? Tasteless?" Colin muttered. The joke had either worn thin, or else he was in no mood to be amused. "You could say that."

"Who is he?"

"Tyler Robards. My anesthesiologist."

Following Colin, Erin watched the compactly built Robards approach the center office, some fifty feet away, until the woman she took for Miles's assistant stalked out from the office.

"Would you keep your voice down?" she nagged.

Robards wore an expensive designer cardigan, white turtleneck and pleated black slacks comfortably, and he obviously knew his way around, but he was taken aback by her aggression. "Why? Are we about to be discovered? Compromised? Hauled off to jail? What?"

"Well, let's start with 'discovered,'" Colin said, making his way into the circle of light from Charlene's office.

The woman jerked around as if she'd been shot, and the color faded in Tyler Robard's face—even after he recognized Colin and stuck out his hand reflexively. "Colin!"

"Ty," Colin greeted. "How was your conference in Amsterdam?"

"Fine—lots of international camaraderie. A few interesting technical papers presented." He glanced around from one to the other, then looked exaggeratedly for an escape hatch. Erin had to wonder if he wasn't assessing the possibility of real damage behind the show of humor. "So... we're busted, huh?"

"Not *we,* Tyler. You," Charlene put in, towering at least six inches over him. He stood only as tall as Erin's five-four, with curly blond hair and blue eyes. He'd likely been an angelic-looking child.

Charlene Babson probably hadn't. She'd pulled her long, carroty-colored hair to the sides so tightly with a pair of combs that her pale scalp blanched, and the glint in her pale green eyes dispelled any cherubic resemblances at all. She turned to Colin, letting her gaze flick from Erin's vicinity to Colin's disheveled tie. "Interesting place to bring a date, Colin. If I'd known—"

"Cut it out, Charlene," he interrupted tiredly, putting a hand at Erin's elbow. "This isn't a date."

"Then you're slipping, old man," Tyler said, eyeing Erin. He held his hand out to her. "This is Charlene Babson—" he indicated "Babs" "—I'm Dr. Tyler Robards. And you are?"

"Erin Harper." She shook his proffered hand. His warmth left her feeling vaguely uncomfortable.

"Charlene is—or rather, was," Colin amended, "Cornwall's second in command. Tyler practices anesthesiology here at Rose Memorial—almost exclusively for me."

Erin assumed by his familiarity that Robard's must be involved with the clinical trials in the same capacity as Colin.

Feeling the intense curiosity of both Charlene and Tyler Robards, Erin thought this entire encounter seemed strained and secretive and hands-in-the-cookie-jar to her. She decided to take it head-on. "If you've been out of the country, Dr. Robards—"

"Tyler," he corrected smoothly. "Any friend of Colin's, et cetera, you know."

"Tyler, then. Had you heard Dr. Cornwall has died as a result of a hit and run?"

"Oh, God. It was ... an accident?"

"Yeah. And it was with my car, Ty."

"Do they know— I'm so sorry... you must be a friend of Miles. Or a relative."

"Neither," she answered. He looked visibly stricken, but Erin couldn't tell whether he was shocked, surprised or struggling to supply the appropriate condolences. "He was a colleague. What did you mean a moment ago when you said that you have another candidate for HemSynon?"

"I..." Tyler began. He must have realized *he* hadn't said "HemSynon," but since she had, she somehow knew enough to ask what he meant. "The computer models, of course."

"Of course?" Erin asked.

"Excuse me, but we're talking about a highly secret project here," Charlene intervened, casting Robards a glance in the vein of I-think-I-hear-your-mother-calling.

He straightened and his eyes narrowed. If looks killed, Charlene Babson would be gasping for her last breath. "She obviously knows—"

"I'll see you in the morning, Tyler," Charlene said curtly.

"Maybe," he retorted. "Colin, Erin, nice to meet you." He swung away as if to go, then turned back and addressed Charlene in a low, warning, silky tone. "Sweetheart, try not to forget where your bread is buttered, huh?"

"Get out, Ty." Her angular, bony chin lifted as she watched Robards until he stormed through the door. She turned to Colin and spoke as if Erin weren't even there.

"Colin, really. Who is this woman? This research is closely guarded. You know better than this."

"Where exactly is your bread buttered, Charlene?" Colin asked, ignoring her reproach.

"What is that supposed to mean?"

"Miles called me in, Charlene," Erin interrupted. Colin's question had occurred to her, as well, but it reeked of finger pointing that would only put the woman on the defensive. "He was convinced that the project had been somehow compromised," she went on. "Would you know anything about that?"

"Nothing," Charlene said, still so icily expressionless that Erin felt chilled. "But let me bring you up to speed. Miles Cornwall was nothing more than a figurehead around here. He's dead, and that's too bad, but HemSynon is mine—and I don't care if he called in the National Guard. I won't tolerate any interference. Is that clear enough?"

Chapter Five

Provoked by Charlene's insolence, Colin stepped forward. "You're wrong. Miles had already arranged with Delvecchio and Sabbeth for his replacement. That's why Ms. Harper is here."

Charlene's thin lips flattened. "Oh, and when did he do that, Colin? Just before he got run over with your car?"

Colin looked as if he wanted to deck her. "The fact that it was my car is totally beside the point—"

"Is it?" she returned, somehow implying in two words that he had designs on the project that only began with getting rid of Miles.

"Don't be ridiculous. I don't have the time for conspiracy, and I sure as hell don't have the inclination. Delvecchio and Sabbeth believe an outside director is what is necessary now. For the good of the project—"

"Spare me your version of what's good for the project, Dr. Rennslaer," she interrupted tonelessly, shedding her cardigan. "I'm the only one in a position to know that."

"I think that's true," Erin answered. She stepped closer, physically aligning herself with Charlene—willing Colin to shut up. "Personally I'm relieved."

If Charlene Babson was the ringleader of the sabotage Miles feared, as his assistant director, she was also the person controlling vital information Erin would undoubtedly rely upon. The last thing Erin needed was to alienate so powerful a player. "I tried to tell them that it would be unproductive to replace Miles from the outside, but—" Erin explained.

"But what?" Charlene pressed.

"Delvecchio is convinced otherwise."

"Why?"

"I don't know exactly." Erin shrugged. "I understand the board of directors trusted Miles. Delvecchio just wants to deliver them Miles's handpicked replacement and get on with the project."

"It's just the way things go, Charlene," Colin said placating her now. "You know that. No one in-house is ever qualified, ever good enough. . . ."

"Don't give me that line of bull, Colin," she snapped. "There's a succession planning document in place naming me as Miles's replacement." She snatched a comb from her hair, scraped her hair into order and rammed the comb back into place. "Miles had *no* business recommending anyone else, the slug," she muttered furiously.

"I agree," Erin answered. "Remember, I worked with him, as well." However disloyal to Miles, she could easily empathize with Charlene's anger, and hope that their common experience with Miles would lend credibility to her ploy.

"If you know," Charlene said, "then enlighten Delvecchio and let me get on with this project."

"I've tried."

Colin appeared ready to confirm this. Erin shook her head. His testimonial would not convince Charlene Babson that the sky was blue. "Delvecchio thinks Miles walked on water."

Charlene's narrow nostrils flared. "Delvecchio is a fool."

"Unfortunately he's the fool calling the shots—and he'll bring in someone else if I leave." Acid had begun to etch entire landscapes in her stomach. Was Charlene buying into any of this? "The only solution I can come up with is to stay and let you carry it all off."

"You'd do that?" Charlene asked.

"As long as you support the illusion. Delvecchio will have to be convinced that I'm in charge." *Choose, Charlene,* Erin thought. *The devil you know or the one you don't.*

"Why?"

Erin gave a half smile. Charlene's cooperation depended upon being convinced of her harmlessness.

Erin wasn't harmless. She intended to salvage the project and stop the sabotage, but she still felt like a child trying to pull off a walloping lie. Colin was watching her like a hawk, as if he knew her stomach already ached and tension wreaked havoc with her ulcer and if this went on much longer the pain would be out of control. Fortunately Erin thought Charlene was too self-absorbed to notice.

Right now, before everything fell to pieces, Erin knew, she had to gain Charlene Babson's support, however grudging. And her best hope of doing that was to echo and affirm Charlene's central attitude.

"The project is too important to suffer fools. Say the word, Charlene, and I'll stay. Otherwise I'm gone."

Charlene squinted at Erin, then gave Colin a dirty look because he was shaking his head. He couldn't believe Erin would defer to anyone when she had the power of the administration behind her.

It occurred to her that there was at least this one woman at Rose Memorial whose bed would never suffer the crumbs of Colin Rennslaer's crackers. But her amusement was thwarted by the acid ache in her stomach.

All expression had gone out of Charlene's pale, freckled face, and her voice went flat as EEG tracings in brain death. "You'll stay out of my way."

Right up until you make a wrong move. "I can't imagine it any other way."

ERIN LET OUT a breath after Charlene had gone, and the control she'd been exercising over the pain in her stomach shattered. She felt tiny beads of perspiration breaking out on her brow. She felt hot and cold at once. Her bluff had worked, but with the price of her ulcer acting out.

"Erin?"

She started at the sound of his voice. A thick, sweltering silence had descended, miming the sensations her ulcer had begun to generate. "What?"

"That's it," he murmured roughly, pulling her against him before she fell down. "You're breaking out in a sweat, Erin, for God's sake."

She thought she'd hidden her pain better than that. "Colin—"

"Be quiet." He cradled her head against his shoulder with one hand and settled the other at her right hip. He let his fingers mold to her side and his thumb probe the space between the ribs just beneath her breast. He found his mark when she winced, and as he pressed steadily, nausea roiled up in her and she shivered. He drew her body tighter to him and applied more pressure to the trigger point. "Relax, Erin. Be still."

The pain in her stomach got blindingly hot and painful, but then it began to subside and Erin obeyed his command, letting her body sink into his. He held the pressure for several seconds until the nausea and burning sensation subsided. Still he held her close, his cheek resting on the top of her head. "Better?"

"Mmm."

"When is the last time you ate something?"

"I don't remember."

Still he held her close, and when the last vestiges of pain had gone, she began to notice other things. His scent. The hardness of his body against hers. The way his hand felt with his fingers threaded into her hair. The gentle scrape of his whiskers against her scalp. The subtle shift in his purpose, from holding her to ease the pain to holding because he wanted to hold her.

His thumb began to caress the underside of her breast. In the far distance a phone rang, four times, but new sensations replaced the doubling-over pain Colin had eased with his fingers. Sharp pleasure, a dull, feminine ache low in her body. He curled his fist in her hair and pulled her head back.

"You're a wreck, Erin Harper."

"I am not."

"You should go home. These are not your problems."

"How many times are you going to tell me that?"

"Until you listen." Then he kissed her.

She had never been kissed like that in her life. Never felt the sudden burst, the frightening, exhilarating mix of anger and gentleness, power complicating real tenderness. Everything in her cried out to return the kiss, every nuance, every feeling. But when he gave her the chance, she backed away because she didn't want to be Colin Rennslaer's next conquest.

And as she stood there facing him, seeing his dark eyes, tasting him on herself, feeling the moisture of his kiss evaporate from her lips, she knew she wanted to be his last conquest if any.

She had made herself sick with anxiety, and he had fixed her with some voodoo Oriental acupressure. She didn't want to be vulnerable and healed by him and not to have him be her conquest, as well.

She backed away because the prospect of all of that was so ridiculously thin.

"Colin." His hazel-blue eyes were so unforgettable, his black lashes so thick. "Please. I've made up my mind."

He took his hand off her waist and jammed it into his pants pocket. He started to say something, but her beeper went off.

She took a deep breath, pulled the beeper from her waist, looked at the number and showed it to Colin.

He shrugged. "Six-oh numbers are administration."

Erin turned to the phone on Charlene Babson's desk and dialed the number.

Alexa Sabbeth answered. "Erin, where are you?"

"In the labs."

"I just dialed Miles's number and got the voice mail."

Erin swallowed and looked at Colin. If he'd stopped looking at her, she didn't know when. "What is it?"

"Your luggage has arrived. I've had it sent around, but I thought you might want to come yourself to get your cat. Priscilla, is it?"

"Yes. Priscilla."

"Well, she's not in a very kindly mood."

"I'll be right there." Erin hung up the receiver. "My cat is here."

He dragged his tie loose again and leaned back against the doorjamb into Charlene's office. "I guess that means you're staying." He took her silence for assent. "I'll walk back with you."

"I'm a big girl, Colin."

He looked down. When he looked back up at her, Erin knew that he'd been studying gold-flecked white asphalt floor tiles to avoid staring at her body as he spoke. "It never occurred to me that you weren't all grown-up, Erin Harper.''

The more studiously he avoided such crass, clichéd behavior, the more she craved it. Colin Rennslaer had all the moves, cultivated to the level of fine art.

FRIDAY NIGHTS Colin usually played the oboe, and once in a while an alto sax in a chamber-music group. After that six or eight of them would head down to some hometown Chicago pizza joint or Swedish diner and drink beer or vodka as the occasion demanded. But suddenly there was Erin Harper in his life, and he knew when he was willing to forgo his music on a Friday night, things were pretty serious.

He'd known her less than twenty-four hours.

He couldn't stay away from her. He wasn't a great believer in love at first sight, but his attraction to her was the closest he had come in years. Circumstances being what they were, he already knew more about Erin's values than he knew of any woman's he had ever been near. And it was painfully obvious that Erin already knew his.

His reputation mattered to him more than anything. He wasn't proud of such a shallow-sounding thing to pin his values on, but you didn't grow up on the seedy side of Chicago, bust your butt to get a track scholarship through college and further bust your butt in med school because an "M.D." after your name didn't give you some interest in your own reputation.

He was regarded as one of the top five transplant surgeons in the country. He'd earned the kudos. He'd taken pains to develop the qualities and skills to merit them.

Admittedly he sometimes played the game of an overweening, status-seeking, arrogant ass to cover his real limitations—which began with still feeling inside like the chump child of a blue-collar alcoholic and an overworked woman who, to this day, had never figured out her own value. Bless her soul—she'd given him every ounce of love and admiration and approval she could muster.

Better to play the arrogant ass than face the other music, style but no substance. Take away the scalpel, take away the horns, and what have you got left? A shell.

He wanted Erin Harper to find more, but he was afraid she wouldn't. He never had. Or at least he'd never been convinced. So he wanted her and he wanted to run.

Walking her back to the administration offices, Colin decided he wanted her more than he feared her finding him out. They'd backed up Miles's entire computer hard drive, and Erin had the disks. Sabbeth had a high-speed 600 dpi printer in her office, and by morning Erin would have reams of data to begin examining.

In the meantime Colin intended to feed her and see where that led.

THE LIGHTS in the hallway leading to Alexa Sabbeth's office had been dimmed for the evening, but her doorway stood open. Sounds of an argument spilled out.

"You did *what?*" came Alexa's angry, disdainful voice.

"I told you I was splitting with him, but he wouldn't take no for an answer. I just threw in a little added incentive."

Erin didn't recognize the scratchy female voice, but she thought the frown furrowing Colin's brow indicated he did. He held her back a moment.

"He was going to—" the voice continued.

"You've lost your nerve and jeopardized— Hold it," Alexa ordered. "Is someone out there?"

Colin gave Erin a light nudge toward the doorway. She crossed the threshold into the room. "It's me, Alexa. I've come for Pris."

Alexa began to nod, then did her best to disguise a double take. Because Colin had arrived with her? Erin wondered. Across the desk from Alexa stood another woman. Both of them radiated hostility. And Pris, still caged in her travel kennel, was not happy, either.

Erin formed several quick impressions. Ginger Creedy had probably been very pretty twenty years ago. She had dark brown hair shaped like a pixie's, blue eyes and a wide mouth. Her complexion was leathery from too many years in the sun, and a little puffy.

Compared to Alexa's cool, controlled, bone-thin demeanor, Erin thought, Ginger Creedy just looked spent, used up. Her lashes were spiky with mascara that had deposited on her lower lids. She clapped her mouth closed, but her baleful eyes betrayed her agitation—but at Alexa or the interruption?

"What are you doing here?" she demanded of Colin. "Aren't you supposed to be rehearsing with your chamber-music group tonight?"

Colin gave a sardonic smile. "Erin Harper, meet my scrub nurse, Ginger Creedy, who delights in controlling my schedule to the quarter hour." He gave a long-suffering smile. "She and Alexa don't always see eye to eye."

Alexa recovered quickly and mimicked Colin's smile. "Actually we do, Colin, more often than not. Probably more often than I agree with you."

He shrugged. "Peas in a pod..."

Watching the dynamics among Alexa, Colin and Ginger, Erin decided the sudden silence that had descended between the two women hinted that they were in league. And she couldn't dismiss the feeling that the abrupt end to their heated conversation had to do with Miles. Was it because Joyce had mentioned breaking off a relationship?

What were the chances that the Miles's breakup had been with one of these women?

Pris didn't stop fussing even after Erin rescued her from her small prison. The cat wanted to bolt, and it took Erin a few moments to realize why. There was a subtle scent in Alexa's office, and apparently it was similar to the perfume Erin's niece had once sprayed on Pris, nose to tail. The cat still hadn't forgiven the child or Erin. Pris was scrambling hard toward Colin, always preferring men to women. He offered to take her, and she buried her face in his suit coat.

Erin tried to remember if she had noticed the perfumed scent in Alexa's office the night before, but couldn't. Then she remembered where she'd encountered the scent before.

"Have either of you been into Miles Cornwall's office in the last day or so?"

The two exchanged glances. "Of course," Alexa answered swiftly. "I met with him almost daily. Why?"

"I thought there was a trace of perfume in the air," Erin answered. Ginger hadn't answered one way or another. "Miles was allergic," Erin explained. "And Pris acts like she is. I think that's why she's behaving so badly. Was there something wrong, Alexa? We didn't mean to interrupt, but—"

"No." Alexa glanced at Ginger. "Our discussion had nothing to do with you. Turf battles in the O.R., is all."

Colin's hands dwarfed Pris, who hadn't peeked out more than once. Stroking her fur, Colin gave an incredulous noise. "What turf battles?"

"Oh, for heaven's sake, Colin!" Ginger snapped, her puffy face flushed. "Since when are you interested in petty squabbles over—"

"Only since Miles Cornwall was run over and left for dead." He looked speculatively at Ginger. "Did you know

Miles's daughter thought he was broken up over some woman. See how everything is taking on a new significance?"

"I'm not even going to dignify that with an answer," Ginger huffed. "In case you'd forgotten, I was playing handmaiden to you in the O.R. when Miles was run over."

"It's a good thing you are such a talented scrub nurse, Creedy," Colin said in an agreeable tone, subtly chiding her disparaging handmaiden remark. "Otherwise I'd sack you in a heartbeat."

"Is there something I can do for you?" Alexa interrupted wearily.

"Yeah," Colin answered. "Have the gourmet kitchen send a meal up to Erin's suite. Pasta Alfredo with chicken, or something. And a bottle of wine." He reached around Erin for Pris's traveling kennel, asked her for the keys, took them. "Make that service for two," he added, and winked, then walked out consoling Pris.

"Men," Ginger muttered under her breath. "Can't live with them, can't live without them." She smiled ingratiatingly, but the message Erin took was that Colin Rennslaer was her meal ticket and therefore the one irritating man Ginger Creedy couldn't live without. "Don't keep him late, Erin," she added waspishly, sailing out the door. "He's due in surgery at 6:00 a.m."

Alexa just shook her head and made the call to the dining room, then sank into her executive chair. "Looks as if you've made a conquest, Erin."

The word made Erin flinch inside. "He just knows I haven't eaten," she answered, dismissing the possibility. "He said you have a high-speed printer. I have a couple of disks off Miles's computer that I'd like printed out."

"No problem." Alexa took the disks. "Anything else?"

"Yes." She sat down opposite Alexa. "I ran into Charlene Babson and Tyler Robards in the research labs. She apparently hadn't heard that I'd even been asked to replace Miles."

Alexa nodded. "I left a message for her, but—did you tell her?"

Actually Colin had, but Erin sidestepped that one. "We talked. She's very resentful, feels overlooked, surrounded by incompetents, undervalued, possessive."

Alexa sighed. "She has been a thorn in Miles's side for months."

"Then why didn't he fire her?"

"She knows too much. He thought he could control her." Alexa paused thoughtfully. "Erin, I don't want to unduly influence your findings, but I will say this. No one knows as much as Charlene Babson knows—and she works at keeping it that way. But I'm sure you've already figured that out."

Erin didn't know which possibility troubled her more. That Alexa Sabbeth was such a cultivated tattletale with her I'm-sure-you-already-know-this-but line, or that she was willing to point a finger at all. Neither tactic was very professional, and it didn't do anything to enhance her integrity in Erin's eyes.

"Anyway, I am glad you dropped by." Alexa turned to the credenza behind her and picked up a pile of papers bound into several books. "These may be among the documents saved to disk that you've brought, but I thought you might like to get a start."

"Fine," Erin responded. "What are they?"

"This one—" Alexa handed over the top document "—is the original HemSynon proposal, which Miles used to generate board approval and financial support for the project."

She continued, handing Erin one document after another. The stack was quite impressive.

"The final approval letter is what Miles was to have presented to the board night before last?" Erin asked.

"Yes." Alexa frowned. "Except that only his resignation was found in his briefcase, along with his recommendation that you—"

"Then you already had a copy of the proposal to the FDA?"

"Yes. As a security measure, though, the rest of the board members were required to read, sign and return all copies in the course of the meetings. Naturally my copies were kept under lock and key."

Erin approved of the guidelines designed to protect the confidential nature of the research. Assuming the measures worked, there wouldn't have been any leaks through administrative channels, unless they came from Alexa Sabbeth herself.

It wasn't a leak that Miles had feared in any case. She wondered if Miles had trusted the Rose Memorial administration as much as they seemed to have trusted him. "How would you describe your rapport with Miles?"

Alexa gave a thoughtful look. "Professional, certainly. One of mutual respect. He was an attractive man, we went out to dinner once or twice years ago. On the whole he knew I would back him. I think he appreciated that."

"I'm sure he did. It's always an enormous benefit to have administration behind you. I'm counting on that kind of support, as well."

"You may, absolutely," Alexa answered. "You were Miles's choice."

"Charlene described a succession plan that says she was to assume Miles's responsibilities."

"Well, obviously Miles never foresaw any real need. Unfortunately succession planning is often treated like a fill-in-the-blank nuisance.... Have you decided how you're going to handle her in that regard?"

"I told her I wouldn't interfere with her work."

Alexa's eyes widened. "What a masterful stroke! Charlene believes she's in charge, then?"

"She is."

"But what if she's the one sabotaging the project?"

"She'll make a mistake." Erin believed that, but Alexa's features tightened unbecomingly. "Why does that annoy you?"

"It just seems hopelessly naive to me, Erin. The good guys don't always win. If you're planning to wait until someone slips up—"

"Don't count on it?" Erin finished.

"Exactly." Alexa got up and stood with her fingers balanced delicately on top of her desk. "I'll have the disks printed out. And—"

"Could we get a security guard assigned to that?" Erin asked. "Everything on that disk is confidential. I don't want anyone reading the material or making copies as it's being printed."

Alexa held up a hand to indicate she understood Erin's concerns, and although she arranged for the necessary security by phone, Erin thought she had a pinched look around her lips.

"Anything else?"

"Not that I can think of," Erin answered. "Thanks again for compiling these reports and all your help." She rose from the chair facing Alexa's desk and made her goodbyes, but at the door she turned back. "Is there anything I should know about Ginger Creedy?"

Alexa tilted her head. "Why?"

Erin decided that despite everything the two of them had in common, she didn't like Alexa Sabbeth very much. "Because I also thought—as Colin did—that when I came in, the conversation between you died sort of...unnaturally."

Alexa laughed. "Don't go looking for trouble, Erin. I'm sure you'll find enough without inventing it."

Chapter Six

It didn't escape Erin that Alexa's response was not an answer.

The question remained on her mind as she walked back to the suite of rooms Jacob Delvecchio had provided for her. But she set the issue aside when she ran into Sister Mary Bernadette leaving her guest suite, a little girl clinging to her hand.

The child wore a darling print, gathered at the neck and waist like a peasant dress, and sandals. Her coloring was dark in a Mediterranean sort of way with exotic, dark eyes, white teeth flashing a brilliant, shy smile. Beneath it, though, Erin sensed a reserve.

Mary Bernadette smiled in greeting. "Erin! Meet my grandniece, Stephanie Mastrangelo. Her mother, Zoe, heads the medical-records department here at Rose Memorial. Stephi, this is Miss Harper."

"Hello."

Erin winked at the sister and knelt down. The child was flawlessly beautiful, with black hair streaming down her back. "Hi, Stephanie. Were you here to visit me?"

"Dr. Colin said I could, 'cause you have a pretty cat named Priscilla. And anyway, we had to bring the candles. The kitty wouldn't come out, though. Dr. Colin didn't know where she went. Does she hide all the time? How can you ever hold her? Does she come out to—"

"Stephi!" her aunt interrupted, seeing the child might well go on all night with endlessly curious questions.

"What candles?" Erin asked, already suspicious of Colin and candles and a dinner ordered from the gourmet kitchen.

"For the dinner table," Stephi piped in. "Me and my mom always have candles at suppertime. Dr. Colin just wanted to borrow some, but my mom says he has to bring back the candlestick holders."

Erin nodded. "He'll bring them back. Maybe you could try again tomorrow to see Pris. I think she's just crabby because she had to ride in a plane to get here."

"I've been on a plane," Stephanie said. "When I was a tiny baby. From Sicily. I—"

Mary Bernadette scooped the child up into her arms and kissed her before she could launch into that story, as well, then put her back on her feet. "Child o' notion, will you run down the hall and push the button for the elevator?"

Stephanie took off skipping and waved from the elevator. "Bye, Miss Harper. C'mon, Auntie Mary B!"

"Coming, sweet pea!" Sister Mary Bernadette turned to Erin and reached up to pat her on the cheek. "She's a darling thing, isn't she? She's just getting over a serious bout with the flu. Well, anyway, I wanted y' to know I've arranged with Miles's daughter for the funeral to take place this coming Sunday."

"Here? In Chicago?" Erin asked.

"Yes. She'll not be coming, however. Too many obligations of her own, I take it. In any case, don't y' be working too hard, now, hear?" She gave Erin a bawdy un-nunlike wink. "Take time to smell the roses along the way."

"Even if they're rose-scented candles?" Erin teased.

"Especially then."

She gave Mary Bernadette a smile, but she was going to give Colin Rennslaer a piece of her mind. The last thing she needed was to have it going all around Rose Memorial that he'd been wining and dining—Miles Cornwall's replacement.

She waited till the nun and little Stephanie Mastrangelo had gotten onto the elevator, then took a deep breath and opened the door to her suite.

"Hi," Colin called out, just lighting the pair of mauve-colored tapers in brass candlestick holders. Erin put down the pile of data on the sofa. Colin uncovered the salad and dinner plates. "Perfect timing. Dinner is served."

Erin straightened.

The sight of the food made her mouth water. The glasses of iced water and white wine sparkled in the candlelight. The warming candle wax smelled of roses, and everything she'd intended to say about the notoriety of hospital grapevines went right out of her head.

Colin stood waiting to seat her, his suit coat discarded, tie properly knotted now, his jaw shadowed, eyes smiling. In all, looking too wickedly handsome to be endured. Which reminded her again of everything she'd meant to say. "Colin . . ."

He held up a hand. "I know. This won't look right, it'll set tongues wagging."

Erin clasped her hands together. "It's a little disconcerting for you to be reading my mind all the time."

Colin shrugged that off. "You just can't spend your entire existence worrying what other people will think."

"For someone whose highest value in life is his reputation—which by definition *is* what other people think—"

"I know, I know. But I like to think I'm..." he hesitated, then smiled, obviously pleased with the term he'd lit upon, "evolving."

"Evolving," Erin repeated, unable to defeat her smile or his appeal. "As in tadpole to toad?"

"Sure. And you can be the princess who kisses me. Relax, Harper," he chided, sliding the chair in as she sat. "I'm hungry, you're starving, and we're just sitting down to a civilized meal. Okay?"

Erin laughed. "Okay." It seemed sometimes as if she spent every waking moment humoring someone else. *Everyone* else, Sidney would say. It felt so inviting to let go and be humored that she gave in to the temptation.

Colin sat down beside her. She picked up her fork and started on her salad. "I met Sister Mary Bernadette and her little niece on my way up. Was it the candles you borrowed?"

"Yes. Do you approve?"

"Such a *civilized* touch," Erin murmured agreeably, teasing, thinking how easy it was to fall into such casual intimacies. "I gathered Stephanie didn't get to see Pris, though. I haven't even seen her."

"She's here," Colin assured Erin. "A little on the touchy side." He sipped his wine and began attacking the Alfredo. After a few moments savoring the dinner, he asked Erin, "Did you learn anything more from the dragon lady after I left?"

"Not really. She had prepared that stack of project documentation for me—and I asked if there was something about Ginger Creedy that I should know."

Colin grinned and took another swallow of wine. "Clever girl. What did she say?"

"That I'll probably find enough trouble without looking for it."

"Sounds just like her," he said, cutting into the chicken breast.

"Is there something there, Colin?"

"Oh, yeah. An armed truce on the verge of daily collapse."

"Really? That bad?"

Colin shrugged. "Turf. Men. Occasionally the same man."

"Really... like who?"

Colin grinned. "No, not me. Tyler Robards. He's married and expecting a baby in a month or so, has an ex-wife with two kids, but he still hasn't learned when—maybe even *how*—to keep his pants zipped."

"With the dragon lady? And your nurse?" Erin asked incredulously. "All at once?"

Colin nearly choked on his wine. "That's a little debauched even for Ty. And it's all just background. History."

"Then why didn't Alexa just answer my question?"

Colin twisted a couple strands of fettucine on his fork. "Maybe she did. We've all been around a long time, Erin. Since before Miles ever showed up. So if you ask what's going on behind the scenes, you're asking a loaded question that probably has nothing to do with HemSynon."

"What about Charlene Babson?" Erin asked. "Has she been around as long?"

"No. At least not that I'm aware of. You handled her brilliantly."

"I'm not so sure." She put down her fork. She hadn't quite managed to finish the exquisite pasta before the mention of Charlene made her stomach feel knotted. "She worries me, actually."

"Why? Because she had so little regard for Miles?"

"No, not exactly. I resented him nearly as much. I can't blame her for despising him." She folded her linen napkin carefully and laid it beside her plate. "Miles was the most single-minded man I've ever known, but not in any flattering sense. Even when he thought he was in love, what he was really in love with was controlling and manipulating."

Colin was eyeing the remains of her fettucine. She offered him her plate. He smiled endearingly, took the plate and began twirling noodles through the Parmesan-and-cream sauce.

"What worries you about her, then?"

"I think she's every bit as single-minded as Miles was, more so, maybe."

Colin's brows drew together in a frown. "Are you saying that's not an asset?"

Erin made a poor attempt to smother a smile. "What have we here? One of Colin Rennslaer's hot buttons?"

"Not at all—"

"But you are being just a little defensive of single-mindedness—"

"I'm just saying, in certain situations, especially—" He caught on to her teasing. "Well, okay. But the point is, where do you draw the line? In a research environment, being focused isn't necessarily a bad thing."

"Focused? Is that what you call it? Colin, I'm talking seventy or eighty hours in the lab—"

"And I suppose," he interrupted, brandishing his fork at her, "that you've never put in seventy or eighty hours a week?"

"Fair enough," she granted. "But I'm talking about an added dimension, I guess. Haven't you ever known a person who's so sure of himself that he can't be wrong, even if he has to invent evidence to convince lesser mortals?"

Colin gently swirled the wine in his glass. "Sure, but I'm not convinced Charlene Babson is in that league."

"She's not, of course," Erin admitted. "But it's the *attitude,* Colin. She believes she's surrounded by fools. People who believe that will throw accepted moral standards right out the window—and they'll believe they were justified."

He put down his glass and stretched out in his chair. "If you really feel that way, why did you go to so much trouble to align yourself with her? Why not just get rid of her?"

"Several reasons." She took a deep breath and let it out slowly, considering. "She may well have the loyalty of the staff—and she's certainly in control of the project data. Mostly, though, because Miles was many things, but he wasn't a fool. If Charlene thought he was, and she was absolutely clear on that, then she underestimated him." Her chin went up. "Right now she's underestimating me, too."

Colin smirked. "I have a feeling she's going to regret that. You're looking a lot better than a few hours ago, Erin. There's a little color in your cheeks."

"Thanks." Erin felt a warm glow, pleasure all out of proportion to his commenting on the difference in her when she wasn't looking nauseous.

He caught a glimpse of Pris strolling out from the bedroom and put a hand down for her. She went straight to him and leapt gracefully into his lap. He fed her the one remaining piece of chicken from Erin's plate, which left Pris preening and purring.

"Now you've done it," she warned, finding herself irritated that the beastie was cottoning up to Colin. She glared right at Pris's beautiful, haughty little face. "Ungrateful wretch. I should fly you right back home to Sidney."

Pris just turned her head away from Erin's threat. Colin sat there stroking Pris's silvery fur, pointedly not looking at Erin. "What about Sidney, Erin?"

He might have framed the question into a casually conversational inquiry, but he didn't, curse him. That would be too easy. Too...respectful.

Colin Rennslaer had probably spent his entire life knocking down fences women put up to protect their hearts—whenever and wherever he wanted, with impunity. He meant her to know *What about Sidney?* wasn't a disinterested question.

"We live together," Erin answered, deliberately misrepresenting the truth.

Pris snarled cutely and hissed and stuck out her tiny claws.

Colin grinned and brought Pris up to nuzzle her nose.

Erin laughed and shook her head. Pris laid an adoring paw on Colin's neck. "Maybe I should put this shameless behavior into perspective. She adores all men, you know. Indiscriminately, without regard to brains or personality or—"

"You live with your therapist?" he asked, ignoring the diversion of the cat's behavior.

"He's not *my* therapist, and I don't live *with* Sid, we just live in the same house."

Pris leapt down and ran off into the bedroom.

"So. Sid isn't your therapist, and he only lives in the same house. Are you in love with him?"

"No. Not that it's any of your business," Erin added, pointing her empty goblet.

"Half in love with him?"

"No."

"Only half in love with me, then?"

She recognized the trap. Heat spread like wildfire from her scalp to her throat, down to her breasts, and she was tongue-tied because either answer confessed she was in love—or half in love—with Colin Rennslaer.

"You're joking."

"I'm not."

"Would it help if I say it first, Erin?"

"No." She loved his voice, she loved his eyes, she loved his five-o'clock shadow and she loved the offer. But no. Her security and her peace of mind and her heart were every bit as vulnerable no matter which of them said the words first. All the same, she *was* half in love with him, and more when he said it first anyway.

"I *am* half in love with you, Erin. More than half, probably."

The echo of her own thought, *more than half,* made her ache with misgivings, but all of a sudden he looked so weary. He slouched far down on his chair and rubbed his eyes, and when he opened them again, he blinked and fixed on her.

"Why is it that you're always lobbying against yourself, Erin?"

She shivered. "I don't know what that means."

"Has it even really penetrated you yet, that Miles is dead?" He could see that it hadn't. "I didn't think so." He believed she knew exactly what he meant, but he was tired. "You feel things and then deny them. You want one thing but you do another. You needed to go home but you stayed."

She lowered her gaze and stared at the white linen napkin in her hands. She loved his voice, loved his eyes, loved his razor-cut hair and his dark whiskers, but none of that accounted for feeling as if she had stumbled upon the one man on earth who might possibly understand her—and loving that.

She gave a tiny smile. "Could I just point out here that if I had gone back to Arizona to... um, to follow my bliss, so to speak, that...I wouldn't be sitting here falling in love with you?"

She loved the sin in his smile, too.

TYLER ROBARDS had a real problem with secrets.

Romantic assignations were one thing. The candle flame of clandestine kisses, the fire of invading a bedroom not his own, the blaze of undressing a woman who wasn't his wife. These were his style, and he knew he was among the damned. He liked to think of it in the politically correct jargon of "the salvationally deprived," which always brought a smile to his lips.

This HemSynon thing was something else altogether. Until tonight he'd told himself to grow up, to get beyond his fear, that if he didn't do what he was doing, someone else would. That's where he'd gotten the bloody idea in the first place.

Someone else would walk away with the fortune Hem-Synon was worth on the open market.

To hell with that.

But his hands were shaking so badly by the time he managed to unlock his Mercedes and get in that he couldn't get the key in the ignition.

Miles Cornwall was *dead*. And Tyler Robards was scared.

He managed at last to switch on the engine. He buckled his seat belt as he always did, then pealed out of his parking place, laying burnt rubber all the way. The shrieking echo in the parking structure fueled his fear.

Miles Cornwall was dead and that was one pretty huge coincidence. Ty didn't believe it was any accident at all. For an hour, maybe two, he'd holed up in his office trying to figure out what had gone wrong, and there was only one answer.

Cornwall was onto them, and Babson had literally done to him what she'd figuratively threatened a hundred times. She'd cut him off at the knees, which in Ty's competent imagination was exactly where the car would first strike him. But the fact that it *was* Rennslaer's Jag led to the next ugly, inescapable conclusion. Babson and Rennslaer had been in it together all along, playing him for a fool.

Now it was Babson calling all the shots and Rennslaer in bed with Miles's appointed replacement, dazzling the dame long enough to ensure no one would ever discover what had become of Cornwall and why. Then they would retire to some island paradise with blood money to burn from the sale of HemSynon on the rich black market.

Ty drove in a haze of angry panic. Even the traffic lights seemed blurred to him, and then the streetlamps when he'd gotten out of the city.

He had a history as long as his arm of not knowing when to cut his losses and get out, but not this time.

He had to see Alexa. Tonight. Confess the whole thing. Make a clean breast of it. She'd know what to do. She was the only person he could think of who was both powerful and smart enough to stop them.

Sheet lightning out of nowhere lit up the sky. He heard the clap of thunder—felt it, really—as he turned down the unpaved country lane and the downpour began.

Swell. *Ty, honey, how did the car get all muddy?* He swore out loud. His wife, Clarie, was a world-class ostrich, able to bury her head in sand three feet deep when it came to his peccadilloes, but she was fastidious, his Clarie was. Not one to overlook mud splattered all over the car.

He swung into the yard, knowing the electric eye at the gate would alert Alexa that he had come. She would open the converted barn door, he'd drive in, and she'd close it behind him.

Only none of that happened, which could only mean that she wasn't home yet. Tyler swallowed, clamped his mouth shut and switched off the ignition to wait for her.

The rain sheeted down the windows of the Mercedes, cutting him off from the larger world. He sat miserably in the cocoon of torrential rain and his own fear for a long time. Slouched behind the wheel, he drummed his thumbs. He heard the killer dog barking its fool head off from inside the barn, and a few seconds later he saw the rain-distorted beams from the headlights of a car turning into the drive. Still the barn door didn't open.

The car pulled up next to him. Alexa got out and dashed from her car to his, and the rain poured in with her. Clarie wouldn't like the passenger seat being wet, either. He'd just have to make sure she didn't ride with him.

"Ty. What a surprise. Don't you want to come in?"

Suddenly he didn't. Her place was thick with reminders of their brief affair, and he didn't want to be confronted with pieces of himself he'd given her. "Thanks, Lex . . . but no."

Tell her. Tell her now.

But he couldn't just spit it out, and maybe that was the best thing. Keep his mouth shut. He could just split, steal the dosages of HemSynon he needed to cut his deal and get the hell out. Leave Babson and Rennslaer holding the bag.

Alexa didn't have to know one damn thing. He wouldn't have to humiliate himself—

"Ty? What's wrong?"

"Nothing." That's it. He would get out. He could still make things turn out all right with all that money. Pack up Clarie and Ty Jr., try on a little fidelity and forget he'd ever had anything to do with this or any other woman. A fresh start.

"Are you sure, Ty?"

"This thing with Miles," he blurted, then clapped his mouth shut. Why had he said that?

"I know," Alexa murmured. She reached out to give a gentle massage to the taut muscles in his neck. "It's set everyone on edge."

"It makes me sick, Lex."

Alexa shook her head. "How can people believe the universe is a benevolent place when this kind of thing happens?"

His fear rose up again, that it was possible for a woman as bright as Alexa to consign Miles's death to some random piece of rotten luck.

He wanted to tell her things don't *just happen*. That Miles had been murdered. But to tell her that required betraying his own role in the scheme. His mind filled with the sudden image of Judas sitting around whining that he'd been betrayed.

"You'll stick with the project, won't you?"

"Lex, I don't—"

"You have to, Ty. We all do—otherwise Miles's death will have gone for nothing."

Too late. Beads of sweat broke out on his forehead.

"Ty, you don't look well at all."

"I'm not, Lex. I think I'm going to have to take some time off. You know. Get out...get out of here for a while."

"Ty, I'm sorry. You always take these things so personally. Go home. Have Clarie fix you a hot toddy and go to bed. Maybe you'll feel better in the morning."

Ty swallowed. "I'll do that."

But he knew a hot toddy wouldn't cure what ailed him. Not tonight. Not any time soon.

Chapter Seven

Sabbeth and Delvecchio called a full meeting of the board of directors for 4:00 p.m. the following day. Its purpose, Alexa told Erin, was to update the board members on the status of the HemSynon project and to take a vote that would officially recognize her as the new director.

Erin left the labs at two-thirty. She'd been there in jeans and an oversize peach-colored sweater—the first things out of her luggage—since dawn. She showered, did a quick blow-dry of her hair and dressed in a straight skirt, white silk blouse and a single-buttoned black blazer.

She sat a few minutes with Pris, calming herself, but by the time she found the conference room, she could have used Colin's voodoo touch.

He arrived at the refreshment table just inside the door at the same time. Straight from surgery, he explained, and so freshly showered that his hair was still damp.

"Did you get the computer-file printouts from the dragon lady?"

Stirring cream into her hot tea, Erin gave a nod. "A team of security people delivered them this morning. Seven box loads. I've spent most of the day going through them." She tossed the stir stick into a trash basket and sipped her tea, scanning the gathering.

"Nervous?" he murmured, stroking the knot in his tie. "A little," she answered, watching his knuckle for a moment. "More...disturbed."

He opened a carton of juice and downed the whole thing. "Why?"

"Security paged me this morning around five. One of the project supervisors had come in to clean out his locker."

Colin's expression sobered, but before he could ask anything further, Alexa tapped on her glass with a spoon. "I think we're ready to begin here."

Erin added another creamer to her cup. "I'll explain."

Still concerned, Colin nodded and took the seat opposite Erin, across the polished mahogany conference table. She took a deep breath and gave him a brief smile, then took stock of the assembled board. Twelve members, including Sabbeth and Delvecchio, had gathered.

A stocky, dark-complexioned, powerful-looking man smiled tersely at Erin and introduced himself as Frank Clemenza, the CEO of the Rose Memorial Foundation and Hospital Corporation. She had heard he was extremely wealthy and ruthlessly powerful.

Introducing the others, he frowned. "Where's Robards?"

"I spoke with his wife this morning, Frank," Alexa answered. "He's apparently not well at all."

Colin and Erin exchanged glances. He'd seemed well enough the night before.

Unhappy didn't begin to describe Clemenza's expression. "Note the absence," he ordered, then went straight to the heart of the issue before the board.

"You all know Miles Cornwall was struck down and has died of the resulting injuries. The police investigation is continuing. No warrants, no arrests. They believe Cornwall was hit secondary to the theft of Dr. Rennslaer's car."

Not everyone had heard that the car was Colin's, but Clemenza cut off the murmurs of surprise.

"The succession planning document names Assistant Director Charlene Babson to the post in the event of Dr. Cornwall's departure, but his demise is out of the scope of what may have been foreseen. I am given to understand that he personally solicited the services of Ms. Harper to succeed him."

He frowned, tugging repeatedly at a scarred earlobe. He dominated space and wielded words like a switchblade, and Erin thought he could have more successfully played the Godfather than Brando. "I'm open for discussion," he concluded, "but I am of the opinion that Dr. Cornwall's recommendation should stand."

Indicating the stack of documents prepared for each seat, which included photocopies of Miles's resignation and his recommendation to the board, he thanked Alexa effusively for her efforts in putting together the summary of Erin's qualifications for the post. He turned to Erin. "Do you really jump tall buildings in a single bound, Ms. Harper?"

Everyone laughed, and Clemenza cracked a smile.

"That would depend." Erin laughed, as well, but her stomach ached. The résumé was as effusive as his thanks to Alexa. By mocking it with such great charm, Clemenza had not only defused the tension, but he'd indicated point-blank that he wished to know how highly—perhaps how truthfully—she regarded herself.

"Upon what would it depend, Ms. Harper?"

Erin smiled sweetly. "Upon whether you want me to wash the windows on the way down."

Colin broke into a smile, but it seemed for a long moment that all the other board members hesitated, anxious to take their cue from how their CEO would respond. Clemenza smirked, smiled broadly, then roared with laughter, his great bulk heaving.

"I guess that answers all *my* questions," he said, passing his glance over everyone at the table. "Anyone else?"

There were a few serious questions. Erin answered them in the same vein. Clemenza asked Alexa for an update, which she gave, including a summary of the responses required by the Blood Products Advisory Council of the FDA. He turned again to Erin. "Do you have any questions or concerns about assuming the directorship, Ms. Harper?"

"A few. I know this is all highly unusual, and I know that you've all taken precious time from your personal lives to be here. Miles would have appreciated that. But I am concerned for the HemSynon project. Miles felt that it had been sabotaged in some way—"

"Do we know why?" the woman to Clemenza's left asked. Her question implied that someone had better know. Gray haired, stylish and extremely well preserved, Elsa Wentworth appeared to have already read the FDA response papers cover to cover.

"No," Erin answered. "Not as yet."

"Then why are we evaluating a replacement for Miles instead of looking into the sabotage?"

Delvecchio glowered at the woman. "Elsa, we don't have time to pantywaist around this thing. The product is red-hot. The time is now."

Elsa's light blue eyes fixed on Erin. "Do you agree with that, young woman?"

"It is vital. But if there has been sabotage of any kind, it's just as important that we find it. Up until this morning, I felt the project must be kept on line—that if someone were engaged in sabotage, that they could best be caught in the act."

Colin stopped doodling on the pad in front of him, Alexa's attention sharpened, and Delvecchio threw his Cross pen down on his pile of papers. "What happened this morning?"

"One of the project supervisors resigned."

"Who?" Alexa demanded.

"A man named Randy Waller."

Responding to the call from Tony Bugen, who had pulled a double shift on security, Erin had walked in on the man filling a sport bag with the contents of his locker. Bugen had recognized Waller, introduced Erin as the new project director and left soon after.

"Randy was extremely reluctant to talk to me," Erin said. "I'm sure he didn't expect to encounter anyone in the labs at that time on a Saturday morning. I had the distinct feeling that he didn't want anyone to know he was taking off."

"What was his role in the project?" Clemenza asked.

"He was in charge of figuring out how to remove the artificial blood cells from the circulation."

"In simple English, Ms. Harper," Clemenza ordered, "if it's important that we understand."

"It is, yes." She searched a moment for a clear, concise explanation. "But only so far as you know this—the HemSynon cells carry oxygen, but after a while they break into pieces that will clog your kidneys—and if your kidneys can't filter your blood, you will die."

"Then you're saying that HemSynon will kill people?"

"Yes. It would be like taking aspirin for a headache, only to find out the aspirin would poison you afterward."

The seriousness of her example quelled even Jacob Delvecchio's enthusiasm. "I thought these problems were resolved."

Erin nodded. "That's why Randy Waller's defection from the team is so alarming. He suspected that team members were beginning to confuse real patients with the hypothetical research models—and that someone had tampered with his research results to prove that Hem-Synon was safe when it isn't."

"Will you be able to verify that, Erin?" Colin asked.

"It will take time. Randy Waller was scared, Colin," she answered. "He was the expert, and he wanted out before somebody was killed."

"He said that?" asked Delvecchio, flushed with anger.

"Yes."

The rest of the board sat silently digesting Erin's explanation. Colin leaned back and hooked an arm over the back of the padded chair. "What do you suggest?"

"That we suspend operations for at least a few weeks."

"Impossible!" Delvecchio snapped.

Clemenza swore. "You're beginning to sound like a broken record, Jacob," he warned softly. Erin thought of men talking softly, carrying big sticks.

Delvecchio swallowed whatever retort he might have made. "I'm just telling you we cannot afford to shut down entirely!"

"And I'm telling you, I get the picture." He turned to Erin. "Are you suggesting the response to the FDA not be sent?"

"Yes." Erin laid her pen down. "We must have all our ducks in a row. The FDA is not a forgiving bunch, and in their little corner of the world, they're more powerful than the IRS. We have to be sure our own research has not been tampered with."

"I see," Clemenza answered. "What about you, Sabbeth? Are you comfortable following Ms. Harper's recommendation?"

"Yes." Alexa gave a curt nod, though her expression had soured. "Miles would have insisted we wait on her findings as a consultant."

"That doesn't mean we have to suspend research," Elsa Wentworth put in, siding with Delvecchio now. "We have an enormous investment in this project—"

"And we'd hate to see it go down the tubes," Clemenza concluded in irritation at yet another iteration of an argument going nowhere. Frowning, he turned to Colin. "What about you? Any problems with knocking off temporarily?"

"Not in general," Colin answered, deliberately avoiding Erin's eyes.

"Specifically?" Clemenza glowered.

"Specifically I think the whole thing is a lot more serious than we knew coming in here this afternoon. I think Waller beat it out of here for a reason. I have my own issues with the way that my patients' cases have been involved in the findings without informing me. But mostly I think the honorable thing to do is dismiss Ms. Harper for her help to date with our thanks to make sure her reputation isn't destroyed by this thing."

Erin started to protest Colin's latest attempt to get her to leave, but Delvecchio beat her to it.

"Rennslaer, I've about had it with you," Delvecchio interrupted heatedly. "Nobody twisted Erin's arm, and she can say so herself if she wants out."

"Looking for a scapegoat, Jake?" Colin asked, leaning in to speak directly at Delvecchio before Erin could so much as register an opinion. "Because that's what it looks like, my friend."

Alexa kneed Delvecchio to silence under the table. "Aren't we being a little overly dramatic here, Colin?" she asked. "The project doesn't need a scapegoat. It needs leadership, and Erin is eminently qualified."

Erin cast Colin a very peeved glance. She wasn't about to get into it with him here, but a few more squabbles did break out around the table. Clemenza cleared his throat and squelched them all instantly.

"I've heard enough. I'm directing that Ms. Harper be officially retained, that the FDA communications be withheld for one month and that the research labs be off-limits to all but the top levels of supervision. Call it an executive order. We'll reconvene one week from Monday. Until then, the discussion is closed."

THE ROOM CLEARED in Clemenza's ample wake. Erin sat right where she was. Colin had gotten up, but seeing that Erin wasn't leaving, he hung back.

"Are you two coming?" Alexa asked from the door.

"Later," Colin answered. "Close the door on your way out, will you?"

Alexa shot him a glare, but he ignored her and waited until the solid door had swung silently closed.

"Okay, Erin. What's going on here?"

"I thought we had an agreement, Colin. I thought you understood—"

She was interrupted by his beeper, which he snatched up and poked several times, reading the message. He expelled a breath in frustration. She waited patiently, though she was angry at him and scared of how powerfully attracted to him she was even in her anger.

"Erin, I want to clear this up with you, but I have to go see my patient. Will you walk with me?"

She got up and pushed her chair beneath the table. "Colin—"

"Please."

"All right." She placed her papers into her briefcase and slid the long strap onto her shoulder.

He held one door after another for her and put a hand at the small of her back when they reached the sidewalk. Fifty feet away was the precise location where Miles had been run down. Erin had the feeling Colin paused because he wanted to remind her of the stakes, that Miles was dead. And that this was no ordinary volcano she had chosen to throw herself into this time.

Erin swallowed and turned away.

The weather was balmy and comfortable, the sky a cloudless blue. The Rose Memorial Flight for Life helicopter, which had recently landed nearby, could still be heard winding down. Colin guided her across the intersecting street in the direction of Rose Memorial's main entrance. "This way." He cleared his throat. "You're right. We did have an agreement, but—"

"What room is there for 'buts' in an agreement, Colin?"

"Plenty, Erin, and don't tell me you can't see it, because I know better."

"I didn't expect things to get *less* complicated, you know."

"Did you expect resignations?"

"Resignation. One. And it's not unexpected in a situation where there's a shift in the power structure of a project like this."

Colin grimaced. "Spare me the management psychobabble, Erin. Waller wanted out. Packing up his gear on the sly is not a good sign, and you can bet Delvecchio is covering his butt six ways from Sunday. If someone goes down with this, Erin, it will be you."

"Delvecchio doesn't need a scapegoat," she argued. "If he did, he'd just shut down and stick the blame on Miles."

They had reached the glass-and-chrome facade at the front door of the hospital. The doors slid open. The operator was paging Colin to the surgical ICU. He headed down the hall, still with his hand at the small of her back.

His mind was already on the patient he'd been paged to see—she could see that—but he wasn't done with her. He stopped at the doors outside the unit where Miles had died, at the exit into the gardens.

"Look. I don't think this will take long. If I'm wrong, I'll send someone out to let you know. Wait for me here," he said, gesturing to the gardens.

"Colin, I need to go to Miles's place. You know where I am on this . . . let's just let it go."

Glancing distractedly toward the SICU doors, he took her hand. "Wait for me, please. We'll grab a bite to eat and I'll go with you."

Erin dug in. "I don't need anyone to go with me."

"I know that. Please." He backed away, his eyes holding hers until the last possible minute. He turned, finally, banged on the metal plate to open the automatic doors and disappeared.

Sighing, Erin shoved through the garden exit. She hadn't promised, but the truth was she didn't want to go alone to Miles's silent, empty apartment.

She had absolutely no proof of it, but in the same way she knew Randy Waller was the smartest rat on the ship, she knew Colin Rennslaer knew before she had that she didn't want to go alone.

Part of her insisted there was something terribly sinister about that, while another part argued that he couldn't have kissed her, that he couldn't have admitted to being half in love with her, that he couldn't look at her the way that he did and still have ulterior motives she couldn't recognize.

She started to sit on a bench in partial shade when she spotted Sister Mary Bernadette sitting alone on a stone bench in the sunshine near the center of the garden. Erin made a deal with herself. She would wait for Colin only so long as it took to visit for a few moments. After that she'd go.

Mary Bernadette clutched a few pieces of folded dime-store yellow stationery in her gnarled fingers with the hand-addressed envelope at her side on the bench.

"May I sit with you, Sister Mary Bernadette?"

The tiny woman startled. "Erin. Aren't you looking sharp as any tack! Of course. Please do." In the sunlight she seemed more fragile than ever, but perhaps that was due to tears glistening in her plain brown eyes.

Erin sat and put down her briefcase, letting the shoulder strap slip down her arm. "Bad news?"

The sister's lips flattened in emotion. "I pray not, but…" She shrugged jerkily. "The letter is from the mother of a little girl who got a new heart here a couple of months ago. Molly Beecham. Audra is the mother. A waif herself. Thin as a stick. Poor as a country mouse, but smart, you know?"

Erin nodded. "How is Molly doing?"

"Oh," Mary Bernadette began, her sad lilt wavering. "She's failing. HVGD, it says here. At least that's the only explanation given Audra." Her chin pruned up. "Sad to say, I can't even remember what that is."

"Host-versus-graft disease," Erin supplied. "Usually everything that goes wrong in a transplant is chalked up to that."

The sister nodded, birdlike. "I'll be prayin' for the child. Colin will be upset, as well, I think. I must remember to tell him."

"He was Molly's surgeon?"

"Yes. Audra traveled here from St. Louis to have him operate on Molly." The nun smiled. "He took nothing for the case. He doesn't know I know, and he'd most certainly throttle me for sayin' so, but the dear man put up over half the rest of the money, too."

Erin shook her head slowly.

"You don't believe me?"

"No, I do," Erin said, pulling her briefcase into her lap, jerking her shoulder strap back into place, thinking that if she were premenstrual there might be some excuse for the lump in her throat. "I'd better be going now."

Mary Bernadette patted her hand. "You're in my prayers, as well, Erin. Perhaps we could ride together tomorrow to the cemetery?"

To the funeral, Erin thought. Miles's funeral. "I'd like that very much."

"Me, too."

She gave Sister Mary Bernadette an encouraging smile, then made her way back into the hospital. Colin caught her at the entrance asking the portly old black doorman—A. Jackson, his badge read—to summon a cab.

"Make it a limo, Abel," he said, putting his arm around Erin. "Trying to get away, my sweet?" he crooned in some Transylvanian-sounding accent, exchanging winks with Abel, drawing her closer.

"Yes. And besides, a limo is a ridiculous expense."

Abel shook his head mightily. "Lady's got a point there, Doc."

"True enough," Colin argued reasonably. "But I'm falling ridiculously in love with her, and I need somewhere ridiculously plush to land."

"Whoa!" Abel rolled his eyes and broke into one disgustingly huge smile. Erin was being had and she was falling for it faster every time.

"So, what do you say, my man? Do I get a limo or do I—"

"You get your limo, sir," he returned, signaling to a uniformed driver reading a newspaper, "unless you want me to use what's left of you to mop off the rest o' my sidewalk when you land."

"Abel, could you really do that?" Erin asked, wide-eyed and sweetly. The limo was already pulling into the circle drive. "Could I watch?"

Abel chuckled. "You better mind your p's and q's, Doc. This little lady can take care of herself."

Colin looked at her as if that one quality was exactly what had him falling so ridiculously in love with her. "I'll do that, Abel. Say goodbye, Erin." He handed her over to the driver, turned back to Abel, then followed her in and directed the driver to a five-star restaurant where they also played some serious blues. "To take your mind off things for a while." He closed the window separating them from the driver.

She looked at him while he angled his lean, powerful body to put his money clip back into his rear pants pocket.

"Have you thought about how we'll get back?"

He cocked one heavy, beautifully shaped brow. "Are you worried?"

Erin tossed her head. "No. I just don't want to have to indenture my firstborn to cover the debt."

His eyes held hers for an eternally long moment, then strayed low on her body, low where she would carry her firstborn, and at her breasts. He swallowed. He had been fantasizing that her firstborn child would be his, as well, and his voice was thick. "I have the money, Erin."

She studied her hands. "I know." And the generosity to see that a little girl with a stick-figure mother and a damaged heart got her surgery. "This is very nice, Colin, but I have a lot of work to do."

"Okay. What's Miles's address?"

The address and keys were in her briefcase, but she hesitated.

"Erin...do you want to do this alone?" His tone implied she might have reasons. Personal reasons to do with having once been involved with Miles.

She regarded Colin steadily. "No. I mean I don't...it's not that." She took a deep breath and plunged in because she knew he wouldn't leave it alone. "The thing is, I don't want you to feel like you have to be...looking out for me all the time."

Muscles along his jaw tightened, and his eyes grew dangerously dark. "Looking out for you, Erin, or looking over your shoulder?"

Chapter Eight

Erin's mouth went dry. She had made him very angry by implying she still didn't trust him not to be watching over her shoulder, checking up on whatever she discovered in order to protect his reputation from the project going bad.

"You still think I'm in this to save my own skin, don't you? I thought we'd covered this territory, Erin."

"Do you know how unnerving it is when you do that?" she said.

"Read you?" He knew exactly what she meant. She'd called him on it once already. "I'm not going to get into defending who I am, Erin."

"I'm not asking you to defend anything. I'm asking you to stop it."

Colin laughed but it wasn't with any humor. "Can you stop throwing yourself into the nearest live volcano?"

She lowered her eyes.

"No. I didn't think so," he went on, his voice low and hard edged. "Somebody always came to your rescue, and you will always be going to someone else's rescue. But when you grow up in a family as screwed as mine was, Erin, you learn there's no one to depend on. No one. And you better hope you learn to read the signs so you can get the hell out of the way before you get knocked senseless."

She felt tears pricking at her eyelids. She stared for a moment at the thick, choking traffic around them. "Colin, *any* rational person would have to question why an incredibly busy transplant surgeon has the time for this."

"Or a motive, for that matter," he added, expanding on her argument for her. As if he hadn't already clearly stated his reasons for caring how Miles's death impacted him—or the fate of the HemSynon research.

"We've been over this, too. You know what my reasons are—but let's tally up the hours, Erin, just for the hell of it. I've spent thirty-five of the past seventy-two hours in the O.R., maybe fifteen sleeping, another ten or twelve in my office or on teaching rounds. If we count this meeting, I've spent six with you—maybe eight. So how does that add up to watching over your shoulder?"

Erin swallowed. "It doesn't," she admitted. But somehow he'd nevertheless managed to be present when it mattered, for every encounter but the one with Randy Waller. Less than an hour ago he'd sat in front of the entire board recommending that she be thanked and kindly dismissed. She felt cornered and outmaneuvered.

"No. It doesn't," he repeated, his voice gritty, his eyes intense on her and dark as sin. "The truth is, even if this whole thing blows up, the scandal would barely make a ripple in my career—so *get* this, Erin."

He put his arm along the backrest of the deep limousine seat and faced her as deliberately as if her heart were deaf and she must somehow read his lips to understand.

"If I had the six or eight hours over again with you, I could think of one or two better ways to spend the time."

She shivered, unable to take her eyes off his lips, unable to mistake his meaning. She wished with all her heart that she had never heard of HemSynon, but she had, and it didn't matter how far beyond half in love with Colin Rennslaer she was. The project was her first responsibility.

And the pity was, none of her usual ethical, exacting conscientiousness changed how charged she felt with him anywhere near her, how alive and aware of him she was. "I'm sorry things are so...complicated," she said at last.

"Yeah." His jaw angled up, still filled with unrelieved tension. "Me, too."

THE ARGUMENT LEFT her tense and strained, conscious of his every move and of his feelings. Three hours after they had begun, he was still angry, she knew, and she felt defensive with him and defenseless in general.

Surrounded by the clutter of Miles's life, by the dusty collection of inlaid wood boxes he had made, by the jelly jars he used for chives and other herbs that had withered in the past few days, by the sorry jumble of cactus in the windowsill and an old pair of reading glasses...she felt nothing and blamed herself for being so heartless.

If Colin read that guilt in her, he didn't try to assuage it with mindless platitudes. But he offered her no comfort, either.

She found several boxes of files and felt compelled to sort through them in case Miles had tried to conceal whatever evidence of sabotage he might have come up with in the most obscure place he could find.

Her search, hampered by her own constant, anxious, greedy glances toward Colin, turned up nothing more recent than late '93.

Miles hadn't been into those boxes in months, possibly years. Colin looked through even less likely files, old tax records, appliance guarantees, car-repair sheets.

She found a pile of job applications on the floor beneath Miles's bed. Straightening the rumpled covers, she sat down and began reading through them.

"What did you find?" Colin asked, wandering into the bedroom.

"Résumés," she answered. "For Charlene Babson's position."

"So Miles *was* trying to replace her?"

"Maybe. But they're not very recent." In fact, they were all dated ahead of Charlene's hire date three years ago. Miles had probably selected her from this batch of applications. All of the applicants had fairly extensive research backgrounds.

Two in particular caught her attention. One because it belonged to Randy Waller, and the other because the applicant listed a John Chalmers for a reference. She'd known Chalmers at the university—his family owned a pharmaceutical company in Wyoming, and he'd always intended to return there to run the business.

She hadn't liked him. He was always taking the path of least resistance, weaseling his way out of any moral argument against lifting someone else's research. His recommendation alone would probably bias her against the applicant, Erin thought, steering her attention back.

Colin was right. The only logical reason for Miles to have these, for the pile to have been at his bedside, was that he *had* been seeking someone to replace Charlene.

"Erin." Opening dresser drawers, Colin had stopped, straightened and then stood aside.

"What is it?" She left the applications on the bed. Colin indicated the open bottom drawer. Lying in a tarnished silver frame, its glass cracked diagonally and shattered in one corner, was an old picture of herself with Miles. She picked up the photograph and held it in both hands so she could blow off the dust, but the grime had hardened on the glass.

She angled it toward better light, staring, remembering. "Here we are," she murmured. "Miles and Erin on a good day." It hit her hard.

So typically Miles to have kept it around, she thought. He was at heart a sentimental man without the taste for it, and he'd have found some biting, alienated comfort in the broken glass. She felt as if the air had been knocked out of her lungs. Miles Cornwall was dead, and she felt...nothing.

"I don't know what I'm supposed to be feeling."

"Do you ever, Erin?" Colin asked, not unkindly.

"What is that supposed to mean?"

"Maybe you should quit worrying about what you're supposed to be feeling and just notice what you *are* feeling."

She stared at the picture again, then at Colin, defiantly. "I suppose you know."

He crossed his arms. "Yes. Angry, frightened. Mostly angry."

"Why should I feel angry?"

"Look at the damn picture, Erin." He thumped at the background of the photo beneath the broken glass. "If standing together in a lab with a bunch of petri dishes and test tubes and chemicals was a good day—"

"That's not fair—"

"Fair? Erin, sweetheart, if that's the picture of you Cornwall framed and saved and threw at something when it was over, what does it tell you? How does it make you feel?"

Resentful, undervalued, taken for granted and angry with herself for feeling guilty. The reality was, there hadn't been much about Miles Cornwall to have fallen in love with.

She swallowed. "The man is dead, Colin."

"Yes, he is. Let him rest, Erin. Let it go."

A tear welled in her eye. "I don't know how." It was true. Colin Rennslaer was far more in touch with her feelings than she had ever been willing to be herself.

"Just do it, Erin." He reached for her. He'd been put out with her for hours, but the tension and irritation in his face eased and finally vanished. "I'll help, but you have to do it."

His fingers rested lightly on her neck, warm and strong, and he wiped the trail of her tear away with his thumb. Erin shivered. His eyes fixed on her lips. His breath came ever so slightly faster. Her heart began to beat harder. He dragged his tear-moistened thumb back across her lips, and his other hand ran up and down her back.

"Oh, God, Erin, let me help."

"Oh, Colin." Looking up, she couldn't see his eyes, only knew they were focused on her mouth. Heat and need and anticipation made her lips ache and her breasts tingle. She gave a small moan that made him pull her closer and move nearer and let his hand stray from her cheek to the collar of her blouse to her nipple.

His breath felt hot and urgent on her face. He touched his lips to her forehead and her temple, to the lobe of her ear and the underside of her jaw—just his lips, passing openmouthed over her face. Swamped in sweetly sexual feelings, she clung to his biceps, willing to wait all night for a proper kiss if it killed her because the lingering was so exquisite.

His hand slid down over her nipple, lifted her blouse at her midriff, dragging it up so when his fingers caught in her bra and pulled it down, the silk fell back into place over her bare breast. He covered the supple fabric and her breast with his hand and brought his mouth to her lips all in the same possessing moment. Erin cried out with the pleasure, and Colin groaned.

She doubled her fists in the scant starched cotton of the sleeves over his biceps and brought the length of her body against the length of his. She felt him, barely, thick and hard and pulsing against her. He sucked in a breath and brought her hips into his arousal for all too brief a moment before he pushed her back again.

"I want you, Erin," he whispered harshly. "But not here, not in Cornwall's bedroom."

His hands went to cup her face, and his kiss grew deeper, more gentle, seeking more, tenderer.

She gave a small cry. He picked up so well on her thoughts, her feelings. He responded unerringly to her needs. She had been foolish to doubt him, crazy to persist in being alarmed at his attentions, to coming back time and again to believing her faith misplaced.

The kissing went on for so long, so sweetly, edging closer and closer to deeper, darker things. His needs stoked hers. She could smell it on both of them. His breathing seemed almost violent, but after he dragged her bra from her breast, he never touched her there again.

If he had, she knew, neither one of them could have stopped, so his kiss was all that consoled her. She wanted it to go on and on, but he ended it at last and let his forehead come to rest against hers. Her lips were tender and wet, and her heart pounded fretfully.

Her pager went off before either of them had regained their senses. Feeling incoherent and confused, Erin bent her head and punched the button. She didn't recognize the number, but she was accustomed now to that.

Colin wrapped her in his arms for another long moment, until she felt the pounding of his heart subside. He let her go then, and pointed out the phone at Miles's bed-side table.

She wiped what moisture remained from her lips, blew out a breath and dialed the number from memory. Charlene Babson answered. "Charlene, this is Erin. You just paged me?"

"Yes. I just heard Randy Waller quit."

Erin sank down onto Miles's bed, facing Colin. "Yes. Where did you hear?"

"Sabbeth told me. I should have heard it from you, Erin. This isn't going to work, I can see that."

"I . . . yes. I should have called you. I'm sorry. I had the meeting with the board of directors on my mind, and—"

"And what? What happened?"

"The board is anxious to get on with the project—" Erin broke off and frowned. "Do you mean to say that Alexa Sabbeth told you that Waller resigned without telling you what the outcome of the meeting was?"

Charlene hesitated a second too long. "I wanted to get your impression."

Erin shook her head at Colin. "Really? I think you wanted to check my story against Alexa's."

"I have every right—"

"You may have, but if you do it again, Charlene, I'll see that Clemenza bars you from the lab, as well." Erin held her breath. She'd bent over backward to safeguard the woman's ego, but a line had to be drawn somewhere or Babson would walk all over her. "I can only work with you if I'm working *with* you—am I clear?"

"Well enough. But I don't like it."

"I understand." She didn't have to like it, only respect it. "Let's have a staff meeting first thing Monday and see if we can pull off a united front. Okay?"

"Fine. Our staff meetings begin at ten."

Erin knew that wasn't true—every staff-meeting announcement she'd seen indicated a nine-o'clock start time—but Charlene had already broken the connection. Erin stared at the receiver in her hand, then laughed. "I'm beginning to get that rejected feeling."

"With no small reason," he added, smirking. He smiled at her. "I'm willing to take a shot at making it go away."

"Okay." She abandoned the pile of applications on the bed and went to Colin. She was not inexperienced, but it felt to her like the most forward thing she had ever, ever done, knowing it was certainly not the most forward behavior he'd ever seen.

His smile widened by slow degrees, and she put her hands on his chest.

He covered her hands with his, clasping them tight against him. She caressed the back of his hand with her cheek.

His throaty noises of pleasure made her feel as if the most forward thing she had ever done was the sweetest gift he'd ever been given.

Maybe it was.

SHE AGREED to go to dinner with him. To put everything else away, forget the project, forsake the hospital and just go away. Colin had instructed the limo driver to return them to Rose Memorial long enough for Erin to lock the résumés in Miles's safe while Colin walked around to get his new Jag.

She wanted to know if she could drive to dinner.

"My new Jag? My brand-new hunter green convertible Jaguar XJE?" he asked, covering his heart.

"Sure. It'd be fun."

"You're kidding."

"No, I'm not. I drive a clutch at home. A little VW bug."

He took his arm from around her, looking pained, standing out of the limo when the driver pulled up to the research-labs entrance, looking even more pained. "It's not the same thing."

"It's the principle of the thing, then?" Erin asked, smiling, playing with his tie when she got out.

"Yeah! It's like . . . I mean a man's Jag. . . ."

"You do trust me, don't you, Colin?"

What was he going to say, anyway, Erin thought, darting up the stairs, picking out Miles's office key, laughing down the stairwell. That he didn't trust her?

She hadn't been so elated or happier-go-lucky or more excited since the day her dad brought home her first girl's Flyer bike.

She knew the minute she stuck the key in the lock and Miles's door swung open and the green library lamp went dark and came flying at her head that she should have been a little less merry and a great deal more careful.

COLIN STOOD in a daze for a few minutes, staring up three floors to Miles's office, wondering how things had gotten so out of hand. Drive his brand-new Jag? Did the woman have the smallest clue what she was asking?

But he was so charmed—so ridiculously pleased that she trusted him, so idiotically happy at seeing this almost magical side of her—that he didn't care.

If she burned out the clutch or dented the fender, hell, if she totaled the car, seeing her eyes light up like that would still have been worth it. Besides, he hadn't owned this one long enough to get too attached.

He started off down the street, the melody of a Debussy piece he'd begun practicing playing in his head. But he hadn't gone half a block when some streetwise instinct kicked in. Things weren't quite as they should be. Why were there lights on in the building?

He looked around but saw no security men, then glanced back up in time to see the third-floor lights go out—about the time Erin should've arrived on the third floor.

"Erin!" He took off running. Where the hell was security? He looked up to the end of the third floor, trying to convince himself that he hadn't seen some muted, suspicious light ahead of Erin. He had. Worse, there was no light now, and she'd had plenty of time to get to Miles's office and turn on his lights.

Desperate to get to Erin, Colin took the stairs by threes, punched in the electronic-lock numbers and jerked the door open.

The building was silent as a morgue, dimly lit, smelling hot and dank, feeling sinister.

"Erin?" he shouted. "Answer me!" He lit into the stairs three at a time, using his left hand on the railing to propel himself faster. But when he rounded the second-story landing, he heard the crack and splinter of glass and everything went dark above him.

He pulled up short. He had to get to Erin. The whole building was deathly silent. If she were okay, she'd have heard him, would've answered. But if he went on hurtling carelessly up into the dark...

He had to be prepared. He withdrew and crouched in silence, giving his eyes a chance to adjust to the darkness and his ears to the silence. He heard a movement, then another, approaching him—he thought from above, but the stairwell masked the direction of the sound.

He stood slowly, balancing with his hand on the painted concrete wall. A scraping sound came, and then the bulk of something like a backpack hurtled down the stairwell between floors, crashing into the railing, falling farther. Refusing to be distracted by the ploy for even one crucial instant, he focused hard ahead and above.

The glare of a thousand-candle flashlight in his eyes blinded him. He never saw the intruder or the vicious kick coming, connecting with his precious left wrist, blinding him again with explosive pain.

Chapter Nine

Erin struggled beneath the broken library lamp and chair the intruder had overturned on her. She forced herself to think, to decide what to do. The lamp had come hurtling at her head. She'd ducked, but the base of the lamp had caught her forehead anyway.

She had lunged at her attacker and caught hold of something like a canvas bag. She heard papers fall—the résumés and things from the bag.

Colin had called out, "Erin! Answer me!" But she'd been too dazed, too disoriented to answer. She'd caught a dim glimpse of her attacker, gaining only vague, fleeting impressions of a small build, a woman's glove—leather, not woolen—a fierce grunt, female maybe, a split second before the chair trapped her where she had fallen, its leg gouging her ankle, the rustle of papers stuffed back in the bag, then . . . nothing.

Cursing her foolishness, tangled in the lamp, she managed to crawl out from beneath the chair and pull the phone from the desk. The receiver fell beside her. She stabbed 911, but the keys weren't lit and there was no dial tone. Angrily she picked up the phone and threw it, crying out in frustration and rage. The cord had been cut.

She heard the slapping thud of something falling in the stairwell in the same instant the phone crashed against the file cabinet and fell to the floor, and then a roar of pain echoing in the stairwell.

She knew it was Colin. She knew he'd been hurt.

"Colin!" She screamed for him and stood, ignoring the threat of her ankle collapsing, climbing over wreckage she couldn't see.

He almost collided with her in the doorway. She reached for the overhead light switch and flipped it on. Light flooded the trashed room. Erin cried out at the grimace of pain on Colin's face.

"Are you okay?" he rasped.

"Yes." God, her ankle hurt. "Colin, your arm!" He was holding it at a funny, protective angle, and the welt on his wrist gave away the vicious injury. "My God, what happened?"

"I..." Staring at her, willing himself not to pass out with the intolerable pain, he let go of his left elbow and lifted her hair away from the gash on her forehead. For all the bloody surgeries he'd ever seen or performed, that gash made him gag. He breathed some obscenity or other and very nearly passed out.

"Colin!" She batted his hand from her forehead and planted her shoulder beneath his. "What happened to your wrist?" The welt, white as bone at first glance, was bright red as the blood rushed back and was swelling hideously.

"Kicked, I think." His features were contorted in pain and rage. "My goddamn left hand, Erin!" He swore again.

She swallowed hard. She understood. Colin was a surgeon. Everything he did, everything he was, was tied up in the use of his hands. "We have to get you to the E.R. Can you walk? Do you think I should—"

He straightened, costing himself a great deal more pain. "Let me see your eyes, Erin," he ordered.

"Colin, I'm all right. I don't have a concussion—"

He drew a terribly ragged breath. "Just do it, Erin, okay? Do we have to have a damn debate over every—"

"Fine," she snapped, sticking her face right in his, her eyes held wide for him. "There. Are you satisfied?"

Excruciating pain shot up his arm in waves. He could barely hold his eyes open long enough to see that her pupils were evenly dilated in the midst of her sultry amethyst irises. He gulped. "Yeah. Is the phone out?"

"It was cut. Should I go into the lab? I could—"

"No." His face drained of color, his lips bitten, he muttered, "Let's just go."

"Will you be able to get down the stairs?"

If the nausea didn't roll over him, Colin thought. "With a little help, sweetheart."

TYLER ROBARDS CROUCHED on the other side of the door to Cornwall's office, listening, paralyzed, as sick to his stomach as he had ever been. He'd just come out of the refrigeration unit when he heard the shouting outside. He had hurried in the dark to the windows and had seen Colin Rennslaer running for the door.

Ty had almost died. All he'd had to do was get in and get out with the half-dozen vials of HemSynon, and things would go swimmingly after. Or not. He hadn't even cared how things would go after.

But no.

He was going to get caught out by the stupid luck of Rennslaer's turning up here. Had he been tipped off by the lights going off? Damn it!

But then a crash had come from Cornwall's office. He'd heard a scream, the sound of something—or someone—falling. Someone else was already nearby.

Ty had been torn. Cold. Paranoid. What to do? Rennslaer would be barreling ass up here next. Ty had run from the window and hidden near the door into Cornwall's office, trying to hear over the roar of the blood rushing in his head. He'd thought he heard someone slamming through a distant door. Colin? Ty had imagined him taking the stairs. He'd bitten his own tongue he was so freaked out.

Colin was coming after him.

He'd sat there, cold and growing colder by the minute, resigned. Part of him wanted to be discovered. He wanted this all to go away. He was going to be caught. Clarie and Ty Jr. and the new baby would... oh, God. He couldn't think about that right now.

He'd heard a roar of pain or rage reverberating nearby. From the stairwell? The struggle on the other side of the door had intensified. He had heard a woman's frustrated cry and the crash of plastic against something harder.

Then he'd heard Rennslaer asking the Harper woman if she was okay, and her anguished cry when she asked what had happened to his arm.

Crouched there in the dark, sweating like a pig, clutching the bag of HemSynon vials he'd taken from refrigeration before any of this nightmare had begun, Ty imagined some horrible injury. Rennslaer was hurt. Badly, Ty thought, because the guy had an incredible tolerance for discomfort and pain and he didn't swear often.

Which, when he realized it, was when Ty knew he was somehow going to get out of this. Colin wasn't in any shape to come after him now if he'd ever intended to in the first place.

Ty laughed soundlessly, desperately, recognizing himself on the brink of hysteria. His imagination had been in hyperspace somewhere. Colin had never been onto Ty and his petty theft of the HemSynon.

He had never been in danger.

He blotted the sweat from his face with his sleeve and breathed deeply over and over again. He hadn't the stomach for this. He had no stomach at all, which was why he'd become an anesthesiologist. He wasn't the one who had to look at bleeding, mangled flesh. Not him. Not so much as a chicken pock.

He was going to be all right. All he had to do was get his head on straight and walk out of here before Colin and the Harper woman could call the cops.

He made it as far as his freshly washed and waxed Mercedes before he knew he wasn't all right. It hit him like a blow to the gut that he hadn't been the only one skulking around up there.

Someone else was either onto him or gone renegade.

He wondered if he had been followed, if he might have been ambushed next, and the HemSynon dose he'd stolen, stolen from him. If Colin and the Harper woman hadn't stumbled into it...Tyler Robards would be dead right now.

He had collected the price of his blood money this night, but he might never be all right again.

TED BAYLESS TOOK one look at Colin's wrist and ordered a shot of Demerol.

"That's too strong. I don't need to be swacked out of my head. Make it—"

"You may have walked in the back door, Colin, but if you want me to look at that, you'll take what I order."

"Fine, but make it a local." He swallowed eight hundred milligrams of ibuprofen, though, and sank back against the back of the exam table, which had been elevated. Erin sat to the side, holding his other hand, grateful that she'd gotten him this far without his blacking out.

Bayless took the scissors from the nurse and snipped the button off Colin's cuff. His wrist was badly bruised and swollen, but Colin decided that it might not be as bad as the pain indicated. The nurse handed Bayless a 5-cc syringe and a vial of two percent lidocaine. He delivered the anesthetic as close as he could to the injury. The relief was almost instantaneous.

Bayless glanced balefully at Erin. "You're a dangerous woman to be around, Miss Harper."

Colin caught the stricken look in her eyes and swore. "Just shut the hell up, Ted, and fix it, would you?"

"Sure. Somebody get me a Band-Aid," Bayless cracked humorlessly. "Colin, my friend," he said, plying the scissors, exposing the extent of the damage. "We'll get X rays, of course, but the swelling will take a few days to go down, and we can't even begin to evaluate nerve damage till then."

Colin shut his eyes. His wrist felt as if it was on fire. "Anybody call the cops?"

Bayless put three stitches into the gash on Erin's head while Colin and the radiologist and an orthopedic-surgery resident conferred over the X rays. There were no fractures or any evidence of permanently debilitating damage. Colin was euphoric. Erin watched Bayless administer more lidocaine, then immobilize Colin's wrist in a disposable cast and gauze.

The police waiting to interview them both in Miles's office were thorough, efficient and gone within an hour, armed with the few vague details Erin could supply about the intruder.

She took Miles's desk chair, and Colin sank into one opposite her. Erin had retrieved a phone from the labs to replace the one that had been cut and thrown around. Colin paged Ginger Creedy to cancel all surgeries for the next few weeks. By the time he had explained to her what had happened, he was slouched in the chair, resting his head back.

"Can I drive you home, Colin?"

He groaned. "I'm too tired to move. You know, I really, really wanted dinner."

"Are you hungry?" Erin smiled wearily at his disinterest. "It's almost ten-thirty. I'd forgotten."

He rolled his head and glared at her. "Why doesn't that surprise me? That's why you have an ulcer, you know."

"Oh, please! I have one from hanging around with people like you."

He let his head loll back. "That would be impossible."

"Because there's no one remotely like you?"

"Well, that is true." He laughed, holding his head up and massaging the back of his neck. He adjusted his left arm in the sling. "But that's not exactly—" He broke off, staring at the floor. "What's that?"

"What?" Erin asked, following the direction of his gaze. The office had been mostly restored to order, but a scrap of paper caught in the carpet lay tight against the side of a file cabinet.

"The corner of an envelope, maybe?" She picked it up and turned it over. Part of a return address was legible: "'mers Pharmaceuticals, Casper, Wyoming, 80214." She went very still, feeling suddenly cold and light-headed.

Alarmed, Colin sat up straight, cradling his arm. "What is it?"

She handed him the scrap. "I just remembered something. I told the police there was nothing missing as far as I could tell, but I had those job applications with me."

"They're not here?"

"No." Erin shook her head. "I remember . . . whoever it was grabbed everything out of my hands. It was a woman, my size, I'm almost certain. Her bag must have fallen open in the struggle." The same bag the woman had thrown down the stairwell a few seconds later, they had decided, piecing together what had happened for the police. "I remember it sounded as if she were cramming papers back into something—but they must have been my papers."

Colin concentrated on the scrap of envelope. "Do you think this came from her bag?"

Erin shuddered. "It must have. And the interesting thing is, there was an application in that stack with a reference from Chalmers Pharmaceuticals."

Colin frowned. His wrist throbbed dully despite the ibuprofen and lidocaine, and he wasn't concentrating very well. "It's way too wild a coincidence, isn't it? The odds must be a million to one that the papers you had in your hands were exactly the ones this woman wanted."

"That's true." Erin rubbed her forehead. "I'm not being very clear, am I?" Her reasoning *was* intricate, but she couldn't afford to ignore the link between someone who had applied for so sensitive a research position and an intruder breaking into Miles's office two days after his death.

Chalmers Pharmaceuticals was the link, and the company was run, as far as Erin knew, by John Chalmers—a man she had never liked or trusted, and who was known in research enclaves as a shark without scruples.

"He's connected with this woman, Colin, I know it. And I wouldn't put it past him to have offered her any amount of money—a cut of the take, for instance—if she could deliver the HemSynon synthesis research."

Colin shook his head. "He could never gear up for production in time to—"

"No, listen…" Seeing how uncomfortable Colin was, she helped him up and they moved to the sofa. She switched on the lamp at the end of the couch and went to the outer office to put on a pot of hot water. Colin settled into one corner and stretched out his legs. Tucking hers beneath her, she sat close to him and continued.

"Suppose you're a musician—star caliber. You're rich and famous, and people send you material as fast as your agent can shovel it out the door. Scribbles, tapes, jingles, melodies, whole songs, whole albums worth of songs. Johnny C. is one of them."

"C. for Chalmers. Okay."

Erin nodded. "So you write your own music—you always have—and you come up with a melody you love. You record, you hit the lists and you finally go platinum. But guess what? Johnny C. thinks your melody is *his* melody. He claims that you stole it. He has proof your people got the tape he sent. And by anybody's standard, your melody is substantially the same. So what happens?"

"I'm screwed."

"And you settle."

"*I* don't settle."

Erin shrugged. "Well, that's a personal call. And it's where the analogy to HemSynon falls short. The beauty of it, for Chalmers, is that he doesn't have to produce one vial. Given enough information, he could make a case that HemSynon had been stolen from him. The validity of the patents, the origin of the HemSynon research—all of it winds up in some legal never-never land."

"And Rose Memorial bites the bullet, deciding to settle with him because if they don't they'll be tied up in court till Hell freezes over. Extortion by any other name."

"It happens. It's easier—and cheaper in the long run—to pay him off than to fight his claim." She rose to pour herself a cup of hot water for tea. "Can I get you something?"

"I wouldn't mind a couple of those chocolate milks."

She set her tea down on the coffee table, then went back for the milk and opened both half-pint cartons for Colin.

He drank an entire carton in one long swig. "So, what can you do about it?"

Erin sipped from her tea cup. "Call John."

"Oh, sure." Colin laughed, miming the call. "'John, Erin. Would you like to confess to attempted extortion now or at some later, more convenient date?'"

But Erin was already on a WATS line to Wyoming information, then Chalmers's residence. He wasn't home, but his wife expected him in the next hour or two.

Erin thought quickly. The last thing she wanted to do was sit around this office waiting for the call, and Colin couldn't hold together much longer. "Colin, why don't I drive you home? I'll give her your number—"

Downing the other carton of milk, he nodded his assent and gave her the number. She relayed that and her name to John Chalmers's wife, who understood the urgency and promised to have him return the call as soon as he came in.

"You honestly think he's going to call you back?"

"John?" Erin asked, offering Colin a hand up. "He won't be able to resist."

IT WAS A SHORT DRIVE to Colin's penthouse condo overlooking Lake Michigan—nowhere to open it up with the Jag and just let go. But Erin was too keyed up to appreciate more than the scent of a new car and the luxurious feel of the deep leather seats.

Tired, distracted and aching, Colin was preoccupied, as well, and beyond giving her directions, didn't say anything. Handling the Jag as easily as if it were her little VW,

Erin pulled into the underground parking after no more than eight minutes, and they walked together to the penthouse elevators, which required Colin's key.

"So is this it?" he said at last. "Do you think this industrial espionage is the scheme Miles had discovered?"

The elevator was a glass one, affording a view toward the lake. Her gaze fixed on the lights of Chicago sparkling off the water, Erin shook her head. "I wish I could believe that. But if Miles already knew about the theft, why the attempt tonight?"

"Good question." Colin grimaced. The painkiller wasn't even taking the edge off anymore.

The elevator doors opened to a foyer carpeted so thickly that their steps left prints. A fabulous gilt-edged, baroque-framed mirror hung over a marble sofa table flanked by a pair of satin brocade Queen Anne chairs. Colin guided Erin to the left and picked out the key from his ring for her.

The condo lay in darkness but for moonlight streaming through the floor-to-ceiling windows. The living area was all open, marble floored, with a kitchen at one end, an eating area in the middle and a living room at the other.

Colin turned on the lights and showed Erin where to leave the keys.

"Wow."

Colin smiled. "It is kind of nice, isn't it?" He went immediately to the kitchen and took out a few more-potent painkillers. He'd wanted to take her to his music room her first time here, but he couldn't play for her with his wrist like this anyway. "Do you mind if I show you around some other time?"

"Not at all." She wandered in. Placed at angles along a gorgeous Persian carpet to the fireplace and entertainment center, two deep leather sectional sofas beckoned. Seriously. She slipped out of her jacket and laid it across the back of a chair, then kicked off her shoes and sank into one of the sectionals.

"Nice?" Done in rich greens and autumn reds, complemented by the polished marble, the condo and its furnishings were exquisite, but it was hard to imagine anyone actually living here. "Colin, this is . . . rich."

He switched on the CD stereo player to a Miles Davis set, then turned out the rest of the lights and handed her a compact cordless phone.

"I am rich," he said, easing himself between her and the arm of the sofa, pulling her close with his one good hand. She leaned into his shoulder, and he rested his head on hers. "That wasn't exactly meant as a compliment, though, was it?"

Erin smiled because she could hear the wry humor in Colin's voice, and sat up a little to face him. Freshly shaven at four, seven hours later he was whiskered again and achingly handsome despite everything that had happened. "Not an insult, either, though, you know."

Feeling pensive, he gave a bittersweet smile and began to toy with her hair. "Not unless rich is all you are."

She could never understand his penchant for occasional self-mocking, but she didn't want to hassle him. "How do you feel?"

"Like somebody put my arm through a meat grinder."

The lines had deepened around his hazel-blue eyes, she saw. "Did I thank you for coming to my rescue?"

"Not properly," he answered, circling his arm around her neck, drawing her close enough to receive his proper thanks.

"Thank you." She kissed him, letting her lips linger for a few moments, teasing herself with his whiskers. "It was a stupid risk, Colin...playing hero. You should have called security."

"How else am I going to keep up with a woman who leaps tall buildings in a single bound and washes windows on the way down?"

"That's so absurd—why do you even say things like that?"

"Come on, Erin," he groused. "A guy wants to feel like he's at least up to his woman's character."

"Oh, stop it. I don't even know what that means."

Colin rested his head back and closed his eyes. Things with Erin had progressed so far so fast that he didn't know what to say. He had fallen in love with her. He knew that. So in love that he wanted to take her to bed without that being what he wanted most.

He'd asked if she thought the theft was what Miles had been in such a frenzy about because he half wanted her reasons for staying in Chicago to evaporate. Half wanted her to go away before she began to uncover his less admirable traits and learned what a skilled pretender he was.

"You don't know me very well, Erin."

"So what?"

He sat there threading his fingers through her hair, letting it fall over and over again, distracting himself fairly successfully from the aching. "I could be some lakeside slasher."

"Are you?" she asked solemnly. His eyes were deep in shadows.

"No."

"I didn't think so." She rested her head on his shoulder again, sinking into him. She was always surprised at the heat his body emanated.

"I'm a glory-monger, Erin. I want to be admired. I'm a show-off. I want constant attention. 'Ordinary' scares the hell out of me. I've avoided commitment like the plague, I hate opening up, I can't stand rejection and I have never put a wet towel up to dry in my life."

"You're right. A total wastrel," she murmured, content to listen to him talking no matter what he said because his voice resonated deep inside her. "Why are you telling me these things?"

He went back to stroking her hair. "So you'll know the worst up front. I don't want you to have any nasty surprises.... This feels pretty serious to me, Erin. If I'm wrong," he said, closing his eyes, letting his hand stroke her back as if it might be the last time, "I'd rather you tell me now."

She almost missed his meaning in the numbing pleasure of his touch. He didn't want her to leave, now or any time, not Rose Memorial, not him. *Us* seemed so suddenly, gloriously right. Her heart was knocking crazily. Was it possible to *know* that?

She sat up once again. Though she couldn't see the expression in his shadowed eyes, she wanted to see him smile.

"Erin."

"I'm a perfectionist, you know," she confessed. "My way or the highway. Impersonal, critical and opinionated. I have to be right all the time, and you've *no* idea how annoying that can be."

He sat there cracking the most supercilious smile.

"Stop me whenever you've heard enough. You were right about never letting myself have my own way. I do that all the time. I might fall into sin and sedition—I might even have fun if—"

Colin laughed, then, a lovely, masculine, throaty laugh, and kissed her, cutting off her stream of confessions. His lips, like his body, were hot and firm.

Protecting his left arm, he lay back on the sofa, pulling her with him, cradling her in his right. "You'll be sticking around, then?" he asked between mind-numbing kisses.

"Just try to get rid of me," she whispered.

Colin groaned and kissed her deeply, his tongue tasting her, his lips consuming her, and he shifted again. His wrist throbbed, and his head was spinning as much from Erin's scent as the painkillers. He had never ached so much in so many places, or been so hard for a woman as he was for her, and the combination staggered him.

The position of his arm in the sling brought his fingers naturally to her breast. His fingers grazed her nipple, then his knuckles, then his fingers again. His knuckles. Her nipple tightened and thrust toward his touch. Deep, deep within herself she felt her womb clench, as well, and she uttered a small cry of his name. "Colin."

"Touch me, Erin. Touch me."

Her hand strayed from his hip toward the center of his body, her fingernails trailing, her palm leading to fill itself. Her thumb edged nearer, nearer, and she sensed the rise, the strength and length and rock hardness.

She hesitated. Her breath caught in her throat. Fear rippled through her. Of him. Of herself letting go, letting his heat unfurl in her hand. Of her need, and honesty and passion distracting her. But she itched with the soft fabric stretched so tightly across him, and her breast ached with his touch, making her hot and restless and urgent, and she covered him with her hand only to discover that her hand wasn't nearly adequate to hold him.

A growl of fierce pleasure tore from Colin's throat. She felt its vibrations, its intensity, to the very center of her nature. Her fingers tightened around him, and she stroked him, far enough down to cup him, far enough up to sense the moisture seeping into the fabric of his clothes.

Desire ripped through him in waves, but he controlled the nearly overwhelming need to surge into her touch and took her mouth again as he wished to take the center of her. The tip of his tongue traced the fullness of her lips, the satiny texture of her tongue, the dark, wet depths of her mouth until her breath caught and she gave a sound so thick with desire that his own breath broke.

She arched her head back to capture his kiss, to lead him to the harder, deeper kiss she craved like a starving innocent child craves scraps of food and drink—anything to fill the yawning need, a hunger far greater than the one to protect herself, to tether herself with reason and authority. His whiskers scraped her neck, sending spasms of primitive, unfathomable heat rushing unchecked through her body.

Colin felt the break in her, the yielding, and knew the immensity of her yielding and surrendering her flawless control. The sweet, unschooled cadence of her hand and the rhythm of her tongue answering his made his whole body tighten and hum like a bow drawn across the string of a cello.

"God, Erin," he groaned. "I'm burning."

For a moment she lay utterly still and silent. His harsh, whispered words appealed to her heart and mind, reassuring her, putting her fears to rest, all of them.

His fingers went to buttons nestled between her breasts, but he couldn't manage them. He stretched his arm and curled back with the throbbing renewed in his arm. He swore in frustration and commanded her, "Undo these, Erin."

She slid her hand beneath his to do his bidding, but his fingers caught her hand and pressed hard, making her palm meet her own swollen breast, feel her taut nipple thrusting, absorb her own heat. The shock of such a forbidden thing made her jerk her hand back, but he trapped her with surprising strength and held her hand there, threaded his fingers savagely in her hair and pulled her hair so that she must meet his turbulent eyes.

"Feel that, Erin. Feel it. And think what it does to me."

Images flashed through her mind, of his blood surging to only one place, of the pulsing and pounding, images of his mouth watering, his tongue aching for the taste of her, impressions of his gut tightening and of need shaping his face in sweet, unrelenting tension. Of desire rippling and muscles bunching in his back and buttocks and powerful thighs...

He saw that she understood, that she *knew,* and seeing it so made his jaw clench tight and his words feral. "Make it happen, Erin. Let me watch you make it happen, just like that."

She nodded, rising up, feeling the sensual power he sensed and returned to her. She stood and caught her skirt in her hands. She lifted it, hiking it higher by slow bunches, and she watched him staring at her, unbuckling his belt with one hand, unzipping his pants, pushing them down, freeing himself while she stripped off her panties and panty hose, discarding them at her bare feet.

She reached behind, and her skirt fell, then unbuttoned her blouse and let it slide from her shoulders. All that remained was her camisole. Colin's eyes went darker still in darkness relieved only by stray moonlight.

He shifted his weight to the center of the deep cushions. "Erin, come here. Let me."

She straddled him, one knee to either side, sinking inexorably into the cushions. He urged her lower with gritty pleadings and his hand on the swell of her hip until her flesh met his.

The sensation of cradling the awesome heat and strength of him cast her into a daze. He closed his eyes tight, wanting to feel more than see. If his wrist still ached, he no longer knew it. He slid his good hand beneath her camisole, let his thumb linger in the slight depression of her navel, then splayed his fingers and forced the satin and lace higher, beyond her breasts.

He felt the flow of her heat in the same instant that she reached high, and he stripped the camisole beyond her fingertips. And then he was into her. She lifted, he thrust, and she took him deep inside her. He took her, as well, so long and so completely that in the rampant, trembling aftermath of her last climax, Erin knew the woman she had been would never be again.

He had tempted her beyond control, forever altering her notions of herself, setting her free of her own harsh judgments about what it meant to wield real power and what it meant to yield to something even greater.

Setting her free, body and soul.

SHE LAY WITH HIM for a long time, but when the call finally came—which she had forgotten to expect—she had risen to get Colin another painkiller and a throw cover for them both. She wrapped herself in the coverlet. Colin took the pill and a glass of water, then held out the phone to her as she sat beside him on the couch. "It's Chalmers."

"John, is that you?"

"Erin? Erin Harper? What a pleasant surprise. I had no idea you had it in you to be crawling into bed—and so fast—with the enemy."

Chapter Ten

Despite the warmth of Colin's body, a chill passed over her flesh.

"Are you drunk, John?"

"No, just pleasantly tuned."

"Why don't I call you back—"

"Why? Won't you be there in the morning? It's hardly in the spirit of the current social climate to run out in the middle of the night. That's just my opinion, of course, but—"

She gripped the phone with both hands to keep from lashing out at something. "I'm really not interested—"

"More's the pity," he interrupted, intimating they might have had something together if only she were interested. "What do you want, Erin?"

"I want to know why I happened across an employee of yours ransacking my office."

He hesitated a fraction of a second too long. "Oh. You mean Miles Cornwall's office."

"Miles is dead, John, and you know it."

"Which is why the thought of obtaining your product has palled for me."

"Am I to imagine that anyone's death stands in the way of your greed?"

"Erin, I'm truly dismayed," he said, imbuing his tone with contempt. If he had been drunk, he'd sobered very quickly. "I've been known to steal candy from a baby—in fact, that's exactly what all this amounted to—but I have never killed the baby. It would appear to me that you are sitting in a nasty little nest of vipers all your very own."

Erin swallowed uncomfortably. "I wouldn't want to discount your part in this, John," she returned. "I didn't hear you deny the woman was your employee."

"Well, I wouldn't know about that. I have a great deal of free-lance help these days. People go off on their own accord altogether too often in this kind of situation."

"A situation of what kind?" She'd had it. "Theft followed by harassment and extortion?"

"I prefer to think of it as free-market competition. You're swimming with the sharks, Erin. Get used to it."

"Why don't we just cut to the chase? I know what you're capable of, I know how the racket unfolds and I'm warning you now. Your scheme can't work once an associate of yours has been caught with her hands in my cookie jar."

"I wasn't aware that an associate of mine had actually been apprehended."

No one had in fact been caught. Erin didn't care. If planting the seed of doubt in Chalmers's mind made him back off, her purpose would have been accomplished.

"Don't miss the point, John," she said softly. "Rose Memorial Hospital has the resources of private investors committed to the research. You don't want to take us on—I promise you that."

"Invoking the private sector! Oooh. Erin, please, give me a little credit here."

"I mean it, John. I want you out of this."

"Well, you know what, darlin'? I couldn't really care less what you want. On the other hand, despite my admittedly larcenous soul, I wouldn't take your goods now if you paid me—not if you emptied Fort Knox into my lap."

Erin began to shiver. Colin pulled her against him and held her tight.

"You still there, darlin'?" He went on without waiting for an answer. "I guess you must be. Let me tell you this. For old times' sake. There are things going on around you which you haven't even begun to imagine. But don't you let that worry you. You just go on back and bed down with the enemy, Erin. And have yourself a few sweet dreams before your nightmare unfolds."

Erin trembled again and felt the onset of yet another attack of her ulcer. Chalmers hung up softly. She handed Colin the phone and pulled the blanket tighter around herself, thinking she must get control of her shivering. She had called Chalmers, expecting to make him back off, but he had neatly, cleanly, efficiently, cold-bloodedly turned the trick on her.

"Erin." Colin held her from behind, his arm enveloping her shoulder to shoulder. "Tell me what he said. Did he deny any of it?"

"Not really."

"What's got you so spooked?"

Erin shrugged in his arms and tonelessly recounted the conversation. "He said that I'm sitting in the middle of a nest of vipers. He said things were going on that I haven't even thought of yet. He said he wouldn't take HemSynon now if I paid him. He insinuated that you are the enemy and...he wished me sweet dreams."

Her voice left even Colin cold. "Do you believe him?"

She angled her head back to rest against Colin's chest and laughed shakily—Colin thought more bitterly than sweet.

"That's the thing about John Chalmers. You can believe most of what he says, but you have to pick and choose very carefully."

Colin bent his head near to hers. "Erin. Answer me. Do you believe that I am your enemy?"

Tears gathered in her eyes. How could she believe that, when she was so spent from loving him and so loved as she had been by him?

"No." She took Colin's arm from around her and bent to pick up her clothes. She began to get dressed again. His question would have pleased Chalmers enormously. Even though she denied believing that Colin was her enemy, the question of her faith in him was one she had planted over and over again herself.

Colin ran his right hand up her back. "If you mean that, Erin, you'll stop what you're doing and stay here with me."

She had no choice. She wanted none. Time and again Colin's actions had served to dispel her doubts, and she would not succumb to Chalmers's poison.

The other questions remained. How did he know what he knew? Which among her staff were the proverbial vipers?

And what nightmare lurked that a few sweet dreams might forestall?

MILES CORNWALL had achieved the level of a lieutenant colonel in the army medical corps. The memorial services were held in the hospital chapel, followed by a funeral procession to an immaculately kept military cemetery. Erin and Colin rode with Sister Mary Bernadette in the same limousine that Delvecchio had first sent for her and that she and Colin had used the day before to go to Miles's apartment.

Every gravestone was lined up with the next in precision rows of pristine white arch-shaped markers. The cemetery reminded Erin in many ways of photographs she'd seen of Arlington in Washington, D.C.

A twenty-one-gun salute was given, but as no family members were present, Sister Mary Bernadette accepted the flag that had covered Miles's coffin on their behalf.

Relatively few people went to the cemetery, but among them were Charlene Babson and a small cluster of lab employees, Jacob Delvecchio and a woman Erin assumed was his wife, Alexa Sabbeth, who stood with Frank Clemenza, and Zoe Mastrangelo, Sister Mary Bernadette's niece. Erin recognized her because she stood arm in arm with the sister, and because she was the picture of her daughter Stephanie grown up.

Exotic and lovely, very small, Zoe stood five-two and could have weighed no more than a hundred pounds. Her hair was a lustrous black, long and full, curling naturally, and her irises were as dark as her pupils.

Sister Mary Bernadette joined the priest in a quiet conversation on the way back to the limousine. Colin, his arm resting in the sling, stayed with Erin. He exchanged kisses on the cheek with Zoe and introduced her.

"Erin, my aunt has told me Miles was a friend of yours for many years. I'm so sorry." She accepted Erin's thanks, then turned to Colin. "What happened to your arm?"

"Wrist, actually. Erin and I interrupted a thief in Miles's office last night."

"That's terrible!" Zoe frowned. "Will it be all right?"

Colin told her that no bones had been broken and, Erin thought, something about keeping it immobilized to protect his wrist, but she lost track of the conversation.

A woman, alone and uphill from the burial site, her face a mask of utter malice, stood silently staring at Erin.

Alexa made her goodbyes, and Frank Clemenza pulled Colin aside to discuss a pediatric transplant surgeon coming to Rose Memorial. Erin was left alone with Zoe and the woman on the hill behind Zoe's back.

"Erin, I hate to trouble you at a time like this, but the medical-records department is still missing a few patient charts which I had signed out to Miles. Do you know what became of them?"

"I don't, no," Erin answered distractedly. "There haven't been any patient charts in Miles's office since I arrived."

"So your intruder could not have taken them?"

Erin shook her head. "It's possible Charlene may have them."

"I'll ask her, then. They were patients of Colin's."

"We only just discovered that Colin's cases were being used for retrospectives on the HemSynon project. Computer models, projections." Scenarios.

Nodding, Zoe gathered a handful of hair and shoved it back over her shoulder. "Yes. Miles talked about that often. Actually I spoke to him about them only a few hours before the accident."

"You did?" The timing Zoe alluded to seemed critical to Erin, triggering her recall of the patient charts Sister Mary Bernadette had spotted in a bin outside medical records—but the woman glaring daggers at her looked ready to turn and walk away, and suddenly Erin knew who she must be.

"Zoe, I think he did return them." She took a step and indicated that she must go. "Check with Alexa in the morning. I think the files may be with her."

"I will. Thanks." Zoe nodded, then glanced doubtfully behind her. "Erin, are you okay?"

"Yes. I just need to speak to this woman. I'll get back with you in the morning."

Zoe nodded uncertainly, but Erin had already turned toward the woman who stood uphill, slapping a pair of black leather gloves into the palm of one hand, her frame rigid with loathing.

The female intruder in Miles's office had been wearing black leather gloves.

Suddenly Erin understood the gloves were a deliberate taunt. The woman wanted Erin to know she was the one who had invaded Miles's office. She had shoulder-length, mousy blond hair cut as blunt as her features and hands— and she was fearless enough of any consequences to willfully intrude on Miles's funeral, as well.

"Leather gloves are rather unseasonable, aren't they?" the woman remarked, staring into the late-summer sun, as brazenly unconcerned as if the lack of fashion acumen were her greatest shortcoming.

Erin stared numbly at her, almost at a loss for words. "Do you *want* to be caught?"

"Let's just say I'm not worried. I have an alibi." The woman shrugged and stared down her unbecomingly thick nose at Erin. "I came to pay my respects. Dr. Cornwall was a brilliant scientist. His loss is a detriment to us all."

"Including people like you who steal research secrets, who stand to profit from the theft of his work?" Erin asked, the heat of anger rising in her.

"Yes," she answered flatly. "Including me. Including John Chalmers. But you must understand—when poor, dear, unwitting Dr. Cornwall surrounded himself with flawed players, the temptation became too great to resist."

"What are you talking about?"

"Flawed players. Flaws. Character flaws. *Fatal* flaws. Miles surrounded himself with people who would sell out their grandmothers for a song. I exploit them."

Or the HemSynon project for a great deal more than a song, Erin thought. The woman's implication was no different than Chalmers's had been: a research project is only as invulnerable as the people involved.

Sickened, Erin felt her ulcer reacting. "If you have a snitch, if you're already paying someone on the inside of the HemSynon project to sell you its secrets, what was there to gain by breaking into Miles's office last night?"

"To plant the evidence of a link between Chalmers Pharmaceuticals and Rose Memorial's research." The woman smiled contemptuously. "But follow the bread crumbs, Gretel. Dr. Cornwall was murdered."

STUNNED AT THE BLUNT statement that Miles had been murdered, Erin recounted the conversation twice. Once for Colin and Sister Mary Bernadette as they drove from the cemetery, then again for the head of security at Rose Memorial in addition to half the other hospitals in the area. Erin had never met Albert Hastings, nor had Colin, but Hastings and Mary Bernadette went back over twenty-five years.

Mary Bernadette was skeptical of the cursory police investigation into the break-in of Miles's office and as upset as Erin by the intruder's appearance at the cemetery. She phoned Chief Hastings from the limo, obtained directions and insisted that they drive straight to his apartment building.

He turned off the Chicago Bears in preseason football on television. His apartment was very ordinary, but the electronics—a computer, fax machine, modem, cameras, even the TV—were state-of-the art. Very slight in build, Hastings had a thatch of graying dark hair and perceptive, intense, steely gray eyes.

After all the introductions the sister settled herself in an easy chair. Erin and Colin took the worn upholstered sofa, and Hastings sat at the edge of a vinyl kitchen chair. Erin told Hastings, beginning to end, what had happened and finished by handing over the piece of paper on which she'd written the make and license plate number of the car the woman had gotten into at the cemetery.

Hastings cocked one brow. "Accommodating, wasn't she? Always an interesting type," he mused, "the ones who want to make sure you know who they are. They say John Dillinger went around picking gunfights the day he died, making sure everybody in town knew who he was. She impress you like that?" Hastings asked Erin.

She nodded. "Very much like that."

"Let me try to summarize," he said. "This woman breaks in, steals a handful of papers which may well be meaningless to her, manages to leave proof of her connections to an industrial competitor and then shows up at the funeral of the man she purports was murdered. That about cover it?"

"Yes."

"So, what can I do for you?"

Erin exchanged glances with Colin. "I think she must have believed Miles was onto her snitch and whoever it was who murdered Miles."

"Why?"

"Because John Chalmers hinted at it, as well," Colin answered. "What was his phrase, Erin? 'Like taking candy from a baby'?"

Erin nodded. "Chalmers was willing to take the candy, but he drew the line at—as he put it—'killing the baby.'"

"So it was at first a simple case of industrial espionage," Hastings said. "But now it's murder, and the customer is no longer interested?"

"That's right."

"So why does the woman bother breaking in?" Hastings asked.

"She must have been fairly angry, don't you see?" Mary Bernadette mused, her brogue richly evident in understatement. "Chalmers was paying her for information. She's out a great deal of money now because Miles is dead."

Hastings grinned. "That's why I love you, Sister," he said, beaming at Mary Bernadette. "You've always seen straight to the rotten core and plucked a perfectly fine apple out after all."

She flushed with the pleasure of a long history with this friend, and her appreciation in turn gave Hastings an undeniable satisfaction.

He turned back to Erin and Colin. "But she obviously knows who her snitch was. Why wouldn't she just tell you who it was instead of breaking in?"

Erin couldn't explain that. "I've no idea." She looked to Colin.

"Chalmers said it, Erin," Colin supplied grimly. "He called the research team 'a nest of vipers.' If Miles wasn't onto Chalmers and this woman, he was onto something else—or *someone* else."

"But for now you need to know which of Cornwall's minions she bribed, bullied or seduced into betraying the project?" Hastings concluded.

Erin stood. "Yes."

"Consider it done."

THE LIMOUSINE DROPPED Sister Mary Bernadette at the entrance to her quarters, which were in a former nurses' dormitory, then dropped Colin and Erin a block and a half away, at Erin's suite of rooms. Between spending the night at Colin's penthouse and the funeral, Erin had forsaken Pris for too many hours, and the snotty little cat would have nothing to do with her.

Colin got her by default as much as by her fickle nature. Oddly, seeing the beastie curl up with Colin seemed to do as much for settling Erin's nerves as if she had Pris in her own two hands.

Colin called the pharmacy to get a medication to ease both the swelling and the pain lingering in his wrist. As soon as it was delivered, he showed Erin exactly where to inject it, and afterward, after a long, sweet, tender kiss they shared on the sofa, Colin stretched out and fell asleep.

Pris threaded herself between his left forearm and the back of the sofa instinctively, as if she knew her body heat would conduct itself into his wrist and, by herself, she would make it all better.

Erin wasn't opposed to any voodoo that worked. She broke a piece of gourmet baby Swiss cheese from a chunk stored in the small, old-fashioned refrigerator and fed it to Pris, who accepted the treat and then settled back.

Erin settled quietly into the rocking chair with a bite of cheese for herself and small glass of chardonnay. She began reading in succession from the top file of the Hem-Synon project personnel assignments in preparation for the staff meeting she had set up with Charlene in the morning. At ten.

She would be there no later than eight-thirty.

By the time she was forced to turn on a light, she had all but four files completed, notes taken and names matched with assignments. She read through the final batch, unaware that Colin and Pris lay awake, watching her.

"I didn't know you wore reading glasses, Harper," Colin murmured.

Erin shoved them up and let her papers fall into her lap. "There's a lot you don't know, Rennslaer."

"Less than you might imagine." He yawned and scraped at his whiskers with his knuckles. The motion intrigued

Pris, who sharpened her attention and writhed closer to inspect. Colin stared her down, but she didn't stop, and he didn't move her.

Envying in some secret, dark corner of her heart Pris's uninhibited behavior, Erin cleared her throat. "For example?"

"How fast you read."

Erin smirked. "I don't even know how fast I read."

"Seven hundred words per minute, give or take," he said. He blew gently at Pris, and she batted a paw at his lips. He grabbed her paw and laughed. Pris jerked it away and batted again, catching her claws in his whiskers. Erin could almost feel the friction. "Want another example? You lick your finger to turn every second page."

Her eyes darted to Colin's and held. She shivered, swallowed, looked away. "Noticing things I do isn't the same as knowing me," she responded breathily, at the level of a whisper.

"No?" His voice seemed throaty and tense, too. He stroked beneath Pris's jaw, and her purring swelled. "Licking your finger is a very sensual sort of thing to do, Erin. It reveals you. More than you know."

She wondered why there suddenly seemed so little oxygen in the room. "It's your imagination."

"Well, that's the point, isn't it?" Pris was sublimely tangling her whiskers with his.

"I . . . what point?" Erin asked snappishly out of feeling so exposed, jerking her gaze off his whiskers.

"It's *my* imagination, Harper." His eyes fixed on her fingers, then her eyes. "And everything you do feeds the fire." Her hand went unconsciously to her throat. His gaze followed. "Everything."

Pris went so lax on Colin's chest that in the exact same instant that Erin blushed and huffed some ridiculous denial, Pris rolled off, scrabbled to land on her feet at the floor and snarled in her embarrassment.

Colin laughed out loud and put his hand down for Pris, but she stalked off. To Erin he said, "You're exactly alike, you know that?"

"That's not true," she protested without thinking where it might lead.

Colin led. His voice was thick with desire, evoking her memory of what they had already done and been to each other. "It is true, Erin. You know it is. You've just forgotten. Pris just naturally goes after what she wants."

Erin's heart hammered. "Are you saying I should take a leaf from her book?"

Colin grinned. "At seven hundred words per minute, Erin, take them all."

"Could we take a picnic dinner to the beach?"

"Would a yacht do?"

Erin stared at him in amazement. "A yacht?"

He shrugged. He was no longer making an effort, as he had only two nights before in the lab, to avoid looking exactly where he wished to look at her body. "I'm a co-owner. September happens to be my month."

Erin put aside her papers, lifted the receiver from the phone and called for a cab. She no longer gave any effort over to staying the course of her gaze, either.

THE YACHT WAS SMALL, a fifty footer, and it required very little attention to take them several miles out into what felt like the middle of Lake Michigan. With Colin's help and a lot of disruptive, stolen kisses, Erin lowered the anchor. Colin switched off all but the lights necessary to stay at anchor in the night.

He hauled half the bedding aboard to the upper deck, and they made a bed and spread it with a picnic of canned ham and olives and artichoke hearts, a bottle of wine and a can of pie cherries, shared with one spoon, licking fingers.

Sated and turned on, Colin fell back on piles of pillows. Sitting cross-legged beside him, Erin saw in the moonlight the grimace he made as he loosened and removed the splint. She took the splint away and put it aside, then began to massage his wrist. He endured her touch until it became far less endurance than pleasure.

Water lapped gently at the sides of the boat. The night air was fragrant and richly pungent and sultry warm, and from the far distance strains of Zydeco reached them in their cocoon.

She knew, because he had freed her to please herself about where she let her gaze wander, that he was aroused and he had been for a long time. Her own body hummed and grew heated. Damp. Still, she rubbed his wrist, treasuring the degrees of need rising like fever afflicting them both.

"Can you move your thumb and fingers?"

"Let me see." He opened his eyes and focused on her blouse in moonlight strewn with wisps of dark, gilt-edged clouds. Her breasts rose. He reached for the small shadow of one taut, aching nipple straining against the polished linen.

Her breath caught, and when he touched her, when his fingers worked so perfectly in opposition to his thumb, closing on her tenderly, she gave a cry that inspired his groan and made him reach for a button.

"Erin." But he wanted no help and she offered none. If the tendons and sinews in his wrist protested, he never noticed. With his damaged hand he opened one button after another. She shed the blouse, which covered only a white fitted silk camisole. His hand splayed at her abdomen and slid with the grain of the silk until the tip of his thumb and the tip of his little finger caressed the nipple of each breast.

"Colin." She uttered a sharp cry of pleasure. He growled, and his perfectly working fingers came together clutching at the center top of her camisole, and he dragged her down to kiss her.

He gave up all thought of testing how adept he could be with but one damaged hand. His lips moved over hers, as did his tongue, and the taste of her plunged him beyond desire into the desperate need to couple with her.

Erin succumbed to the joy of having experienced once again what it was to ask for what she wanted and the wicked, newly sacred act of letting herself have her own way. And in all of that dim awareness, she took a deep breath and sank into the sweet, poignant morass of making love with Colin Rennslaer in the moonlight.

Chapter Eleven

Colin spent the night with Erin, but had risen at some ungodly hour, "dark-thirty" he'd grumbled, to go home, shower, shave and dress for his morning teaching rounds at 6:00 a.m. He grabbed a bag of fresh croissants and ran into Al Hastings climbing out of a Midtown Hospital Security vehicle at Erin's building at 7:20.

He shook hands with Hastings, and the two of them went in and got on the elevator. "Are you onto something already?"

"Sundays are a great time to scout around," Hastings answered, shrugging. "You're gonna find this interesting, I think, but let's wait till Ms. Harper can hear about it, too."

Colin rang the bell at the door to Erin's suite. She answered with a pencil between her teeth, a file folder in hand and her reading glasses propped on her nose. She snatched away the pencil. "Colin, Mr. Hastings—"

"Al," he supplied, interrupting her. "Is this a good time?"

"Of course." She shoved the reading glasses on top of her head and stepped back to let them in, then put down her papers and reading glasses on top of them. "Let me get you a cup of coffee."

"Black. Thanks."

Colin divvied out napkins and croissants from the bag, and they all sat around the living room coffee table.

"Well, your intruder has a name, a reputation, a rap sheet, an attitude, with a capital *A,* and an incriminating family tree. Where would you like me to start?"

"With her access into the HemSynon project," Colin said.

"Dr. Tyler Robards."

Colin stiffened. If Hastings had named him personally he could not have been more stunned. He threw a half-eaten roll back into the empty bag and got up. "Al, maybe you should start at the beginning."

Hastings's eyes followed Colin's pacing. "Look, Doc. I didn't say Robards was guilty of anything, just that at first blush he's the one with ties to your intruder."

Colin halted, blew out a breath and scraped a hand through his hair. "Okay. What have you got?"

"The vehicle belonging to the woman who presented herself at the cemetery is registered to one Lonna Clark. According to property-tax records, she owns a farmhouse almost into Indiana. Run-down place, according to the local cops. All the valuable farmland has long since been sold off from the original property.

"Neighbors aren't fond of her. She's forty-three, single, never married—and, it turns out, her mother's cousin's son is none other than Dr. Tyler Robards."

Colin took a swallow of coffee. A part of him stood detached, pleased by the fact that his brain wasn't buzzing around figuring out how all this was going to reflect on him. Feeling a little awed, in fact, because it felt as if it was Erin's influence that reassured him.

Still, he didn't want Ty to be responsible. "I don't know my mother's cousins. I don't even know if she has any cousins."

Al nodded, as if to say the extent of Colin's family knowledge was neither here nor there. "The class of '72 high school yearbook, class size of two hundred and eighty, lists Lonna Clark and Tyler Robards as the pair most likely to own a small island nation in the Caribbean."

Colin wasn't amused, but Hastings's point was made. Ty had known his cousin. "Well, he was in a position to do some damage."

"Especially if he was in league with Charlene," Erin mused softly. The only place she'd even seen Tyler Robards was in the lab a few nights ago, telling Charlene Babson he had a new candidate for the blood substitute. "You said Clark had a reputation and a police record?" Erin prompted.

"Two things relevant to her actions here," Hastings responded. "One. Farm people always resent the hell out of good land going to development, and I gathered she sold right out from under a couple of leases. And two, she has a couple of tax-evasion convictions. She is fearless—not many people have such a devil-may-care attitude where the IRS is concerned. Couple that penchant with selling off the family plot, and you begin to get why she's into shady deals and quick-money schemes."

"Which someone spoiled," Erin concluded. "She lost her market advantage when Miles was killed." She frowned. "How can she be so certain that Miles was murdered?"

"She can't," Colin answered flatly. "Unless Ty had something to do with it." His tone dismissed any possibility of that being true. "I've got to talk to him." He reached for the telephone.

"Save yourself the trouble, Doc," Hastings said, rising to go. "Robards is out of the country."

THE SENIOR STAFF of the HemSynon research project gathered in a second-floor conference room at 9:00 a.m. six women, three men. Several of them had not even heard of Miles's death.

Charlene fielded a flurry of fearful questions and then announced that Randy Waller had resigned. She introduced Erin as a project consultant called in by Dr. Cornwall. Erin relayed Frank Clemenza's decision to close the labs to all but management and supervisory personnel. After a stunned silence the conference room erupted in confusion.

With the exception of Charlene Babson, who sat sullenly, smugly refusing to help ease the difficult situation, Erin felt badly for all of them. Every person present and everyone down the line was bound to feel personally and professionally threatened.

The meeting was long and difficult, but the staff seemed reassured that their opinions of the project would be appreciated. Babson scraped her chair and left the room in a huff. Virtually everyone else sat writing their evaluation for well over an hour.

Intending to read them all, Erin first found her way to the medical-records department and Zoe Mastrangelo's office to follow up on the missing patient charts.

Though the door was open, Zoe sat concentrating on computer-generated report. Erin knocked on the door frame. "Could I interrupt you for a few minutes?"

Zoe glanced up from her work. "Erin. Of course. Please come in and sit down."

Erin sank into the chair in Zoe's small, sunny office. "Did you speak with Alexa?"

"Yes. I did, and you were right. She had the patient charts. She said that you and my aunt Mary Bernadette had happened across them sometime during the night Miles was killed."

The night Miles was killed. Erin nodded, struck by the sudden juxtaposition of facts. Was it possible that Miles had been fatally struck down not because he'd discovered evidence of espionage, but because of what he'd found in those charts? "Zoe, could you tell me about those patients?"

"Yes." She laid her pen carefully down on the chart she had been reviewing. "Alexa said you might be interested. They were all transplant cases of Colin's, as I told you before. The interesting thing is that Miles brought all four patients to my attention from the minutes of a monthly morbidity-and-mortality committee meeting."

Zoe lifted a stack of papers in a wooden bin on her desk and pulled from beneath them a manila file folder. Opening the file, she selected the minutes from the April meeting of the committee. "These are four months old. As you can see, there is an addendum to the minutes which comments on the extraordinary success of these particular transplants."

Erin took the notes and rapidly skimmed to the addition Zoe had pointed out. Each patient was referred to by initials, age and sex, date and type of transplant surgery. The cases were cited collectively for breakthrough examples of complex surgeries performed without the necessity of blood transfusions.

They were, in effect, cited as a pat on the back of Colin Rennslaer and Tyler Robards by their colleagues.

Erin looked up. "This is pretty amazing. No blood was ever transfused?"

Zoe's elegant brows lifted and she shook her head. "No. I went through the charts myself—Dr. Cornwall had asked if I would mind following up on the cases before he took the charts." Her expression sobered. "Unfortunately three of the four patients—Enos Polonoski, Candace Hobbs and Ralph Costigan—had already died of late or delayed complications."

Erin felt her heart crowding her throat. *Three of four dead. Late or delayed complications.* By themselves the stats were not terribly sinister or extraordinary. Critically ill transplant patients were always at serious risk of succumbing to HVGD—host-versus-graft disease—at any stage of recovery.

What made these deaths seem so ominous to Erin was that Miles was dead within hours of reviewing their charts. The cause-and-effect logic required an incredible leap—that Miles was murdered because of what he had discovered— but once the leap was made, everything else fell so neatly into place that it was impossible to ignore.

In surgeries such as these, despite the technology of cell savers and oxygenation outside the body, it was virtually unheard of not to transfuse. Yet none of these patients had been given even a single unit of blood.

Erin swallowed with terrible difficulty, and her ulcer seemed to have leapt beyond all warning signs. "Zoe, is there anything else unusual in these charts? Anything at all?"

Zoe shook her head. "Nothing I could see. Erin, you look as if you'd seen a ghost. Are you okay?"

"Yes." She wasn't. "What about the postoperative blood gases?"

"They were dream material, Erin. Better than normal. Only the hematocrits were low. Here. Let's look." She turned to a credenza behind her where the charts she had recovered from Alexa still lay, gave one of them to Erin and kept the another.

Enos Polonoski's chart was three inches thick. Erin turned to the divider marking the section reporting laboratory results and forced herself to focus on her purpose over the nameless fears invading her consciousness.

Transfusion decisions were based upon the patient's having lost a large amount of blood.

Polonoski's blood level was too low, but he'd had quite enough oxygen. Erin searched her mind for some explanation to reconcile the inconsistency. Without the normal amount of blood, his oxygen levels should also be too low—*unless he'd been given a dose of the research Hem-Synon....*

The lab reports proved the same thing for the other two Rennslaer patients, Candace Hobbs and Ralph Costigan.

Erin saw clearly now why Miles had been so profoundly upset. Reading these charts, he too must have pieced together the evidence that Colin's transplant patients had secretly been given doses of the research HemSynon.

And now Miles was dead, as well.

Erin gave a deep sigh and closed the chart. She thought of all the occasions Colin had taken to advise her to go home. The times he had insisted upon being with her, his uncanny ability to read her mood, to adapt himself to her needs, the opportunities he'd taken to warn her with such innate charm that he had no character. She had overcome them all. She had trusted him.

She had given herself to him.

Some small piece of her heart held out, refusing to accept that Colin could have had anything to do with the premature, possibly fatal, transfusions of HemSynon. But she felt very much as Miles must have. Horrified at the betrayal, no matter who had been involved, and the possibility that HemSynon might ultimately have killed the patients it had been intended to save.

"Erin?"

She broke out of her reverie and met the concern in Zoe's dark eyes. "Yes?"

"What is it? What are you thinking?"

"Could I have a copy of the morbidity-and-mortality committee minutes, and the names and telephone numbers of the primary-care physicians for these patients?"

"Of course." Zoe flipped to the back of each chart and copied onto a separate paper the information for all three patients and handed them to Erin along with the morbidity-and-mortality report. "Anything else?"

"Yes." Erin swallowed. "Who was the fourth patient?"

Zoe picked up the last chart and read the name on the cover. "Molly Beecham. A child."

Erin's heart plummeted. Colin had performed and secretly financed Molly Beecham's surgery. And according to the letter her mother had written to Sister Mary Bernadette, the child was now failing, as well.

Numbly Erin thanked Zoe for her help and left. The hallways teemed with Monday-morning activity, orderlies and nurses transporting patients hooked to multiple IV's on gurneys or in wheelchairs to the cardiac catheterization lab down the hall from medical records, or to radiation therapy, or imaging or diagnostic radiology down the other hall.

Fighting to keep control of her emotions, Erin took the maze of corridors that led directly to the building housing the research labs and Miles's office. What if Molly Beecham was failing because she'd been given a dose of HemSynon, too?

Her hands were shaking almost uncontrollably as she faxed a model of the HemSynon molecule to a research colleague she'd known at the university in Arizona. Irv Kartz, she believed, would respond to her questions with a minimum of nosiness.

After looking at the model, he phoned Erin. He knew exactly what the molecule was intended to accomplish. "Looks really promising, Erin. What can I help you with?"

"Irv, I just wanted an unbiased, expert opinion to back up my reasoning. What would happen to the body after the HemSynon cells started to break up?"

He thought in silence for a few moments. In the background Erin could hear the scratching of a pencil against paper as Irv brainstormed the various outcomes. At last he rattled off a set of symptoms Erin had described in the meeting with Miles's board of directors. The kidneys would get so clogged with pieces of the HemSynon cells that they would fail.

"Irv, if you were a physician coming in late to a morbidity-and-mortality committee meeting, what would you assume had been the cause of that particular set of symptoms?"

"Assuming no preexisting cause of kidney failure?"

"Right."

"Well, on that basis, I would say we were dealing with a body rejecting a transplant. The patient would die."

Chronic, end-stage host-versus-graft disease.

Erin's stomach lurched. Molly Beecham would die next. HemSynon fragments were probably collecting in her tiny kidneys every minute, and she was failing—even if her new heart was working perfectly.

Erin spent the next hour collecting and copying bloodbank records. Almost accustomed to the pain radiating from her ulcer, she felt as if she were suffocating. She left the blood-bank labs, shoved her way through a side door into the sunshine and ran across the street to a street ven-

dor. She forced herself to take deep, calming breaths and
bought a plain egg bagel with a thick layer of cream cheese
in the middle.

Consuming her food, Erin sat on a park bench in the sun
for a while. Aware of pigeons bobbing and warbling near
her, and people and traffic surging around her, she couldn't
seem to shake the numbing effect of knowing what she now
knew.

Too many questions clamored for answers. Miles had
been murdered because of what he knew, but whom had he
confronted? Who knew that he had discovered the illicit
transfusions of HemSynon? Who had killed him? Who had
access to Colin's keys?

And the questions surrounding Miles's murder only
scraped the surface. How many people had to be involved
in the original plot to transfuse the HemSynon without
Miles's knowledge? And why had they done it? Where did
Chalmers fit in, and the woman whom the police had
identified as Lonna Clark, third-cousin to Tyler Robards,
who was now conveniently out of the country?

Most of all, what had Colin known and when had he
known it?

Jerkily Erin tossed the last bits of her bagel to the pigeons and brushed off her fingers.

She had to see him, because if there were anything that
could minimize the damage now, it would be to save the life
of an innocent little girl. Molly Beecham wouldn't become
the next victim if Erin could help it.

She forced herself to walk back across the street, then
turned left toward the hospital-associated Medical Office
Building, where she knew Colin's suite occupied the penthouse floor. It was decorated tastefully in soothing shades
of celery green and white, but there were no patients waiting.

A sweet-faced, middle-aged receptionist named Debbie greeted Erin blankly. "May I help you?"

"I'm Erin Harper, here to see Dr. Rennslaer."

She glanced at the calendar. "Did you have an appointment?"

"No, but—"

"I'm afraid he's attending a luncheon meeting at the hospital—"

The telephone interrupted her. Erin watched her push a button separate from the others. The call was coming in on a private line, and from the subtle shift in the receptionist's posture, Erin guessed it was Colin himself.

"He should know that I'm here," Erin said. "Please."

Debbie told him as much, then smiled when he cracked some joke or other. She jotted notes of his requests for a few moments, then disconnected. "He said I should show you around—and that you could wait in his office. He could be a while, by the sounds of it. Here...come through that door."

Debbie led the way past several examination rooms, then stopped and opened the door marked Ginger Creedy, R.N., M.S.N., Nurse Practitioner.

"This is Dr. Rennslaer's nurse's office. Do you know Ginger?"

"We've met. Where is she now?"

"Why, I believe she was called—rather unexpectedly—out of town."

It struck Erin how terribly convenient it had proved for Tyler Robards and Ginger Creedy, both of whom had now gone out of town, that Colin's wrist had been disabled.

She stepped into Ginger's office with the same sense of foreboding that had accosted her earlier, a sense of pieces coming starkly, relentlessly together. The scent of perfume that had driven Pris wild in Alexa's office lingered here in

Ginger Creedy's office, only this time Erin remembered it was in Miles's office with Colin two nights ago that she had first become aware of the scent.

Something about it had troubled Erin at some subliminal level then. She knew what that was now. Although Miles was allergic and the perfume would have disturbed him, someone wearing it had nevertheless been in his office.

"Lovely, isn't it?" Debbie said.

Erin's attention snapped back. "Yes." The loveliness was lost on her. According to Miles's daughter, he had been despondent over some failed relationship. As convoluted and interwoven as everything else appeared, it struck her as no less likely that the woman might have been Ginger Creedy.

"Debbie, does Ginger confide in you? Would you know if she were involved with Dr. Cornwall? I noticed the scent of her perfume in his office, as well."

Debbie smiled, too. "It does linger, doesn't it? But if Ginger was having a fling with Dr. Cornwall, I pity the poor devil. He'd have been way out of his league with her."

She held the door for Erin, then turned to Colin's office, which was protected by an electronic keypad lock. She punched in the combination. "Dr. Rennslaer said you should make yourself at home. Is there anything I can do for you?"

Erin glanced around the office—at the wet bar and refrigerator and slate gray carpet thick enough to paddle through, the black leather sofa and captain's chair, the enormous desk and state-of-the-art telephone system—and thanked Debbie cordially for her help.

"I have a few calls to make. Would you mind?"

"Not at all."

She put in calls to all three physicians whose numbers Zoe had given her. Two of the three were available but not much help. They had already spoken with Dr. Cornwall, and in any case, their patients, both maintained, had not died unexpectedly, but rather of complications arising from HVGD. The third was out of the country on a UN mission to the starvation victims of some Third World country.

Erin stared for a long time at the telephone's automatic-dial button marked Creedy, took a deep breath, lifted the receiver from the cradle and rang Ginger. There was no answer. She really hadn't expected one. She replaced the receiver when Colin walked in.

"Hi." His look said he missed her.

"Hi." She felt instantly the overwhelming sense of fear that he had to have been involved in transfusing Hem-Synon prematurely, and she avoided meeting his eyes.

The force of his personality took her breath away. His black pin-striped suit seemed as fresh as it had this morning when he and Al Hastings had arrived at her door, but it didn't seem to matter how recently he'd shaved. The shadow of his beard gave him the look of an upscale rakehell in a tuxedo.

The immobilizing splint reinforced the sense of danger. His eyes were bright and clear.

Guiltless, Erin thought, her heart straining to keep any rational rhythm.

Guiltless? Or lacking anything faintly resembling compassion or scruples?

Chapter Twelve

He came around the desk, intending to pull her out of his chair and kiss her. Something stopped him, some tiny, wary movement he hadn't expected. Or the guardedness in her deeply violet-hued eyes.

He sat on the edge of the desk instead. "Erin, what's wrong?" She backed up in the captain's chair, away from him. Colin took it for a poor sign.

"Would you tell me how your blood orders are handled?"

He wouldn't have mistrusted the question except that she refused his eye contact. "What is this about, Erin?"

"Your surgery orders. How are they handled?"

"Ginger does the scheduling and places all the cross-match orders." He got up and moved around the desk to the wet-bar refrigerator, pulled out a couple of containers of cranapple juice and peeled off the aluminum lids. "For the most part, they're standard and on file in the blood bank."

"Without exception?"

Colin swallowed, and his head filled with terrible, Gothic-melancholy passages of music. He looked at Erin, knowing this was the woman he'd fallen head over heels for, who knew his gravest doubts and highest aspirations, the woman who had inspired his music even before he met her.

The one woman in creation with whom he wanted to share a lifetime of sex and croissants, bouts of dirty diapers and decades of old age.

But she was looking at him now as if he had invented betrayal. He cleared his throat. It hurt to talk. "Why do I have the feeling we're having another little crisis in confidence here?"

She shook her head. "Don't patronize me, Colin—"

"I'm *not* patronizing you, Erin." He looked hard at her, meaning to convey his anger. "I'm trying to figure out why we have to go through this every twelve hours. And whether it's worth it."

"This is not about us, Colin! These are very serious matters. Please…" She rose from his chair and gestured for him to take her place. "Look at these and explain them to me if you can."

He had no idea what she wanted him to look at. He could think of nothing he had ever done to warrant the look of betrayal in her eyes, but he had seen her read reasons to mistrust him into half a dozen other situations. To be fair, from her point of view, he understood most of them.

He put his coat over the back of his chair and sat and glanced at the stack of photocopies. They appeared to be the cross-match and blood sign-out records of the hospital blood bank. He looked closer and recognized the names of some of his surgical transplant patients.

He felt vaguely threatened, as if he'd been asked to explain someone else's fraudulent tax return, and he didn't like the feeling. "If you have serious questions, Erin, ask them."

"All right." Standing beside him, she pointed to the records for Candace Hobbs. "These show the routine procedure. The blood bank confirmed with the floor nurses your standing orders, cross matched thirty units of blood, assigned as many single-donor platelets and signed them all out to surgery. But here—'' she pointed out another copy ''—all of them were returned to the blood bank.''

Colin nodded. "Okay." He sensed this was just the beginning and didn't bother asking her what the point was. "Go on."

Erin set the Hobbs documents to one side and went onto Ralph Costigan. "Here, although the same procedure was followed, no one ever came to the blood bank to sign out the units of blood. The technologist remembers the case very well because they go to a lot of trouble to have the blood ready for surgery staff to pick up. The tech called the O.R., but—as she noted in the computer—the units were never sent for."

Colin stared at the final entry, which indicated that all units for Costigan had been released from cross match after forty-eight hours, as was the usual procedure. But he had no clue as to why the units were never on hand in the O.R.

He swore softly. "If Costigan's pressure had dropped out of sight…" He didn't even want to contemplate how badly compromised the man's life would have been. "Erin…"

He couldn't go on. What was there to say? *It's not my fault?* That Creedy should have seen to it that the blood was on hand? Any court in the land would have to absolve him of the slightest responsibility. He'd written the orders and, as the physician, he had to be able to expect that they would be carried out.

But where would that have left Costigan?

Colin shook his head and pitched the photocopies back onto his desk. "Where is this going, Erin?"

"Look at Polonoski, Colin," she answered softly. "Even the cross-match orders were suspended. The techs in the blood bank were really baffled, and they wrote it up six ways from Sunday. 'No cross-match orders rec'd. Call by AJK to Dr. Rennslaer's nurse confirmed: No blood ordered.'"

Colin leaned back in his chair. "I don't get it."

She turned to face him, leaning against his desk. "You knew, didn't you, Colin?"

He frowned. "Knew what? That these three surgeries came off without transfusions? Yes. That Ginger had suspended orders? No." He grimaced in pain and readjusted his left arm in the sling. "Thank God nothing happened."

Erin's chin went up. He went very still. "What?"

"Something happened, Colin."

Colin expelled his breath. "I'm not in the mood for riddles, Erin. Spit it out."

At her sides her fingers clung to the edge of his desk. He could see the tension in her. He knew from the peculiar little wrinkle over her left eyebrow that her stomach hurt very badly. What could possibly have her wound up so tight?

"I'm convinced all three of these people were given HemSynon."

He almost laughed but he knew better. Her ability to keep her faith in him seemed pretty damn grievous to him, but he could not fault her intelligence or her reasoning. "That's what you were asking if I knew, isn't it?"

She swallowed. Her breathing was shallow. "Did you, Colin?"

He shook his head. "There was nothing—" He broke off because he wanted her full attention. "Erin, *look* at me." She complied defiantly. He knew she was in pain. "There was *nothing to know.*"

She bit her lip. "That's not true."

He threw up his one good hand. "What's the use? Tell me that, Erin. You won't believe me. What do you want me to say? That this was all one big conspiracy? That we all went behind Miles's back and transfused the stuff? That I handed my keys over to some lowlife with orders to run him down when he caught us?"

"Colin, please—"

"Please *what*, Erin?" He surged out of his chair and towered over her. "You're right, aren't you? Isn't that what you told me? Erin Harper, God bless her soul, is always right."

"And you told me that you would do anything to enhance your precious reputation."

He regarded her angrily. "Right again. I did." He stared at his relatively useless left hand for a moment. She had no idea how sucker punched he felt. He wasn't used to defending himself, but under attack he wasn't used to pulling his punches, either. "I guess I thought it went without saying that my pursuit of glory is tied up in saving people's lives, Erin. Not risking them."

"But if you believed there was no risk..."

Colin's shoulder slumped. She knew the drill. She knew that the anesthesiologist handles all meds and transfusions in the O.R. It blew him away that there was any possibility that Ty Robards could have transfused HemSynon, but she had to know he had nothing to do with it.

Apparently she didn't.

"So where does your 'scenario' end, Erin? With me screwing your brains out so you wouldn't catch on?"

"Oh, Colin, stop it."

He knew the image was vulgar and upset her. He meant to make her wake up and see how ugly her own accusations were, but she was clutching both arms beneath her breasts now to somehow ease the pain in her stomach, and he hated himself for giving a damn.

"I'll quit anytime, Erin," he answered more gently. "You just tell me when I've rounded out the conspiracy well enough—"

She cried out and doubled over in the same instant, and he couldn't help reaching for her. He couldn't stand her pain.

She jerked away from his touch.

"Erin, stop it and come here."

"Just leave me alone!" She didn't dare move away from the support of his desk for fear of collapsing.

He swore at her and raked the sling from his elbow and down beyond his wrist. His left arm was free before his intention penetrated the fog of her spasms. He circled her shoulders and dragged her to her feet against him with the strength of his left arm, and with his other hand he searched for the pressure point to ease the attack.

She cried out and struggled for a moment like a wildcat trapped and chained. It finally hit Colin how desperately trapped she felt, caught between the damning evidence she had uncovered, of actions he knew nothing of and couldn't explain and Lord only knew what else . . . and her feelings for him.

His throat thickened. Her soft cries wounded him. "Shh, Erin. Shh." His wrist throbbed dully, but he held her closer still and laid his cheek down on the top of her head. Massaging the intercostal space between her ribs, he murmured her name over and over again. "Erin. Erin. Take a few deep breaths. We'll work it out. Relax."

He began to gently rock her, and she began to settle down in his arms, to feel the pain subsiding. She could breathe again, but every breath was suffused with his scent, every wave of sickness defeated by his healing touch.

There were things that required explanations—terrible things—but she could no longer summon the energy to fight her attraction to him or imagine any scenario but one that would somehow exonerate him.

The phone began to ring. Colin ignored it as long as he could. He punched on the speaker phone, and Debbie connected Frank Clemenza.

"Rennslaer. Are you there?"

"Yeah."

"What about Harper?"

He wanted to lie. He wanted to put her on a one-way flight to the South Seas and he wanted to follow her there. "She's here, as well."

"Good. I want to see you both, in my office. Now." The line went dead, and eventually an obnoxious warning beep blared out of the speaker.

Colin let go of her to disconnect. She backed away, straightening her skirt, drying her cheek, fluffing her hair, better now by the smallest margin.

Colin winced as he replaced his splinted wrist back in the sling, which was not particularly better at all. He hung his head for a moment, letting the ache ease off, then looked back up at her. "Erin, you look like hell."

She swallowed and gave a brief, sad smile. "Got a mirror?"

He angled his head toward a door. "In the bathroom."

"Thanks." She turned to go repair the damage, but Colin caught her hand.

"Do you know what Clemenza wants?"

Erin shook her head. "No." She knew what question he meant to ask. *Who else knows what you suspect?* "For what it's worth, Colin, I came to you first."

BUT SOMEONE DID KNOW.

It shouldn't have come as a surprise to find Charlene

Babson, Alexa Sabbeth and Jacob Delvecchio already waiting in Frank Clemenza's office. With its thick beige pile carpeting and mahogany enough to denude a small rain forest, Clemenza's office rivaled the richness of Colin's.

Despite Clemenza's smile, the gathering gave Erin the impression of a lynch mob waiting to happen, and in some strange way even Sister Mary Bernadette's presence made it all seem worse—as if divine forgiveness she might call upon were to be the only sort doled out.

Erin steeled herself and nodded at Charlene, whose expression betrayed her continuing contempt, then greeted the sister and the power brokers. "Mr. Clemenza. Mr. Delvecchio. Ms. Sabbeth."

Clemenza gestured to the remaining empty club chairs. "Please, sit down."

Erin sat, but Colin refused, taking a more aggressive stance. "What's this about, Frank?"

"We were hoping you might tell us, Dr. Rennslaer," he answered. His tone conveyed a reluctant deference to one of his premier surgeons, but his smallish eyes were sharp and hard as a scalpel blade as they flicked toward Erin. "One of you, at least, should have the... intestinal fortitude, shall we say, to come forward."

Colin hooked his fingers in the sling holding his splinted left wrist. He didn't like Clemenza and never had, and he would not return the reluctant respect. "I'm afraid I'll need a clue."

Charlene uttered a sound of disgust, but Clemenza gave Colin a blank look, then turned to Erin. "And you, Ms. Harper. Will you require a clue?"

Erin placed her arms along the top of the chair, affecting a calm she was far from feeling. "If you want an intelligent dialogue, yes."

Clemenza laughed and tossed a gold-plated pen onto papers littering his desk and rocked his hulking body back in his chair. "An intelligent dialogue," he repeated. "That's rich. Tell me this. It's true that you worked with Miles Cornwall years ago, is it not?"

"Yes."

"And isn't it also true that you were once engaged to Miles Cornwall?"

"Yes."

"And that Dr. Cornwall occupied the scientific seat on your Ph.D. jury? That in that capacity he denied your—"

"Oh, now this *is* rich, Frank," Colin interrupted in disgust. "Are you suggesting that Cornwall would deliberately sabotage his own project by recruiting Ms. Harper?"

"That's exactly what he's saying," Erin said, her focus pinned on Clemenza, a deep-seated resentment taking hold. "Miles Cornwall had uncovered evidence of sabotage to the project which he could never cover up or fix. He needed out, and he needed a patsy. Is that how the thinking goes, Mr. Clemenza?"

"Please. Continue. You make a fascinating case."

"All right." Despite the force of Clemenza's disdain, Erin went on. "The board," she said, "including you, Mr. Delvecchio, and you, Alexa, had recognized and expressed faith many times in Miles's expertise. But rather than dealing with the problem directly, in a manner befitting his talent, you're suggesting Miles's answer was to get out as fast as he could and exact his own revenge by leaving the project in the bumbling, vengeful hands of a former protégée and jilted lover."

Clemenza brought his hands together, clapping once, twice, three times, the sound cracking loudly in the cloistered silence. Sister Mary Bernadette gave the gesture a look of distaste, but Alexa took a deep breath and stared at her hands. Charlene refused to meet Erin's eyes.

"Do you think it might have been appropriate to reveal at the board meeting the details of your rather...checkered past, Ms. Harper?"

"Why?" Colin asked before Erin could reply, his question ringing with sarcasm. "Do you think she would have taken on your dirty little assignment if she thought the extent of her flaws would come out?"

Again Charlene started to say something, but backed off when Clemenza let his chair fall forward, as much to intimidate with his formidable body as his words. He pointed at Colin. "When I want your opinion, Rennslaer, I'll ask for it."

"Why, Frank," Colin returned, unfazed and in Clemenza's own belligerent vein, "you got me, you got my opinion. Is there more to this witch-hunt, or are we coming to the crux of the matter?"

"Actually the picture Ms. Harper painted is the less likely of two possibilities, " Clemenza answered, glancing pityingly at Colin, "which you might have picked up on had you been thinking with the organ between your ears, Colin."

"You've a filthy mind, haven't you, Frank?" the sister put in, but for a moment Colin ceased to breathe. The rich irony of Clemenza's remark hit him like a fist in his gut. An hour or less ago he'd mockingly suggested that it was Erin who was supposed to have been blinded to the sabotage by his seduction. Now Clemenza considered it was Erin seducing him against the possibility of discovering *her* complicity.

Seeing in Erin's eyes a recognition of the same bitter piece of absurdity, he knew the implied accusation was beneath a response from either of them. "Which possibility is that, Frank?"

"Here's the picture Ms. Babson paints." If Clemenza had been offering clues and innuendos to force a confession, he left off the strategy and went for the jugular now.

"Cornwall was getting desperate. For months he lied to the board about his progress. Someone was trying to steal his work, and he became convinced that he had to move quickly. He began an affair with Ginger Creedy to gain her cooperation in recruiting Robards to the plot, and convinced the two of them to transfuse the HemSynon he handed over to them."

Erin started to interrupt. In a million years Miles would never have compromised his beloved project, but even if he had become so desperate, Miles Cornwall had never had the confidence in himself as a lady's man to conceive of an affair leading to cooperation. If any part of that were true, it was the reverse—that Ginger had gone to Miles.

But Clemenza held up a hand to forestall anything she might add, and delivered his pronouncement. "The scheme worked just as he'd planned, but he had no idea the guilt that would consume him. He called in the one person most likely to fail in uncovering his treachery. That would be you, Ms. Harper."

"So much guilt," Erin asked, ignoring the accusation against her, "that he threw himself in front of the first convenient speeding car?"

"Your insight continues to astonish me," Clemenza said.

"Perhaps you've misjudged, Frank," Sister Mary Bernadette offered from her position at the window. Her arms were folded, her hands hidden in the folds of her wimple, and her steely tone lacked any hint of warmth or her usual charming brogue. "You've based this entire spectacle on nothing more than vicious innuendo and haphazard speculation. Rubbish, in short.''

"Need I remind you, Sister, that you are present here only at my sufferance?''

"Likewise, Frank," she returned softly.

Clemenza turned to her, stared hard for a moment, then deferred. Erin assumed Mary Bernadette must clearly yet be a force to contend with in the political life of the hospital.

"Perhaps, Sister," he said. "Perhaps. But a project manager's highest obligation is to the integrity and confidentiality of the project—and it is not speculation that Ms. Harper faxed an accurate, detailed model of the Hem-Synon molecule to a colleague in blatant and reckless disregard of that obligation."

Everyone present stared at Erin. She turned to meet Charlene's smug expression. Of those present, only she could have examined the fax machine in Miles's private office, determined what number was the last destination and followed up.

Irv Kartz would never willingly have betrayed Erin's consultation with him, but if Charlene had called to ask if he had received all of Erin's transmission, he could have easily been tricked into describing what he had received.

Curiously, smack in the middle of the worst straits of her professional life, Erin felt no twinge of protest from her ulcer, only a kind of distant regret at the expressions of dismay surrounding her.

"Did you really think you'd get away with it?" Charlene taunted.

"No, Charlene. But then, I never hoped to get away with anything." She exchanged glances with Colin, turned to Clemenza and took a deep breath.

Her only defense was the truth. "The project was compromised. I'm not certain yet of all the players, but you should know the extent of the damage. In all likelihood Dr. Robards was funnelling information to a competitor. I believe now that HemSynon has been transfused to transplant patients against all accepted research protocol, and that—"

"That's a lie!" Delvecchio thundered from behind Erin, rising angrily from his chair to confront her. "A complete fabrication—"

"And that as a result," Erin persisted over Delvecchio's outburst, "three patients are now dead."

Every scrap of color drained from Charlene's already pale face; Delvecchio's only turned more red with his anger. Alexa and Sister Mary Bernadette were stunned to silence, and Clemenza's bulk seemed to deflate.

Colin was staggered. He swallowed, fighting to stay in control. "Who is dead, Erin?"

The plush office erupted in accusations and protests and denials. Charlene, from Delvecchio, from Clemenza, who warned in the most coldly menacing tone Erin had ever personally heard, that she had *damn well* better have the proof to substantiate such charges.

"Surely you're mistaken, Erin," Alexa said.

But though Erin registered the turmoil surrounding them, it was Colin's question that tore at her.

He stared at her. "Who died?"

She rose from her chair. This was the point she had been getting to when their own argument had hurtled out of control. The point she had never gotten to.

She approached Colin, unhappily aware that though she had gone to him before anyone else, he didn't yet realize that his patients had died as a result of the illicit transfusions of HemSynon.

He looked pale, beyond the flush of anger, and his whiskers seemed still darker, more primitive. "Who died, Erin?" he demanded harshly.

"Hobbs and Costigan and Polonoski died, Colin. All three of them."

"No! It's not possible." In the same moment Sister Mary Bernadette uttered a Mother of God, crossed herself and flew to Colin's side. He expelled a breath in shock and dragged his right hand through his hair. His throat locked up, and his mind reeled and cold dread flooded through him.

Charlene began to rant and rave about his act, *as if he didn't know*, the miserable lowlife. Clemenza told her to shut up, but Erin's eyes filled with tears for the torture in Colin's, the dismay that must surely be a hundred times worse than her own.

Those people had been his patients, and though they had been turned back to the care of their own physicians, Colin must feel the brunt of suffocating responsibility. Dozens of puzzling events had begun to come together, to find answers, to make a desperate kind of sense.

Knowing now that HemSynon had already been transfused, Tyler Robards's remark concerning another candidate to Charlene Babson took on a terrible new meaning. But Erin had many more-immediate concerns.

Like the life of a child, failing now in a hospital in St. Louis, Missouri. A child under the care of physicians who had no idea what they were dealing with.

Though Clemenza was taking Delvecchio apart with rapid-fire questions, everyone but Colin and Sister Mary Bernadette seemed to fade to some black-and-white background.

"How, Erin?" the sister asked, her hand at Colin's arm, voicing the question he couldn't get past his lips.

"Renal failure," Erin answered, "attributed to chronic HVGD."

Alexa came into their small circle. "Colin, you didn't know?" she asked softly.

He gave a bitter, disbelieving sigh. "No, Alexa. I didn't know."

Erin reached out to touch his hand. She glanced at Sister Mary Bernadette. "Colin, there was one more."

"Mother, no!" the sister moaned, clutching at the crucifix resting above her heart.

Her stricken cry tore through Colin, and he knew. Molly Beecham was the last of the transplants he'd performed in May.

Chapter Thirteen

The Flight for Life helicopter pad atop the tower of patient rooms at Rose Memorial buzzed with activity. The chopper pilot was on the phone, figuring the most expedient flight plan to St. Louis and the county hospital where Molly Beecham lay fighting for her life.

Erin got on a cellular phone to try to locate Randy Waller. Between his knowledge of the HemSynon cell-fragments trials and Irv Kartz's expertise in kidney function, she hoped to find a way to counteract the damage already being done to Molly's kidneys.

Neither man was immediately available. Erin left urgent messages for both of them.

Colin stood off to one side of the control area, deep in conversation with Sister Mary Bernadette.

"Colin, dear boy. I wish I had brought Audra's letter to you sooner."

Colin's tongue locked in the pit of his mouth, and he looked away. "I wouldn't have known what to do for her." He swore because he didn't know what to do for Molly now, either. "I can't believe this is happening."

"Nor I," the sister agreed.

Nor could Colin remember a place or time when Sister Mary Bernadette's expression contained so little hope or when the light had gone out of her eyes like this.

Or when she'd more fiercely clung to her faith. "I refuse to believe the dear Lord would have sustained her life till now without hope of an answer."

Colin squinted into the late-afternoon sun and cleared his throat. His head was filled with melodies that signified mourning, ones his mother had hummed because she had never once believed she deserved more than the brute she'd married. What was it she used to say? *Things will get better, son. You'll see. Have faith.* Colin wasn't long on faith, except in his own abilities, and Molly needed something else altogether now.

Maybe Mary Bernadette's faith. Maybe the hand of God, plucking that sweet, innocent child from the hands of men.

Deus ex machina. He swallowed. "It may take a miracle, Mary B."

"Well, miracles are the province of Rose Memorial, Colin. Do what you can, but do not be so arrogant as to think that God has yet died and left you in charge."

Colin gave a strained smile. Of all the occasions on which the sister had reminded him that the Spirit moved with him and sometimes without, this was the hardest to accept. Patients in his care had died.

Colin watched the pilot leap inside the helicopter, then turn to assist Erin in. The engine began to gear up, and the chopper blades slicing through the air drowned out everything else. The turbulence plastered the sister's habit to her frail body, and the ground-crew chief motioned.

"Dr. Rennslaer, sir?" he bellowed.

Colin turned to hug the sister, to absorb a measure of peace from her determined faith. Alexa shoved through the

oor with a briefcase of studies she'd collected and handed
em to Colin.

"The meds you asked for are inside." She hesitated.
ooking pale and drawn, as exhausted as Colin had ever
en her, she exhaled sharply and pulled herself together.
You'll let me know if there's anything I can do?"

Colin nodded. "Count on it."

She had already tracked down Molly's doctors, set up a
onference call and made the chopper available. The up-
ar in Clemenza's office had reached unmanageable pro-
ortions when Alexa stepped in. Delvecchio swung wildly
etween outrage and panic. Clemenza was ready to send
eads rolling. Alexa had managed to contain them both
id put herself between Colin and harm's way so he and
rin could get to Molly Beecham's side without delay.

He had never cared for Alexa or her style, but he had to
ve her credit for having moved heaven and earth when the
ed arose. She'd agreed to take care of Pris and even run
 the pharmacy to fill a prescription he wrote for Erin's
lcer.

"Alex?" he prompted.

She turned. A shadow of deep resentment in her expres-
on surprised him.

"Are you okay?"

"No, Colin," she snapped. "I am not *okay,* any more
an you are. People screwed up, and I'm the one who's
aying the price. If people had just—" She broke off, pro-
oked at her own outburst. "This is pointless. Just go do
hat you have to do, Colin, and I will do what I have to
o."

She gave a brief, distracted nod and disappeared through
e doorway to the stairs back down into the hospital.

Disturbed by Alexa's flare-up, Colin touched the sister's
eathered cheek. "Keep an eye on her, will you?"

She stared after Alexa. "She won't thank me." Ma
Bernadette required no thanks, and Colin knew it, whic
made her comment seem somehow ominous. "I'll do it, a
the same."

Colin nodded and ran for the chopper. He broke out th
medications for Erin as they lifted off, and she swallowe
them gratefully. The pilot offered her a box of thick pre
zels, and she gnawed on one as she curled up with th
HemSynon fragment protocols and reports Alexa had d
livered.

Colin watched Erin reading intently, breathing softl
and he envied her the ability to focus her attention like tha
He was capable of it in surgery or when he picked up h
sax, but now he couldn't even relax.

He listened to the pilot pointing out repairs of damag
done by the floodwaters in '93, but his mind was els
where, chasing after clues he should have taken, inconsi
tencies he might have noticed, deaths he might hav
prevented—if only he'd known.

Tyler Robards wasn't the sort of guy Colin would eve
have thought capable of falling in with the kind of schem
ing it must have taken to pull off transfusing HemSynor
But he knew from the insights Erin had provided that a fe
documented surgical successes would make the blood su'
stitute one hell of a lot more attractive—and jack up th
price on the black market high enough to fill the treasu
of a small nation.

Ty was always in over his head financially. Colin tried
tell himself anyone could succumb to the lure of that muc
money, but he still didn't want to believe it.

Then there was Ginger, God love her—no one else di
Whatever respect he'd had for her considerable abilities
his side in the O.R., he couldn't believe that she would c

his, either, or that she could have gall enough to actually suspend his routine blood orders.

He had always believed the two of them reflected well on him. The reflection in his mind now reminded him of his father in one of his alcoholic stupors.

Oblivious.

Colin had never been drunk a day in his life because he detested that consequence so much, but he might as well have been if Robards and Creedy could put this over on him not once but four times.

It might not have been so clear-cut. Colin supposed anyone could have injected the HemSynon after the surgery. And a slick lawyer could probably confuse a jury of laymen, dazzling them with all the opportunities for someone else to have made the injections. But Ginger had suspended his routine blood orders, and Ty controlled all the medication and transfusions given in surgery, so it *was* that clear-cut to Colin. Ty and Ginger had administered the HemSynon and as good as signed Molly Beecham's death warrant in the process.

He took a deep, shuddering breath. If they had planned to sell the secret, the only loser would be the hospital itself because its development dollars would never be repaid. Colin was willing to admit that they had never foreseen or intended people should die, but all the same . . . The way to Hell was paved with good intentions, and Colin was well on his way down a path not of his own making.

He hoped to God there was something he could do.

The pilot indicated at forty-seven minutes into the flight that they were nearing the landing pad at the county hospital. Colin reached out to stroke Erin's cheek, breaking into her concentration.

"We're almost ready to land. Find anything?"

"Oh, there's a lot here," she answered. Some of the re
porting appeared inconsistent, which suggested that Rand
Waller had been right to suspect the studies he'd con
ducted had been tampered with. But she and Colin still ha
to find a way to treat Molly if her kidneys were clogged wit
the lethal little pieces of the HemSynon cells. "I hop
Randy and Irv have gotten their messages."

Colin echoed her sentiment. "They've had Molly on di
alysis. There's no reason she should have gotten worse," h
said, as much to reassure himself as Erin. But the trut
was—and both of them knew it—Molly was failing despit
the dialysis.

The hospital public-relations officer met them at th
helicopter. Tall, blond and outgoing, but studious wit
wire-rimmed glasses, Beverly Patterson introduced hersel
and hurried on. "Dr. Rennslaer. And Ms. Harper?"

"Yes. How is Molly?"

"Critical at this point but stable. Her doctors have bee
paged to the conference room."

Erin slipped a hand through Colin's arm, and they fol
lowed Ms. Patterson from the helicopter pad through th
modern facilities to the meeting room. Dr. Jason Kellog
and a renal specialist, Dr. Anthea Whitlow, awaited them

They went rapidly through introductions, then took seat
clustered at one end of an oak conference table. Kellogg le
off. "What can you tell us about this mysterious transfu
sion of Molly's?"

Colin explained. "We're developing an artificial bloo
product—HemSynon—at Rose Memorial. We believ
Molly was transfused with the HemSynon and that th
fragments of artificial blood may be creating the effect
you're seeing now in her kidneys."

Kellogg swiped a hand at a fly buzzing around his ears
"You're telling me this child was dosed with an experi

mental product? That's quite an unfortunate accident, isn't it?"

Colin sighed heavily. Erin responded. "We don't believe it was an accident. But the important thing now is to see if we can salvage Molly's renal function."

"What is her status report?" Colin asked.

In her strong accent and an annoying penchant for Texan slang, Whitlow described the clinical signs and symptoms—Molly's lack of consciousness and the stabilizing effect of having started her on dialysis. "So this Hem-Synon isn't likely ever to break down far enough to be washed through the kidneys?"

Colin agreed that was the case.

"And you have an answer for this?" Kellogg asked.

"A combination of treatments probably," Erin answered, knowing that Kellogg's hostility and less-than-respectful attitude must be carving holes in Colin's heart. She got out the reports of the various treatments that had been used to eliminate the fragments from the bloodstream and handed them to Dr. Whitlow.

"Which of these would you recommend we try first?" he asked Colin.

He swallowed. Until Erin had a chance to speak with Randy Waller and Irv Kartz, they couldn't choose one. "It's evident Molly is already in renal failure—and it's possible none of the treatments will reverse that."

Kellogg's nostrils flared. "In that case, what purpose did it serve for you to come flying in here?"

Erin wanted to leap to Colin's defense. He had saved Molly's life with a delicate and extraordinarily demanding transplant operation. He had waived his own fees and met the expenses of her hospitalization out of his own pocket.

He hadn't transfused the HemSynon.

Despite that, despite the high value he placed on his stature in the surgical community, Colin wasn't scurrying around trying to protect his reputation. He steadfastly continued to refuse pinning the blame elsewhere—where it truly belonged. Her heart swelled in awe and her respect for him soared.

He cared enough about a child's life and survival that he was willing to shoulder the responsibility and suffer the antagonism of his colleagues. To be here, taking actions that might well sully his precious reputation because a child's life was far and away more important.

She confined herself to touching his leg with her knee beneath the table.

He gave her a quick smile of thanks, then stood to meet Kellogg's glaring anger. "I transplanted that little girl. I fought over her life for fourteen hours. I gave her a new heart and I intend to make sure she survives. Whatever it takes. You can either roll up your sleeves and help me or you can get the hell out of my way."

Tears prickled at Erin's eyelids. Colin's whatever-it-takes attitude had finally cost him in spades, but he was prepared to meet the price.

COLIN'S MEETING with Audra Beecham brought Erin close to tears again. Molly's mother wouldn't have understood the most simple explanation of what had happened, but regard for him shone in the woman's gaunt eyes. As far as she was concerned, things would be okay now. He'd saved her baby once. He could do it again.

They left her with a sympathetic, plump woman who served the hospital as a social worker, and went to the hematology lab.

Erin sat down and put the oldest slide under the microscope. In turn, Colin, Kellogg and Whitlow looked with

Erin through the microscope. The evidence was clear, confirming what she and Colin had suspected. There were HemSynon cell fragments in Molly's blood—fragments that were killing her.

She could feel Colin's tension soaring. Molly was in critical condition, and every second now counted more than ever. "Damn it, why hasn't Irv called? Or Randy?"

Colin shook his head. "Why don't you try calling back yourself?"

"I will." Kellogg and Whitlow took them to the doctors' lounge, and Erin put in a call for Irv Kartz.

Her call was transferred from one location to another until someone found Kartz scribbling notes on a blackboard.

"Irv? It's Erin—"

"Erin, hello. I've been tossing this problem around for hours. How is your patient?"

Erin swallowed. "She's critical, Irv."

"I hear you. Look, I've talked to Waller, and we've come up with a strategy that just might work."

Erin nodded quickly so Colin would know there might be some help here and mentally sent kudos to Alexa, who must have put the two men into contact with one another.

"Go on, please."

"You're dealing here with chemical bonds holding what's left of the HemSynon pieces together." He described a solution that would dissolve the bonds. "I would say you're going to have to go to surgery and flush the kiddie's kidneys."

"Irv, let me have Molly's surgeon talk with you."

She handed Colin the phone, then dug out a pad and pen from her briefcase for him to make notes on. Listening intently, he discarded his suit coat and ripped the Velcro closures open on his splint to free his wrist, then began scribbling notes in his oddly backward, left-handed way.

She could almost feel cautious jubilation building in Colin. His forearm was still creased by the splint, and he seemed to be babying his wrist, but he could write, and Erin would have bet if he had any pain, he wasn't feeling it now.

MOLLY BEECHAM was wheeled to the O.R. in a light coma. Colin and Erin went into pre-op the moment the child arrived, looking like a tiny waxen doll. Her strawberry blond hair was matted and tangled against the stark white pillowcase, and her smattering of freckles made her pallor even more severe. As he stood over her, Colin's throat convulsed.

He had battled the government insurers for the chance to save her with a transplant and he'd worked over her sweet, stick-thin body for the best part of a day. But what he had done was nothing, *nothing* to the fight Molly had put up. She'd gone through more by the age of four than anyone should go through in a lifetime.

He swore to himself she would make it through the night if he had to breathe for her himself.

He stroked Molly's strawberry bangs from her forehead and touched a kiss on his finger to her cheek, then touched her fingers. "How about a smile for your good ol' Dr. Renn, Molly May," he said softly.

Erin watched a tear fall from Molly's closed eyes. She didn't smile but she must have heard Colin. For an instant Molly's tiny fingers closed tight around his... one desperate little plea for help.

BY THE TIME the life-saving solutions were delivered to the surgery department, Molly was prepped and undergoing anesthesia. Kellogg was in the O.R. with her. Anthea

Whitlow, dressed out for surgery, finished scrubbing ahead of Colin and winked broadly at him.

"You pull, this off, sugar," she said, bumping backward through the door, "and you are going to be one celebrated cowboy."

"Yeah." Colin grimaced, disinterested for the first time in his life in being celebrated. "Or, alternatively, there may be some small possibility that I'll be able to live with myself."

Standing at the door beyond which she couldn't go without dressing out and scrubbing herself, Erin reassured him. "You will, Colin. You're doing everything possible. Remember Sister Mary Bernadette's thing. No one has died—"

"—and appointed you God," they finished together.

Colin rinsed forever. Shaking water from his hands, he searched her face. He swallowed and stared at the footies covering his shoes and then at her again.

"Will you come away with me when this is all over?"

He looked so handsome in the unflattering pea green scrubs—handsome and powerful and...infatuated. He shut his eyes for an instant. There was no one around; he would be called in when the team was ready for him. But the glare of full fluorescent lighting felt blatant and harsh and futilely unromantic. Still he made her pulse hammer.

She ached with it. He made her blood run hot. "Why?"

"I want to make music for you, Erin."

He wanted her to hear his music, feel what he felt, know how much he loved her by the way he would play his horns for her. His life as he'd known it hung in the balance. After this, nothing would ever be quite the same again, and he was discovering at last what Mary Bernadette had been trying to get through his skull for so long. Only life mattered. Lives like Molly's.

And love.

He wanted Erin to see him for more than a screw-up who was so enamored with himself that he failed to notice what his surgical team was doing, more than a crack mechanic who was so bloody good that he could snatch a child's life back from a certain tragic end.

But suddenly he realized that Erin didn't even know about the music in his head or in his soul or his fingers or his instruments. The music that even now crescendoed darkly toward the moment when it would stop and he would devote his attention to salvaging Molly's life.

"What music, Colin?"

Suddenly, stupidly, he felt the heat of embarrassment. "My horns. Anything with a reed. An oboe, mostly. And a sax."

He left her tongue-tied. In the next moment, or the one after that, every cell and sinew and intention in his body would be devoted to the life of a desperately ill child.

In *this* brief moment, aware of all the weight of the next one, he was offering her the truth of him, the things that mattered most and the promise of more. He wanted to make music for her. He played an oboe. A sax.

"No wonder you kiss so well, Colin Rennslaer."

A nurse poked her covered head around the swinging door and told Colin they were ready for him.

He backed away toward the door and gave Erin a sweltering look. "Will you do something for me?"

"Anything."

"Hold that thought."

"I will," she whispered, but the door had already swung closed behind him, and his attention had already turned to Molly's life—which was what Erin loved most about Colin Rennslaer.

Chapter Fourteen

Molly's vital signs were not promising when they rolled her out of surgery into the postoperative acute-care unit. Colin dragged the surgical cap off his head and embraced Erin for a few moments before she took him to the waiting room to talk to Audra Beecham.

He spent nearly three hours at Molly's side with Audra and Erin—unprecedented time under unprecedented circumstances. He'd ordered hourly lab tests. When blood-test results finally came back around 2:00 a.m. that indicated Molly's condition had greatly improved, Colin let himself begin to believe.

Molly Beecham was going to live.

The grueling night—the nightmare—was over. He felt exhausted, drained and euphoric at the same time. In the hotel room set aside for them by Beverly Patterson, Colin gathered Erin into his arms and turned her and dragged her onto the bed with him and kissed her hard on the lips.

"Lord, Erin, I'm so whacked out in love with you. You make me feel human again." He kissed her again, slanting his lips one way then another, leaving them damp and tender and loved.

"Colin." She trembled. His touch left her flesh quivering with outrageous desire. She ran her hands down his back and pulled the polished linen shirt from his pants and slid her hands back up the length of curving, powerful muscle and sinew.

Everything he had done this night, from taking Molly to surgery, saving her life, to comforting her mother with such warmth and compassion, even to agonizing over the other lives in the long, hideous hours of not knowing whether Molly would break the pattern and survive, all of it went into seducing her emotions, and she wanted to make love with him, to be part of him in the most elemental way. To share his triumph and ease his bleak heart over the quagmire that awaited them in Chicago.

He lay back, tucking her head beneath his chin, and began to unbutton his shirt, then her blouse, undoing his pants, then her skirt, peeling away his shorts, then her nylons and panties.

And when they lay naked together, at once subdued and exalted, sad and wildly grateful, Colin touched her between her thighs and found her ready and entered her, desperate for release. And for salvation. Whatever there was of that for him, he found in Erin's body.

She quaked and arched toward him and took him into herself and gave him what release she could. He was a powerful lover, creative and potent and gentle and attentive and forceful. And for long hours neither of them was conscious of anything but the sharp, abiding pleasure of their lovemaking.

But for all that, she knew no physical release would ever ease the pain lingering in Colin's soul. Enos Polonoski and Candace Hobbs and Ralph Costigan would never love or make love again, and Colin would never forget.

HE FELL into a deep sleep. Erin slept deeply for a few hours, but awoke around 6:00 a.m. During Molly's surgery, Erin had read over every report ever produced by Randy Waller's team. She'd been troubled by inconsistencies. It should have been apparent to everyone that the HemSynon was not ready to transfuse, that it would eventually kill the people it had been used to save.

She showered and dressed and put on a pot of coffee to brew in the miniature hotel coffeemaker. Sitting down to the reports once again, she pulled sheets from several separate reports and lined them up in a row on the round hotel game table to compare the studies one more time.

Colin woke and sat up, leaning against a pillow he propped up against the headboard. He looked wonderfully disheveled and sexual and male, but Erin was deep in her head into counts of HemSynon fragments.

"Coffee smells good."

"Mmm. It should be done in another minute or so."

Concentrating on the rows upon rows of numbers from one sheet to the next, she was vaguely aware that Colin had gotten up, poured coffee and even showered by the time she sat back in frustration, her own coffee untouched and grown cold. Someone had deliberately made HemSynon look safe to transfuse on paper. She just couldn't see how.

"Damn it, this doesn't make sense!"

He shook his head. "It's probably a pack of lies, Erin. Why do you expect it to make sense?"

"Because I think people do try to make sense. An embezzler tries to cover his tracks. So did whoever produced these reports. Look at this."

He came to stand and look over her shoulder. She pointed out the discrepancies. "The studies don't compare. The first set of tests come straight out of the original reports Waller submitted, while the second set—the one that makes HemSynon look safe to transfuse—come from the reports Alexa had supposedly gotten from Miles. Where did these numbers come from?"

Colin's brow creased as he thought about the reports. All the numbers made him think of music, and an analogy began to take shape in his head. He sat down with her and took one of her sheets of paper and began to doodle on the back, whipping off several music staffs and the signatures denoting four-four time, and six-eight and a few others along with notes of music.

"See if it helps to think about it this way. A quarter note in something like 'Mary Had a Little Lamb' is different than a quarter note in, say, a jazz piece. They look the same, but they're not—the time to hold the note is different. See?"

Erin nodded slowly. "Their value is different."

"Exactly."

Erin saw immediately how the music analogy compared to the bogus HemSynon studies. "Someone went through systematically assigning different numerical values and then let the computers generate false calculations to make it appear HemSynon levels would be safe."

"That's what it looks like."

Erin sighed and rubbed her eyes. "There must have been two sets of records compiled. The first set were probably accurate and true. This one—" she indicated the one from Alexa's reports "—this one is what Miles saw and what he reported to the FDA."

Colin dumped Erin's cold coffee and poured a fresh cup. "Do you think Randy Waller did it?"

Erin shook her head. "If Randy Waller were responsible for this, he wouldn't have even bothered coming back to clean out his locker. He would have been long gone. And he wouldn't have agreed to talk to me."

"So who does that leave? One of his underlings?"

Again Erin didn't think so. "This took someone who not only had the mathematical understanding—it also required the position to make the page substitutions."

Colin looked skeptical. "A secretary could substitute pages." But an unexpected light clicked on for him. "Erin, do you remember what you were saying about Charlene? About people like her who are so convinced that they're right that they'll invent the evidence if they have to?"

Her stomach twisted in sudden anxiety. "Charlene?"

It made perfect sense. Of course. But Charlene Babson had been handpicked by Miles for an incredibly sensitive research post. And the possibility that she could actually have done something so horrendously contrary to every research tenet in existence seemed way too remote. Or it had seemed remote.

Erin swallowed. "It had to be Charlene, didn't it? She's the only one with enough knowledge to pull off the lies— and the power, being second only to Miles."

Colin grimaced in anger. "She wouldn't have had to convince Ty that HemSynon was safe to transfuse, either. As far as he could have determined, these were perfectly safe levels to proceed with transfusions."

Erin shivered. "It's so cold in here!" But though the hotel room was air-conditioned, she knew her chill came from inside herself. So many built-in safeguards had been compromised in the research. So many principles tossed by the wayside. And all it took was a few key people.

The telephone rang. Colin answered. The caller was Anthea Whitlow—Erin could even hear her obnoxious twang. Colin listened for a moment, then gave a terse thanks and hung up.

He broke into a grin. "Molly's kidney function has returned."

"Oh, Colin, thank God! That's wonderful!"

"Let's go see her." He rubbed his hands together. "You're gonna love this. Molly's got the prettiest aquamarine eyes you ever saw."

THEY TOOK A FEW HOURS to visit Molly in her bed in pediatric intensive care. It was as if she were a different child than the one who'd lain on that surgical gurney last night, death so near that she'd looked waxen.

"Dr. Renn!"

Molly's excited aqua eyes loomed in her face, and her tremulous smile when Colin walked in would melt the Grinch's heart, but Erin wasn't fooled and she knew Colin wasn't, either. Though Molly had bounced back incredibly well, she was still one fragile little girl.

"Molly May. How y' doin?"

She gave another brave smile, but her voice quavered. "I couldn't wake up yesterday."

"I know, sweetheart." He lowered the bed rail and sat on the bed with Molly. Erin started to turn aside and go sit with Audra Beecham to let Colin have this redeeming moment with Molly to himself, but he stopped her.

"Oh, no, you don't," he said, catching Erin's hand in passing. "Erin, this is Molly, and Molly, this is Ms. Harper, who figured out what was wrong with you so we could fix it."

Molly looked solemnly up at Erin. "So I could wake up again?"

Erin nodded, smiling. "That's right. No use sleeping all the day long, is there?"

Molly turned her head back and forth on the pillow. "I was s'posed to go to school this time."

"This fall, you mean," Erin asked, "when all the other kids go back to school?"

"To the day care," Molly's mother, Audra, supplied. "Headstart." Molly looked away, and her lips tightened in disappointment.

Colin leaned down and cupped her tiny head, turning her face back toward him. Her beautiful little eyes filled with tears, and her limp curls caught on the dark hairs on Colin's hand. "I'm sorry you couldn't go to school yet, Molly. You got bad medicine while I was taking care of you, and that's what made you sick again."

Her pitifully thin hand reached up to pat Colin's cheek. "It's okay, Dr. Renn. You made me wake up again anyway."

"Thank you, Molly May." Colin swallowed hard, hoping it was true and that it would last for a long, long time. Erin had never seen such devotion or tenderness, or been so enamored by such things in her life.

COLIN SIGNED OFF on notes he had dictated from the surgical procedure before they left the hospital, and Erin called Alexa. There was no answer at her home, and she'd apparently not been at the hospital since the previous afternoon.

Jacob Delvecchio came on the line at Rose Memorial. He knew Colin had taken Molly to surgery because he had personally faxed Colin's credentials to the administration in St. Louis, but he knew more, as well. "I understand the kid's kidney function appears to be restored."

"Yes—"

Delvecchio made an impatient noise before she could say anything more. "Sabbeth called in an hour or so ago. She apparently spoke to some doctor this morning. Kellogg, maybe?"

"Yes. Jacob—"

"Is there any reason you can't wind things up and get back here?" he asked sarcastically. "Because if there isn't,

as you might imagine, there are a few fires to be put o
around this place, and Sabbeth is supposedly sick for th
first time in thirteen years.''

He broke the connection before Erin could respond. H
hadn't offered to send the helicopter to pick them up.

THEY GOT OFF Interstate 55 at Litchfield in the rented Lex
to indulge Erin's craving for an Egg McMuffin.

"You really expect me to drive a Lexus through a driv
up window?'' Colin asked in about the same vein he'
adopted when Erin wanted to drive his Jag.

Erin smiled. "It's just a car, Colin. And yes. You ma
have a champagne appetite, but mine is strictly be
budget.''

"Not to mention ulcer inducing,'' he complained. "Ho
am I supposed to live with a woman who's turned out t
have such a keen appreciation of junk food?''

She stared at Colin, but he seemed not to notice wh;
he'd said about living with her.

"I want a Coke, too,'' she added defensively. He pulle
up to the order squawk box and lowered the window wit
the electronic switch, ordering a large orange juice and
plain English muffin for himself.

"Take your ulcer meds.''

His order reminded her that Alexa Sabbeth had phone
in sick, and she told Colin.

"I'm not surprised. She didn't look very well to me whe
we left yesterday.''

"I can't imagine how she's coping,'' Erin reflected, ta
ing the small sack of food and the drinks. "If anyone's g
ing to turn out to be the scapegoat in all of this, I'd bet
will be her.''

Colin shrugged and headed back to the interstate. "De
vecchio supported Cornwall through thick and thin.'' H

ooked at Erin. "No offense, Erin, but Miles wasn't much
on top of things."

She handed Colin his muffin and unwrapped her sand-
wich. "I won't argue that. Where do you think it all started
falling apart?"

"Another 'scenario'?" he asked bitterly, discordant
snatches of music clashing in his mind. "Okay. Lonna
Clark applies for the job Charlene got. She doesn't get it,
but she keeps an eye on the project for months. Everything goes along swimmingly for a while. Progress is made,
a product is developed. Then Clark gets an incredible
break. Her distant cousin gets on the project." Colin broke
off, shaking his head.

"What?"

"Don't you think it's strange how one random, unlikely
event changes everything? Or some decision you make that
you might as easily have made the other way?"

Erin nodded. "Sister and I talked about that right after
Miles died. 'The road not taken,' she calls it. So Clark had
her piece of luck. She's in. Suppose Robards is taken in by
the quick and easy money, too. He decides he can make the
sale to the black market without her, or else she scrams
when Miles is killed. Suddenly it's too hot to touch. Where
does Ginger Creedy fit in?"

Colin finished up his muffin while he thought about
Creedy's actions. "Actually Ty could have told her I said
to cancel the blood orders."

"Do you think that's what happened?"

"No. But the only other possibility—given that we know
he did suspend my orders—is that he promised her a cut
of the deal."

Erin thought about that. "Then the only thing we don't
know yet is whether Babson was in on it, too, supplying the
HemSynon and falsifying her records to make the product

look better, or if Ginger and Ty were stealing the doses they transfused and Babson knew nothing about it."

"She knew," Colin answered, setting the cruise control so he could relax. "That's why Ty came in the night you and I were there. Remember? He said he had another candidate for the 'most precious blood.' He'd just gotten in from Amsterdam."

Erin eased out of her shoes and curled up in the plush Lexus seat. "That's probably why he's out of the country again, Colin. Someone he met in Amsterdam made him an offer, and he's delivering the goods."

Colin's right hand clinched into a fist on his thigh. "None of it explains who knew that Miles had uncovered the transfusions."

Erin watched the play of expressions on Colin's clean, utterly masculine profile, then stared at her hands. It hurt to look at him, to realize that she loved him irredeemably. To see the turmoil and bewilderment and outright loathing of events and behaviors beyond his control.

She cleared her throat. "I think it was Ginger."

His eyes narrowed in concentration. "Why?"

"Remember how Pris behaved so badly? Ginger was wearing the perfume—Pris had a very bad experience with my niece and perfume. The scent was in Miles's office, too. The other reason is, Miles's daughter told me part of the reason that he called me was that he had discovered what it was to be betrayed by someone he loved."

"Creedy?" Colin took a deep, frustrated breath. Her affairs had been notorious, but she'd never quite connected with the right guy. Or the right combination of man and money. But maybe there had been something. A flirtation that cost her nothing in the interests of a high-stakes deal.

Colin shrugged. "I must have been sleeping through the last year." He looked at his watch. "We should get back about the time Ty gets in from France. I've got to talk to him, Erin. Alone, preferably."

She understood. In spite of everything, he wanted to spare Tyler Robards a little humiliation. "Why don't I drop you off at his house and go pick up Pris from Alexa?"

Colin smiled and reached out to take hold of her hand. His touch, more than ever, stirred her. How very scary, she thought, to feel so in synch, and be so in love and know its worth in the midst of such heart-breaking circumstances.

They arrived at Ty and Clarie Robards's half-million-dollar house at two-thirty in the afternoon. Colin drew Erin a map detailing the route to Alexa's rural farmhouse, then kissed her and held her as though he might not let her go.

"I'll be back, Colin. How much time do you need?"

He gave her hands a squeeze. "I'll be ready whenever you make it back."

CLAIRE ANSWERED the door in a maternity dress and nylons, matching necklace and earrings, with Ty Jr. straddling a hip. Perfectly groomed, a former debutante and airline stewardess, she had light brown hair and a sweet face and a fierce determination to rise above Ty's peccadilloes so long as he provided her the life-style to which she had become so accustomed.

"Colin. How nice to see you."

"Clarie."

"Please come in." Her expression turned anxious in response, Colin thought, to his, and the toddler began to fuss and buck in her arms. "Is something wrong?"

Colin felt for her and curved his hand soothingly over the little boy's blond curls. "I just need to talk to Ty. Is he home?"

"No." She lifted her hand over her ample girth to check her watch. "He should be anytime, though. You knew he was flying in from France this afternoon, didn't you?"

"Yes." Al Hastings had known which flight Ty had reservations for, and by now it all made stark sense. After Cornwall was killed, Ty must have known he had to close the deal quick. "I just thought he might be home by now."

"Oh." Reassured, Clarie turned and began to cross the hardwood entry beyond the dining room toward the kitchen. "Well, I was just about to fix a glass of iced tea. Would you like some?"

"Sure." Colin closed the door behind him and followed Clarie. He sat down at the wooden table in the sunny, expansive breakfast nook. The house smelled of lemon wax and baby wipes. She put Ty Jr. down on the floor at a pile of blocks and filled a couple of crystal tumblers with ice.

Nothing Clarie Robards did was done without class. She poured the iced tea and sliced lemons and served them with a tray of mint cookies. But Colin thought there was something strained and too careful about her behavior.

"Clarie, are you all right?"

She sat, clapped and smiled at Ty Jr.'s little antics, sipped from her iced tea and then looked straight at Colin. "There wasn't another conference in Paris, was there?"

He refused to lie to her. "No."

"What's going on, Colin? Ty hasn't been himself lately. He's sort of…" She paused to think of the right words, but the muted drone of the garage door opening stopped her cold. She swallowed. "That must be Ty now."

Tyler Jr. stood excitedly, bouncing, crying, "Ty! Ty! Ty!"

Clarie frowned and bit her lip, but then smiled at her child. "That's right. Daddy's home!"

Ty came in through the back door. Colin sat watching the small boy clapping, observing Ty and Clarie and the glances that passed between them when Ty saw Colin sitting there, and Ty burying his shocked reaction in frantically gleeful play with his son.

He winked at Colin as if to say he just had to get through this family welcome first, then kissed his wife, stroked her hair, asked how she was feeling, how much the baby was kicking—but Clarie was angry and refused to cooperate with his thinly veiled act. He put the baby down and turned to Colin.

"What's going on here?"

"Don't," Colin warned softly. "Just don't." Part of him wanted to shove his friend's perfect teeth down his throat. Another, larger part wanted Ty to have some excuse, some reasonable explanation for what he'd done, because any way Colin looked at it, Ty had contributed to the deaths of their patients. "Don't act like you don't know why I'm here."

Ty made a strangled noise and angled his head away from Colin. Clarie stared at him as if he'd grown horns and a tail, and Tyler Jr. was whimpering around, whining to be picked up again. For a moment Ty seemed as disoriented as if he'd taken a hit of his own anesthesia meds.

Colin stood, picked up the toddler, cradled the child against his shoulder a moment, then handed him to Clarie. "Maybe you could take him upstairs and get in a nap together."

She stared up at Colin for a moment, searching his face as if she might be able to see how bad this was, then at her husband. "Ty?"

He refused to look at Colin. "Get a nap, Clarie. Everything will be okay. I promise."

She turned jerkily and walked away, crooning comforting noises at Ty Jr.

"Things are going to be okay, aren't they, Colin?"

"I don't see how, Ty. The authorities will have to be involved soon."

"The authorities?" He downed the tea he'd poured, then opened a cabinet and cracked open a bottle of Scotch and sloshed his glass half-full of the amber liquor. "Are you threatening me?"

Colin sank into the ladder-back chair and scraped a hand through his hair. "No threats, Ty. Just the truth."

"The truth?" He stared into his glass and inhaled the scent, then slugged down most of it in a single swallow. "Do you think I haven't figured out your part in this? You think I don't know you're the one—you and that bitch Babson—that colluded to take Cornwall out?"

Colin shook his head, wondering what universe Ty was living in that his reasoning made the least sense. "Ty, put away the liquor. You're not thinking straight—"

"The hell I'm not!" Ty snorted. "Cornwall was onto something, and Charlene found out about it. She'd as soon kill Cornwall as look at him, and now she had an excuse. You gave her your keys, didn't you?"

"Ty—"

"Then you decided to take Nina Tobias to surgery that night. She wasn't on till morning, but you needed an alibi! So if you're thinking about going to the *authorities,* Colin…think again. You're in this way deeper than I am."

"Except that it didn't happen that way, Ty. Tobias wasn't scheduled at all. We had to take her when the heart and lungs came available."

"Whatever," Ty answered. He sat down at the table where Clarie had been sitting and poured more Scotch.

"The point is you knew the organs were coming, and you knew you had an iron-clad alibi."

Colin took a deep breath and blew it out, staring at the baby's blocks on the floor. He could sit here all afternoon trying to reason with Ty. He hadn't given Babson his keys, but he could see the twisted reasoning that led Ty to believe that he had.

"The thing is, Ty, I didn't know you were transfusing the HemSynon."

He shrugged. "Not in the beginning."

Colin's thoughts went very still. Ty was getting drunk enough to brag now. Drunk enough, perhaps, to unwittingly reveal who knew what and when they knew it. "What happened in the beginning, Ty? Was it all your idea or was it your cousin's?"

"Lonna?" He smiled and took another swig of Scotch, then wiped his lips with the back of his hand.

Colin thought it was proof of how witless Ty was when he drank that he didn't even think to ask how he knew about his cousin.

"Yeah, it was her idea," he acknowledged grudgingly. "At least she's the one who said there was a market out there for stolen goods, if I could get her proof of successful clinical trials."

"But then you must have thought—if you were the one who had to risk everything anyway to get her the proof— that you could pull it off without her. . . . She thought you were the weak link, didn't she, Ty?"

Ty made an ugly grimace. "The bitch! She would have cut me out so fast, it'd make your head spin."

It took all the strength Colin had to sit there listening to a man who had been a friend and respected colleague talk about selling out people's lives. "Did you need the money so much, Ty?"

He laughed humorlessly and began recounting expenses, beginning with his ex-wife and children. "Linda's house payment is six grand a month. The child support for Jennifer and Justin is thirty-seven hundred. My old man's in a nursing home for Alzheimer's cases at just under five grand every month. And all that before Clarie and I see a single dime. You figure it out." He shook his head, then shrugged. "This deal was going to happen, Colin. Somebody was going to get the bucks, and it wasn't going to be Rose Memorial. I figured it might as well be me."

Erin would be appalled. Colin understood but he couldn't sympathize. Not at the expense of human lives. "So you created the Scenarios, only they weren't all models, were they?"

"No."

"Who got the HemSynon?"

Ty grew surly because in his drunken state he couldn't even remember the names of the people he'd condemned to die. "Who cares? They got it and it worked. That's all that counts."

"Costigan? Polonoski? Hobbs?"

"Yeah."

"They're dead, Ty. All three of them."

The news had the effect of a bucket of cold water thrown in his face. From one moment to the next, his confidence deserted him. His bravado collapsed, and he began to shake. "That's impossible."

Colin wanted to kill him. "How did you convince Ginger to suspend my routine blood orders?"

Ty swallowed. "I didn't—"

"Was she in on it from the beginning?"

"I don't know! I suppose..." Ty was panicking now, confused and scared, shaking. "Why are you asking me all this? You knew about it! You got the scenarios! You knew those people were the experimental candidates—"

In one concerted move Colin rose and reached over the corner of the table and grabbed a handful of Ty Robards's shirt placket and dragged him to his feet. He'd never been so angry in his life or so ready to choke the life out of another man.

Robards's pitiful whining made him stop and think about what he was doing, and about the use of trying to tell a man with no integrity left that he hadn't known any of it.

He spared himself the effort, took a couple of deep, angry breaths and shoved Ty sprawling back into his chair, then sank into his own and turned so he wouldn't have to look at the pathetic excuse for a man Ty had become.

Erin was right. Everything was so convoluted, so thick with greed and betrayals and finger pointing that it was impossible to see the forest for the trees. How had it all come together?

Ty had transfused the deadly medicine. Ginger had suspended SOPs, someone had hit Cornwall and no one knew anything about anyone else's role. It made no sense. How could a conspiracy exist if the left hand knew nothing of what the right hand was doing?

He kept coming back in his mind to Ty's inconceivable assumption that he had given Babson the keys to his beloved car. That he had needed an alibi. Some ill-defined question kept creeping back. He sat at Ty Robards's table, stroking the beads of condensation from his glass, posing silent questions.

Who even knew Miles had been onto the scheme, or where he would be and when he would be there, or that Colin was in surgery and his keys—

Colin stopped cold. The answer had been staring him in the face from the first. There was only one person who

knew what everyone else knew. One person privy to all the
project data, to everything Miles Cornwall thought and did,
every player's vulnerability... and only one person who
knew where his keys could be found, coupled with the sheer
guts to run a man down in cold blood.

And Erin was walking straight into her deadly clutches.

Chapter Fifteen

Erin missed the exit off the highway to the county road Colin had drawn and numbered on the map. More and more anxious to collect Pris, bring Alexa up to date and get back to Colin, she had to double back on the access road, then turn north.

It seemed to Erin that there wasn't a house anywhere in a hundred-mile radius. The blacktop, two-lane county road ran uninterrupted, straight and true as a ruled line. She shifted up to overdrive and let the Lexus eat up the miles, edging near eighty miles per hour.

Eighty was half what the car was built to do, but ever since they had uncovered the discrepancies in Charlene's reporting of the residue studies, Erin had felt as if she were hurtling toward some unknown, unwelcome territory. And even at half its ability, the powerful engine reinforced the illusion.

Over several small hills and eight or ten miles the countryside began to close in. Maple trees and green ash, oak and sycamore, trees Erin rarely if ever saw in Phoenix, lined the road, growing more and more dense. Pheasants occasionally startled out of the barrow pits.

She slowed down. Alexa's property began where a break in the trees came, lining her drive. Erin turned west, across the oncoming lane. She could see the white clapboard house through the stands of decades-old hackberry, maybe another quarter mile.

By the time she pulled onto the drive, which fronted what must have been—or still was—a barn, Alexa stood on her porch, shading her eyes against the blazing midday sun.

Erin shut off the car and got out. Cradling Pris in an arm, Alexa smiled despite the ugly barking coming from the barn.

"Erin. Welcome back."

"Thanks. How are you? Delvecchio said—"

"Fine." Alexa sipped at some lemonade, then gestured at the Lexus. "Colin pop for that? You two must be getting pretty tight after an out-of-town assignation."

Confused at Alexa's odd tone, not knowing what to say, Erin merely nodded. The barking gave way to one last vicious-sounding snarl. Pris seemed oddly complacent in Alexa's arms, totally ambivalent to the dog and to Erin's arrival. "What's wrong with Pris?"

Alexa handed the cat over. "I'm sorry, Erin. She had a terrible scare with my dog. I've had to sedate her."

Erin took Pris's deadweight in her arms and buried her face in her cat's fur to cover a flash of annoyance—why would Alexa agree to take a cat if she was bound to be terrorized or eaten alive? But though Pris didn't so much as move a muscle, there didn't seem to be any real damage. "Could I come inside and fill you in?"

Alexa shrugged. She looked haggard and disinterested. "I suppose."

She led the way into her house, through the dining room into a kitchen with bleached oak planks and cabinetwork and marble-topped counters. Polished brass pots and pans hung from a wooden rack over an island with a double-wide oven and six-burner cook top.

She poured Erin a glass of the pink lemonade from an antique ceramic pitcher.

Struggling to understand Alexa's indifferent behavior, Erin settled a lethargic Pris in her lap and complimented the kitchen. "Alexa, this is fabulous. Are you a gourmet cook in addition to everything else?"

"No." Alexa sat as well, looking around her as if truly seeing her kitchen for the first time. "I wanted a proper kitchen, so I've bought one, but I don't cook."

Her flat tone gave Erin the creeps. "Alexa, are you well?"

"What do you think, Erin?" But she seemed to shake off her mood. "So, little Molly Beecham is going to be fine. All's well that ends well, I guess."

The remark annoyed Erin. "It's hardly over," she responded. "Molly will survive, but Candace Hobbs is dead. And Ralph Costigan, and Enos Polonoski."

"They were critical transplant patients, Erin."

"Which may be why Dr. Robards chose them."

"He didn't choose them," Alexa snapped, then elaborated in defense of Tyler, "in the way you're suggesting. He's incapable of it."

"Incapable of what? Playing God?" Erin asked incredulously. "Or choosing who will die in the interests of greed couched in scientific inquiry?"

Alexa's lips tightened. "Look, Erin. Those people may have been victims, but no one involved meant to hurt any of them—especially Tyler Robards. He relied on data which led him to believe that those patients could only benefit from the HemSynon transfusion. And we will never know for certain if it was HemSynon that killed those people."

Erin stared for a moment at Alexa's blank expression. She respected Alexa's intelligence as much as her resourceful nature, and though she had sometimes sensed a core of pitilessness in Alexa, she had never seen her display such a deeply callous attitude.

"There is still the matter of Charlene lying to the FDA. The results of Randy Waller's studies aren't what she reported. She indicated the HemSynon would be safe—"

"And it isn't," Alexa concluded in a bored fashion.

Erin sat back in her chair. "You knew that?"

Alexa took a long drink from her lemonade and held the glass to her temple as if to ease a headache. "I've spoken with Charlene. She repeated Randy's tests herself."

Erin felt as if every direction she turned, there was a brick wall. "Alexa. I can't believe you knew the HemSynon would kill."

"I didn't. She came to me after you left yesterday. And no matter what it looks like, Charlene believed HemSynon was safe for transfusion."

Puzzled by Alexa's defense of both Tyler Robards and Charlene Babson—Alexa Sabbeth, who tolerated nothing short of zero-error performance—Erin rose from the kitchen table and stood leaning against the sliding glass patio door, holding Pris. "I suppose Ginger Creedy also felt it was safe?"

"Anything to enhance Colin's reputation," Alexa snapped, "which is an attitude *he* has promoted and encouraged in Ginger Creedy and everyone around him from the word 'go.'"

Erin bent to bury her nose in Pris's fur again, stroking her cheek against the cat's head. That was probably true of Colin, but she rejected the implication that his attitudes had fostered criminal behavior. "Look, Alexa—"

"No. You look, Erin. You're not from around here. You have no history at Rose. You have no idea of the sacrifices all of these people have made—including Colin. But even if you had, even if you were Sister Mary Bernadette herself—I would say to you, *no one* ever intended to harm a patient in our care. If there was a conspiracy, it was one meant to enhance lives. That's what there is to look at. We'll withdraw our licensing application from the FDA, quietly shut down the labs and forget that any of this ever happened."

Erin shook her head. She understood high intentions. She could even appreciate Alexa's loyalty to people who shared her long history at Rose Memorial. She couldn't pretend that nothing had happened.

"You can't simply withdraw. And even if you could, I can't."

Alexa blew out her breath and got up from the table and went to the sink to wash her hands. She stood there turning the soap bar over and over in her hands, staring out into the pasture where her Arabian mare grazed peacefully and a very young filly darted and dashed around.

"Do you know what it's like to want everything, Erin? And then you get it, and you find it's really nothing? Do you know what it is to go for one promotion after another, get there and discover how meaningless it all is?"

Sensing the extent of Alexa's despondent mood, which must account in some way for her coldly indifferent attitude, knowing the question was not meant to be answered anyway, Erin said nothing.

"Do you know what it is to be consumed with need, wanting everything, proving everything, finally getting nothing no matter how hard you've worked? Nothing should have gone wrong. Nothing would have gone wrong if people had been doing their jobs, keeping their noses clean and to the grindstone, solving problems.

"Don't you think I know?" she went relentlessly on. "Now, after the fact? Do you think I don't see exactly how Charlene deluded herself? What a gutless wonder Ty is?

How stupidly self-centered Ginger Creedy is? And Colin—'' She broke off and began to scour at her nails with a surgical scrub brush. "What a fool. But I tried. God knows I tried to handle it all."

"Alexa, it's impossible to oversee every detail—"

"I have always gotten what I wanted," Alexa continued, ignoring Erin's attempt to soothe her. "One way or another I've gotten what I want. I wanted control of this research, and I went to Frank Clemenza and I convinced him to let me administer the project." She scrubbed ruthlessly, focusing maniacally on her hands. "Convincing Frank of anything is like . . . like . . ."

She couldn't seem to find any suitable comparison for whatever feat had been required to persuade Clemenza to let her steer the project, but the mental search had distracted Alexa from her hands.

She put aside the brush and rinsed the lather away. Turning to face Erin across the marble countertop, she dried her hands. Her face seemed cast in ice.

"So you see, I have never *really* gotten what I wanted."

The contradiction jarred Erin, but she suspected Alexa saw no discrepancy. She may have gotten what she wanted, but nothing had ever satisfied her. There must seem nothing now for her to hold on to, nowhere to go.

This woman who had presented herself from the first as capable of taking care of anything had been suddenly, finally, devastated by a flood of anxiety because the people she had invested herself in had ruined everything.

Erin shifted Pris in her arms, her uneasiness growing. Alexa's control and unflinching concentration seemed to be crumbling into behavior so unbalanced that with every passing second Pris's deadweight seemed more ominous.

"Alexa, what did you give Pris?"

Her eyes rested briefly on Pris. "All I had was metocurine. Sorry."

Erin felt the color drain from her face. The drug, which Alexa would have had access to in surgery at Rose Memorial, functioned as a nerve blocker. It was a derivative of curare, infamous as the poison on the arrows of blowguns. It induced total paralysis for up to ninety minutes—more, certainly, at Pris's body weight—without causing loss of consciousness.

Pris's respiratory system could collapse at any second, and there would be nothing Erin could do.

"You gave her metocurine," Erin repeated numbly, disbelief haggling with the sudden certainty that in her rage and frustration, Alexa Sabbeth had become capable of any cruelty.

"Intramuscularly," Alexa answered coolly, as if not having administered the drug into Pris's veins but into a muscle removed any danger. "She's still breathing."

"What if she weren't?" Erin cried.

"Then she would be dead, wouldn't she?"

Erin took a step back. How pointless it was to have asked. Dead or alive, Pris no more mattered to Alexa than a throwaway tissue. Had Alexa wanted to punish Erin—in the most heartless and sadistic way she could dream of—for ripping open the facade, for exposing the rotten core of the HemSynon project? For ruining everything, thwarting what Alexa had wanted so desperately?

Erin swallowed. "I think I'd better go."

Alexa's icelike expression softened. "Erin, if you're worried, perhaps you should stay until she regains movement. Besides, I have something to show you." She turned and left the room without waiting to see if Erin would accompany her.

Erin followed only because the Lexus was also parked outside in front. She intended to leave, but Alexa was right. She couldn't afford to put Pris down because she would never know if the poor thing stopped breathing altogether.

"Please, Erin," Alexa said, motioning inside the garage where the vicious barking had begun again, "you must see this."

Erin stood in the sweltering heat of the afternoon sun, staring at the right front fender of the rented Lexus. "Alexa, I'm not taking Pris in there."

"All right. My dog is tied up, but I understand. Wait a moment. Please. I'll open the garage door."

Erin could hear her pulse pounding in her ears. The blinding white light of the sun, the absolute stillness of the leaves in the trees, the gently rolling landscape—everything around her conspired to present some bucolic picture of rural Illinois, harmless and sleepy and utterly benign. Even the unseen dog ceased its snarling. But Erin felt a dread so strong it nearly buckled her knees.

The garage door motor kicked on. The door itself began to draw upward. Alexa stood in deep shadows, the snarling Doberman to one side. Pris twitched but seemed okay, as if, perhaps, the metocurine were beginning to wear off.

But there in still deeper shadows Erin saw the outlines of a car with an Illinois license plate. Her eyes adjusted to the almost violent contrast of sunlight to dark shadow, until she could see that the plate was custom-made and what it read.

Too Cool.

Chapter Sixteen

Robards's Mercedes had no car phone. Colin shoved the accelerator to the floor, banged the heel of his hand off the steering wheel and swore. He'd lit out of the house—Ty in tow—too fast to even think about calling the cops. Robards had every toy imaginable, but he'd junked his car phone when the cellular models improved so much.

Ty sat angrily slouched in the front passenger seat, chewing at a thumbnail, his elbow planted on the window ledge. His leg jittered. He couldn't keep still. He was panicked and angry and worried.

He knew better now, but he claimed Alexa had scammed him. He thought she'd never been involved, not until yesterday.

Driving hard and way too fast, Colin fought to keep his cool. "What happened yesterday?"

"She called me in Paris," Ty snarled. "She tracked me down. She knew where I was. She'd guessed what I was doing, and she told me flat out I could either get half the fifteen million deposited in a separate Cayman account for her or face arrest at customs when I flew back in."

"What if you hadn't come back at all?"

Ty's expression twisted into one of pure hate. "She'd have killed Clarie and Ty Jr." His jaw clamped shut, and he began to shake uncontrollably. "Come on, Colin. Let's go back and send the cops. She's got the money. Harper is already dead meat...."

Colin kept his eyes trained on the highway. There was no time to go back. No time to call the cops. Probably no time to save Erin. But he had to try, and his brain was flooded with the natural amphetamines of fear, and he had to keep control.

"If she is, Ty, there will be bloody hell to pay."

HORROR RICOCHETING through her, Erin blinked. Colin's Jaguar was still there, and the dog was still frenzied.

In the instant of a single heartbeat, she recalled how desperately Miles had tried to tell her, to get her to stop care-taking and just listen to him. He'd been trying, not to tell her what damage had been done to the HemSynon project, but to name his assailant. He'd only managed to get out the first syllable of *sabotage*. *Sabbeth* was, of course, what he had meant. Poor Miles.

She'd only been prepared to hear what she had expected him to say. Sabotage, Miles? *Not exactly.*

Erin shuddered violently. "Alexa, my God! How could you have done this? How could you?"

She shrugged. "Miles had become something of a liability," she answered indifferently. "He needn't have died necessarily, but those are the breaks, aren't they? But I don't know whether to be flattered or appalled that any of this comes as such a surprise to you. Did you really think *anyone* else had the backbone to do what had to be done?"

Erin shook her head in disbelief. ... *the girl works day and night,* Sister Mary Bernadette had said. *Can't be per-*

suaded to go home. I thought she had, earlier, but she's
back in her office.

Of course. Alexa had left work that night, taken Colin's
keys, run down Miles, hidden the antique Jag away in her
barn and returned to work. The timing wasn't even delicate. She would have had hours to play with over the course
of Colin's seventeen-hour transplant to return the keys.

How simple the truth was, she thought dazedly. Everyone with any motive at all to have killed Miles also had an
alibi. The flaw in her own thinking seemed glaring now.
Alexa Sabbeth had motives Erin had never begun to consider. She had seemed above the fray, too far from the heart
of the project. Too helpful, too willing to provide Erin virtually anything she needed.

"No," Erin answered, knowing it had taken her no more
than a few seconds to stumble over what was now so obvious. "You were the only one who could have pulled it off."

She transferred Pris's deadweight from one arm to the
other and reached for the car door.

"Don't even think about it, Erin," Alexa warned softly,
leveling a handgun she had held hidden at her side in the
deep shadows of the barn. "They use this baby in veteri-
nary practice. The CO_2 cartridge will deliver enough metocurine to drop you cold."

"Alexa—"

"I mean it. Don't move until I've thought what to do
with you."

Erin swallowed and backed off. Everything seemed so
surreal—the stark, blinding sunlight, the shadows embrac-
ing Alexa, the snarling dog, Pris's barely breathing at all.
And a gun, meant to anesthetize animals, aimed at her with
deadly intention.

Colin.

Dear God. He had no way of knowing. She could well be dead before enough time passed that he would get worried she hadn't returned.

She had only herself to depend upon. She bowed her head, then looked at Alexa. "Why did you give those patient charts back to Zoe? Why risk letting me see them?"

Alexa gave a bitter, barking laugh and sank to her haunches, leaning against the barn wall. "Kind of ironic, isn't it? I underestimated you and overestimated everyone else."

"We're alike in that, Alexa," Erin answered carefully. Her arm was sweating beneath Pris, and flies droned on around them, but she had to keep focused.

If she could just keep Alexa talking, she might find some opportunity to escape. "We expect people to do what they've been instructed to do. These past few days must have been hell for you, knowing everyone had screwed up—"

Alexa interrupted her with a disgusted sound, but her attention to her aim never wavered. "You have no idea."

The sun shone hot on her back, and Erin felt the first prickle of sweat between her shoulder blades. "Was it Ginger who discovered what Miles knew?"

Alexa's teeth locked in a savage grimace. "The stupid cow!"

"It was her?"

"You want to know?" Alexa sat on the ground, drew up her knees and propped her wrist so that her aim at Erin held true and steady. "Fine. You might as well hear it all." She regarded Erin with contempt. "Miles called Creedy to his office. The fool had fallen head over heels for her. He thought she was in love with him, too.

"He practically begged her to tell him no one had transfused the HemSynon. He'd read the charts. He must have known, but he would have believed Creedy because that's what he wanted to believe. All she had to do was pat him on the head and croon a few denials in his ear, but she couldn't stand not to fling the whole thing in his face."

All Erin could think to do was to stroke Pris, to get her circulation moving and counter the poison. Alexa started to say more, something about the argument she had had with Creedy in her office the night Erin and Colin had interrupted, when the dull roar of a car tearing up the country lane penetrated the quiet of the afternoon.

"Alexa, listen—"

She rose. "Do me a favor and shut up, Erin. I'm really quite sick of your supercilious attitude. Anyway," she said, shading her eyes, watching the dust cloud stirred up by the approaching car, "it's too late for anything you could say to make the least difference."

She took the chain off her snarling dog and made it sit at her side, then calmly pushed the button to lower the automatic garage door. It had stopped when Tyler Robards's silver Mercedes hurtled around the corner onto the property, and they could both see Colin driving and Tyler Robards beside him.

"The cavalry to your rescue," she remarked expressionlessly. She lowered the dart gun to her side.

"Don't do anything foolish," Erin urged, chilled by Alexa's lack of any emotional reaction to the arrival of Colin and Ty. Was she even human?

Her brows raised contemptuously. "Foolish? Don't think I can't take all three of you down, Erin."

The dog was looking for the slightest excuse to come after anything that moved. Alexa jerked on its collar and smiled thinly at Erin. "And if you go down, I won't be able to keep Donovan here—" she indicated the menacing dog "—from taking you apart."

"Alexa, it's not too late—"

She let go of the dog's collar. "Don't even move. Don't say one word."

Colin screeched to a stop two feet short of the Lexus, shoved open the door and jumped out, but Erin stood stock-still with Pris limp in her arms, and he must have sensed the grave danger she was in without knowing exactly what it was.

Ty cowered in the car. Erin looked at Colin, but there was no way to convey that Alexa had the vet gun, loaded with deadly dosages of metocurine.

"Colin," Alexa greeted him, approaching Erin, ordering the growling dog to stay. She had crossed her arms beneath her breasts. Her hand and the gun were out of sight, hidden by her shoulder. "Do me a favor. Tell Ty to get out of the car."

Colin ignored her. Pris's limp body made his guts tighten. "What's wrong with the cat?"

"Metocurine," she answered evenly. "The same thing afflicting you and your sweetie here, Colin, if you don't do what I tell you to do."

He knew then that it was a gun she held behind her, but she would never come close enough to let him get it away from her. His mind flew, gauging her, figuring a way to jump her. But if he blew his one-time shot at her, if he jumped her too soon, the dog would take him out.

He gestured through the windshield for Robards to get out. Ty complied sullenly, but stood protected by the car separating him from everyone else.

She gestured at the Lexus, then at Erin, standing a few feet away with Pris encumbering her arms. "Put your hands on the roof. If you move, Donovan will take them apart before you can breathe." She turned her attention to Ty. "You couldn't even have prevented *this?*" she asked nastily.

"I hate your guts," he ranted at her, too heated to keep his mouth shut long enough to think what he was doing. "You used me!"

Stroking Pris, rubbing beneath her jaw, Erin watched Alexa shake her head, her facial expression twisting with disdain.

"You're such a babe-in-the-woods. Did you think this whole thing was coming off without someone facilitating your every move? Did you think you were controlling Creedy and Babson?"

Ty's jaw cocked sideways in tension, and he looked away from Alexa. Erin felt Pris struggling to move, her tiny muscles bunching uselessly, protesting the watchful, low growls of the dog. Colin could do nothing.

"Get in your car, Ty. Just get in the damn car and drive away before I kill you."

He looked confused, as if he couldn't trust that her offer was no trick.

"Do it Ty," Colin ordered. "Get out of here and call the cops."

"Shut up!" Alexa snapped. She stared at Ty. "That would be very stupid, you know that, don't you, Ty? No one will ever know how you were involved if you just keep your mouth shut."

He swallowed and his eyes darted to Colin, but he nodded. "What are you going to do?"

"I don't think you want to know that, do you, Ty?"

His eyes darted between Colin and Erin and he gulped. "Get out."

He dove into the car, crawled frantically over the gearshift console and started the car. He threw it into reverse and pulled out of the drive as fast as he could go. By the time the dust had settled, the dog was ready to split himself.

The silence became oppressive. Colin still stood with his hands plastered to the roof of the Lexus, knowing Ty wouldn't have the guts to do the right thing and call the police.

Flies buzzed. The dog paced back and forth. Alexa had leveled the gun once more at Erin. "What are you going to do, Lex? Murder us?"

"Remove the obstacles," Erin murmured. "Isn't that your forte?"

"Yes." She tilted her head, considering. "Perhaps a double suicide."

"For God's sake, Lex, let Erin go. Maybe we can cut some kind of deal."

She smiled. "Nice offer, Colin!" She turned to Erin. "He's really very, very good, you know. Like me. You unfortunately are much more like Miles than you'd like to believe." She sneered. "Willing to be deluded."

Pris mewed pathetically. Erin held her closer. "What are you talking about?"

"You bought it, didn't you? You still believe Colin never knew what was going on. C'mon, Colin. Time to 'fess up."

For one terrible instant Erin feared that she had been duped by Colin. No matter what heroic measures he had taken since the sabotage had been discovered, there was still the possibility that he had played Alexa's counterpoint as a skilled consummate at deception.

The probability was glaringly real to her. Despite everything she had uncovered, she had been duped by Alexa Sabbeth, and there was nothing to suggest that she had not been deceived by Colin, as well.

Nothing but instinct and her faith in Colin. She had fallen for him, but it wasn't only that. She trusted him as she had never trusted another living soul.

Erin saw only one way out of this trap. One small chance. "You slime," she muttered, glaring at Colin and Alexa in turn. "Both of you!"

Colin stared at her, and she knew he was stunned at the violent emotion in her voice. She gave a nearly motionless wink, hoping against hope that he would recognize the ploy she'd used to enlist Charlene Babson's support in the lab that first night.

But Alexa laughed. "Nice try, Erin. Really. But remember, I know how well you handled good old Charlene." Her look turned ugly. "*I* won't be handled. Got it?"

Erin clenched her teeth to keep from crying out in frustration. Pris was getting more distraught by the minute, trying to move, and finding herself clumsy, she yowled. The more stressed she got, the harder she tired, the greater the risk that she would put herself into respiratory failure.

Seeing Erin's own distress, Colin almost hurled himself at Alexa then, but she had begun to move back across the yard. Once again she pressed the button to open the garage door. "Now that Ty is gone..."

Colin saw his beloved antique cherry red Jag parked inside, and the air seemed to come forcibly out of him. "Why?"

"Because it had to be done. Because Miles forced my hand." She shook her head sadly. "Just as you two have forced my hand. Here's what we'll do," she improvised, like a bad-seed child creating a death scene. "The two of you pile in, you'll each take a little shot of metocurine, I'll switch on the car, close the garage door and let the carbon monoxide take over. Painless and easy."

"What's the point, Lex?"

Her face went blank. "The point, dear Colin, is that I will be out of the country long before anyone discovers your bodies. By then I won't care if it looks like suicide or not. Get in the car, Colin."

Neither one of them moved. Alexa gave the dog a sharp order, and its hackles rose. Prepared to attack, it snarled viciously.

Fear unlike anything she'd ever felt flashed through Erin. She cried out, her knees buckled, and she would have fallen to the ground if Colin hadn't moved to take hold of her.

Colin swore. "Get the damn dog chained!"

He held Erin tight against his body and helped her walk with him toward Alexa. If he had to, he'd take the metocurine dart in the gut, but he wouldn't let this go on anymore.

Training the gun on Erin, Alexa jerked at the dog and managed to get the chain back on its collar. As Alexa stood, Pris screeched and her muscles bunched in some horrible parody of real movement, and she leaped at Alexa's face, fury and adrenaline fueling her small body into a clawing, hissing, scratching missile.

Alexa screamed in rage and held her hands up, and the gun fell out of her grasp to the ground. Colin hurled Erin out of the way and dove for the gun and fired point-blank at the attacking dog only a fraction of an instant before Pris fell awkwardly and spent within its reach.

Alexa turned to pick up something else for a weapon, but the dog collided against her, and she fell, cracking her head against the side of the barn.

Alexa lay still as death but breathing, and the dog was motionless, paralyzed and unable to move as Pris had been. The horror was over. The stillness after the sudden, violent battle overwhelmed Erin. She sank to her knees beside Colin and took Pris into her arms.

Colin exhaled sharply a couple of times, trying to blow off the excess adrenaline coursing through his body. He took one more deep breath, then threw the gun aside and gathered Erin into his arms. "It's over," he murmured, as much to make himself believe it as to soothe Erin. "It's all over now."

Tears squeezed out of Erin's eyes, and she dashed them away with the back of her hand. She lifted her face to Colin. "I don't even know how to feel."

His throat closed painfully. Her response was so classically Erin. God, but he loved her. He smiled and tucked her head beneath his chin. "You're going to have to give up trying to figure it out, sweetheart, and just feel what you're feeling."

Enclosed in the protective circle of his arms, Erin raised her head to look into Colin's beautiful hazel-blue eyes, fringed with such indecently thick black lashes. What she was feeling was also pretty indecent with the unconscious bodies of Alexa Sabbeth and her dog so nearby.

"I feel like inventing an ending to this disaster. We have to call an ambulance. And a vet."

Colin nodded, and the lump in his throat tightened. "Then what?"

"Then you'd better take me home and start keeping your promises, mister."

He didn't have to ask which promises or figure out an ending at all. This would require no particular heroic measures, just constant, abiding love.

He would play his music for her, and then he would make music with her, and then he would spend a lifetime of sex and croissants with her, sprinkled with bouts of dirty diapers, culminating in decades of old age, spent together.

"Whatever it takes, love. Whatever it takes."

HARLEQUIN®

I N T R I G U E ®

Into a world where danger lurks around
every corner, and there's a fine line between trust
and betrayal, comes a tall, dark and handsome man.

Intuition draws you to him...but instinct keeps you
away. Is he really one of those...

Don't miss even one of the twelve sexy but secretive
men, coming to you one per month in 1995.

In April, look for

#317 DROP DEAD GORGEOUS
by Patricia Rosemoor

**Take a walk on the wild side...with our
"DANGEROUS MEN"!**

Available wherever Harlequin books are sold.

DM-3

HARLEQUIN®

I N T R I G U E®

**HARLEQUIN INTRIGUE AUTHOR KELSEY ROBERTS
SERVES UP A DOUBLE DOSE OF DANGER AND DESIRE
IN THE EXCITING NEW MINISERIES:**

THE ROSE TATTOO

At the Rose Tattoo, Southern Specialties are served with a
Side Order of Suspense:

On the Menu for June

Dylan Tanner—tall, dark and delectable
Shelby Hunnicott—sweet and sassy
Sizzling Suspense—saucy red herrings with a twist

On the Menu for July

J. D. Porter—hot and spicy
Tory Conway—sinfully rich
Southern Fried Secrets—succulent and juicy

On the Menu for August

Wes Porter—subtly scrumptious
Destiny Talbott—tart and tangy
Mouth-Watering Mystery—deceptively delicious

Look for Harlequin Intrigue's response to your
hearty appetite for suspense: THE ROSE TATTOO,
coming in June, July and August.

HARLEQUIN®
I N T R I G U E®

What if...

You'd agreed to marry a man you'd never met, in a town where you'd never been, while surrounded by wedding guests you'd never seen before?

And what if...

You weren't sure you could trust the man to whom you'd given your hand?

Look for "Mail Order Brides"—the upcoming two novels of romantic suspense by Cassie Miles, which are available in April and July—and only from Harlequin Intrigue!

Don't miss

#320 MYSTERIOUS VOWS
by Cassie Miles
April 1995

Mail Order Brides—where mail-order marriages lead distrustful newlyweds into the mystery and romance of a lifetime!

MOB-1

Harlequin invites you to the most
romantic wedding of the season.

Rope the cowboy of your dreams in
Marry Me, Cowboy!

A collection of 4 brand-new stories,
celebrating weddings, written by:

New York Times bestselling author

JANET DAILEY

and favorite authors

Margaret Way
Anne McAllister
Susan Fox

Be sure not to miss Marry Me, Cowboy!
coming this April

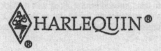 HARLEQUIN®

MMC

HARLEQUIN®

Don't miss these Harlequin favorites by some of our most distinguished authors!
And now, you can receive a discount by ordering two or more titles!

HT#25577	WILD LIKE THE WIND by Janice Kaiser	$2.99	☐
HT#25589	THE RETURN OF CAINE O'HALLORAN by JoAnn Ross	$2.99	☐
HP#11626	THE SEDUCTION STAKES by Lindsay Armstrong	$2.99	☐
HP#11647	GIVE A MAN A BAD NAME by Roberta Leigh	$2.99	☐
HR#03293	THE MAN WHO CAME FOR CHRISTMAS by Bethany Campbell	$2.89	☐
HR#03308	RELATIVE VALUES by Jessica Steele	$2.89	☐
SR#70589	CANDY KISSES by Muriel Jensen	$3.50	☐
SR#70598	WEDDING INVITATION by Marisa Carroll	$3.50 U.S. $3.99 CAN.	☐
HI#22230	CACHE POOR by Margaret St. George	$2.99	☐
HAR#16515	NO ROOM AT THE INN by Linda Randall Wisdom	$3.50	☐
HAR#16520	THE ADVENTURESS by M.J. Rodgers	$3.50	☐
HS#28795	PIECES OF SKY by Marianne Willman	$3.99	☐
HS#28824	A WARRIOR'S WAY by Margaret Moore	$3.99 U.S. $4.50 CAN.	☐

(limited quantities available on certain titles)

	AMOUNT	$
DEDUCT:	**10% DISCOUNT FOR 2+ BOOKS**	$
ADD:	**POSTAGE & HANDLING**	$
	($1.00 for one book, 50¢ for each additional)	
	APPLICABLE TAXES*	$_____
	TOTAL PAYABLE	$_____
	(check or money order—please do not send cash)	

To order, complete this form and send it, along with a check or money order for the total above, payable to Harlequin Books, to: **In the U.S.:** 3010 Walden Avenue, P.O. Box 9047, Buffalo, NY 14269-9047; **In Canada:** P.O. Box 613, Fort Erie, Ontario, L2A 5X3.

Name:_____

Address: _____ City:_____

State/Prov.:_____ Zip/Postal Code:_____

*New York residents remit applicable sales taxes.
 Canadian residents remit applicable GST and provincial taxes.

HBACK-JM2